DISCARD

TAKING THE
WRAP

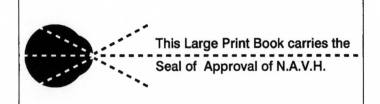

This Large Print Book carries the
Seal of Approval of N.A.V.H.

TAKING THE WRAP

Dolores JOHNSON

WHEELER PUBLISHING

Published in 2005 by arrangement with
St. Martin's Press, LLC.

Wheeler Large Print Compass.

The text of this Large Print edition is unabridged.
Other aspects of the book may vary from the original edition.

Set in 16 pt. Plantin.

Printed in the United States on permanent paper.

Library of Congress Cataloging-in-Publication Data

Johnson, Dolores.
    Taking the wrap / by Dolores Johnson.
      p. cm. — (Wheeler Publishing large print compass)
    ISBN 1-58724-915-4 (lg. print : hc : alk. paper)
    1. Dyer, Mandy (Fictitious character) — Fiction.
  2. Women detectives — Colorado — Denver — Fiction.
  3. Dry cleaning industry — Fiction. 4. Denver (Colo.) —
Fiction. 5. Large type books. I. Title. II. Wheeler large
print compass series.
  PS3560.O3748T35 2005
  813'.6—dc22   2004027065

With love to my grandson, Aaron James Johnson, who'll be old enough to read this dedication before long. For that day . . .

National Association for Visually Handicapped
----------------------- serving the partially seeing

As the Founder/CEO of NAVH, the only national health agency solely devoted to those who, although not totally blind, have an eye disease which could lead to serious visual impairment, I am pleased to recognize Thorndike Press* as one of the leading publishers in the large print field.

Founded in 1954 in San Francisco to prepare large print textbooks for partially seeing children, NAVH became the pioneer and standard setting agency in the preparation of large type.

Today, those publishers who meet our standards carry the prestigious "Seal of Approval" indicating high quality large print. We are delighted that Thorndike Press is one of the publishers whose titles meet these standards. We are also pleased to recognize the significant contribution Thorndike Press is making in this important and growing field.

Lorraine H. Marchi, L.H.D.
Founder/CEO
NAVH

* Thorndike Press encompasses the following imprints: Thorndike, Wheeler, Walker and Large Print Press.

ACKNOWLEDGMENTS

I wish to thank the following people: Stephen V. Cantrill, M.D., Associate Director of Emergency Medicine, Denver Health, for answering my questions on hit-and-run victims, head injuries, and gunshot wounds; Don Oberbeck, owner of Boulder Photo Center, for information on "spirit" photography; Joe and Kaye Cannata, owners of Belaire Cleaners, for dry cleaning information, and my brother-in-law, Ken Johnson, for his expertise and enthusiasm for a subject that, if I mentioned it, would give away the plot. Readers should be able to guess what it is when they finish the book.

Any errors are mine and not the fault of the people I interviewed.

As always, I want to thank members of my two critique groups — Rebecca Bates, Thora Chinnery, Diane Coffelt, Cindy Goff, Donna Schaper, and Barbara Snook; and to Lee Karr, Kay Bergstrom, Carol Caverly, Christine Jorgensen, Cheryl McGonigle, Leslie O'Kane, and Peggy Swager.

Finally, specials thanks to my agent, Meg Ruley, and her associate, Annelise Robey, and to my editor, Marcia Markland.

CHAPTER ONE

"I have a detective job for you, Mandy," Laura Donnelly said when she came into Dyer's Cleaners just before closing time on a stormy January night.

I put up my hands before she had a chance to continue. "Sorry, I'm out of the detective business for good."

Laura, who's a relative of sorts, knew of my involvement in a couple of murder cases. What she didn't know and I wanted to make clear was that I had no desire to get involved in anything even vaguely criminal ever again. She relieved my mind by pushing a long red cashmere coat across the counter to me. The coat was more in line with my real expertise — fabric forensics.

"Okay, that's different," I said. I'm the owner of the cleaners, after all. "What do you have — a mysterious stain that you can't identify? I'll put my crack spotting team on it, but it better not be darkroom chemicals. I warned you that they're almost impossible to get out."

Laura's a professional photographer.

She's also the niece of my stepfather, Herb Smedley, so I guess that makes her my stepcousin. When she first moved to Denver, Herb had asked me to keep an eye on her. I visualized someone I'd have to ride herd on because she would be a little scatterbrained like Herb. As it turned out, she was as independent as I am, and we got along just fine. However, we didn't see that much of each other, and this was the first favor she'd asked of me. Unfortunately, it turned out to be a lot more difficult than stain removal.

"I don't have any darkroom chemicals on the coat," Laura said as she pulled off a tan knit hat and shook out her curly shoulder-length blond hair. "In fact, this isn't even my coat, and I need you to try to track down the real owner. The woman must have taken my coat by mistake Saturday night. I'd like you to see if you can help me get it back."

I pictured another red coat that was similar to the one she'd handed to me. I wondered what she expected me to do: stand on the street corner and yell, "The redcoats are coming," like Paul Revere every time I saw someone in a coat that vaguely resembled this one?

"I was up at this restaurant in the

10

mountains," she said, "and when I went to get my coat, it had disappeared. I finally borrowed the only coat left on the rack because I needed something to wear on the trip home. I'm hoping you can find the owner."

Finding missing persons — even the owner of a friend's coat — wasn't in my field of expertise, either. I started shaking my head.

"It was a good thing I took the coat," she said, "because there was an accident on the way back down to Denver. I was stopped for what seemed like hours because of all the emergency vehicles in the road."

I remembered the snow on Saturday. The storms had been coming in batches this winter, one right after the other, and there was a blizzard again tonight. If I'd been Laura, I would still be wearing the red coat, whether it was mine or not, instead of the safari jacket she had on.

At the moment, the snow was coming down almost horizontally outside the window, and I shivered just watching it. It was almost seven, long past dark, and I was dreading my trip home.

"The coats don't even look alike," Laura said. "Mine's a tan car coat." That put an end to my idea of standing on a street corner and stopping anyone in a red coat. "And whoever owns it is shorter than I am."

That would be eighty percent of the female population. Laura is slender but probably five inches taller than my own height of five-five, and she has the kind of long legs that women yearn for and men flip over.

"Besides, my coat has a lot of pockets," she said.

That probably explained the safari jacket as well as the coat she wanted back. As a photographer, Laura liked pockets, the more the better, for the odds and ends of camera paraphernalia she carried for her trade.

"I took some great shots in the snow on the way up to the restaurant, but unfortunately, I stuck the roll of film in one of the coat pockets when I was finished with it."

So that was really why she wanted the coat back, I decided, as I stared at the two patch pockets on the front of the red coat. "Was there anything in this coat that might help identify the owner?"

Laura grabbed the coat back from me. "Only these." She pulled out a box of matches, a bottle of aspirin, and a business-sized envelope with a stamp affixed.

I guess I reacted to the envelope, what

12

with all the reports about anthrax back in 2001.

"It's okay." She opened the envelope and turned it upside down. "See, there's nothing inside. In fact, it's something the woman must have been planning to mail, because it's a return envelope to the Internal Revenue Service. Maybe she was going to stick her tax return inside and mail it on her way home."

Laura was right. I could see a stick-on label on the front, addressed to the IRS, along with the stamp. The only things missing were whatever was to be placed inside and the sender's address in the upper left-hand corner.

I stuck the envelope back inside the pocket and glanced at the box of matches. It was from a restaurant called the Rendezview, not Rendezvous, which ranked right up there with Dew Drop Inn as a too-cute name.

Laura motioned to the matchbox. "That's the restaurant where I was that night." She must have seen me grimace at the name. "It has a great view down on Denver."

I opened the box. It had three small wooden matches inside. "The owner must be a smoker." I took a sniff of the coat.

"Yep, I can smell the smoke."

Personally, I thought this was about the extent of the detecting job I could or was willing to do for Laura, given the evidence. "Did you check with the restaurant to see if the woman called about the coat mix-up?"

Laura didn't even appreciate my analysis of the matches. She gave me a how-dumb-do-you-think-I-am look. "Of course I called the restaurant."

I returned the matches and the aspirin to the pocket that held the envelope. "I'm sorry, Laura, but the only thing I can suggest is to keep calling — unless, of course, you expect to receive a ransom note and want me to handle the drop."

Laura frowned. "The mix-up was Saturday. Today's Monday, and I've already called the restaurant half a dozen times. Nothing. You're the only hope I have left." She grabbed the coat off the counter and began to poke around inside the left sleeve. "See here. I think this is a dry-cleaning tag." She pointed to a tiny blue strip of paper, stapled to the lining at the bottom of the sleeve, with the numbers "1" and "223" on it. "I was hoping maybe you could tell me the name of the dry cleaners that uses this tag. That way I can track down the person who owns the coat. She has to have mine, and I want it back."

I shook my head again. "It would be practically impossible to find the owner from this. We all use these tags. They're called lot numbers, and they're strictly for in-plant use so we can keep track of garments while they're in our care. The only thing I can tell from this tag is that the customer only had one garment to be cleaned that day."

She gave me a pleading look. "Please, won't you at least try?"

I guess it seemed easy to her, but there was nothing on the tag to indicate what cleaners had used it. In fact, all the dry cleaners I knew removed the tags before returning the clothes to a customer. They had a duplicate copy of the lot number that they attached to their invoice, but what dry cleaner would want to go back through all his invoices to find a matching number for a red coat?

"I'll pay whoever finds the name of the owner a hundred-dollar reward," Laura said.

I was beginning to relent. What were friends for, after all — not to mention relatives twice removed?

Laura and I, who are both in our thirties,

had hit it off immediately because of our mutual interest in art. She considered herself an artist who painted pictures with her camera, and I saw myself as an artist who worked in oils. Never mind that I never had time to do it anymore.

Laura had come to Denver because of the promise of a job on one of those slick city publications, but she'd no sooner arrived than the magazine folded. Fortunately, she'd inherited some money from her aunt, who'd raised her. This was similar to my situation: I'd inherited the cleaners from my Uncle Chet, except that I'd also acquired a not insignificant mortgage.

Laura had decided to go into business for herself, and she'd set up a studio and was busy developing a clientele. I, on the other hand, already had customers and worked six days a week at the cleaners. Our day jobs kept us so busy we seldom saw each other, although we had gotten together a few times for dinner to talk about our respective approaches to art.

"I suppose I could do some checking with other cleaners here in Denver," I said finally, "but I know one thing for sure. We didn't clean the coat. We don't use staples to attach the tags; we use a tagging gun to put on plastic fasteners like department

16

stores use for their price tags."

"I knew I could count on you," Laura said.

I was sure she didn't realize just how many dry-cleaning establishments there were in the Denver area. I'd have to see if any of the owners would be willing to check back in their invoices and match up the lot number and the color of the tag to a red coat. The sequence of numbers and the color of the tags are repeated over and over by us dry cleaners, so it wouldn't be an easy task unless the cleaner had a computer system where the lot numbers were recorded.

I explained all this to Laura and told her that if one of the dry cleaners found a match, the rest of the "detective" work would be up to her. "It'll take some time, and I doubt if we'll get results."

"Thanks, Mandy, for at least trying." She gave me a smile that lit up her rather plain and freckled face. Laura would be quite striking with the right makeup, which she never wore. In fact, it was her complete obliviousness to her appearance that made me overlook the fact that she had legs to die for.

I wrote her name on a slip of paper, pinned it to the collar of the coat, and took the garment through the door to our plant. After I put it on a hanger, I stored it on a rack we use for "orphan" garments that have lost their tags and for items we've removed from our conveyor because customers haven't picked them up in more than six weeks.

By the time I returned to the front counter, Laura had pulled up the collar of her flimsy jacket and slapped on the knit hat and was preparing to head out into the storm.

"I owe you one," she said, tucking her hair up under the cap. "In fact, I'll take you out to dinner soon, but I can't do it tonight. Right now I'm on my way to discuss taking pictures at a fiftieth anniversary party next week."

"Good luck. I'll let you know if I find out anything, but don't hold your breath."

She nodded and opened the front door, sending a rush of cold air sweeping into our call office, which is what we call the customer area of the plant.

Apparently, she'd parked across First Avenue near the upscale Cherry Creek Mall. First Avenue is a busy thoroughfare, even in a storm, and I watched her walk to the corner where there's a crosswalk so she could cross with the light.

18

I was fascinated by her almost surreal appearance as she disappeared into the storm. She became a blurred image, like a photograph that was badly out of focus. She waited for the light to change, looked back toward the cleaners, probably to see if any cars were coming, and then stepped off the curb.

Before she'd taken more than a few steps, a car came out of nowhere and hurtled toward her.

"Watch out, Laura," I screamed as I ran toward the door. She couldn't hear me, and it wouldn't have done any good, anyway.

The driver was going too fast for the icy conditions. He must not have seen her in the swirling snow; I could hardly see her. But the driver also had a red light. He should have stopped whether there was a pedestrian in the crosswalk or not. Maybe he hadn't seen the light, either.

Just as I opened the door, I heard the impact as the car hit her.

"Call 911," I shouted back to Theresa, my afternoon counter manager, who had been waiting on another customer.

The car skidded on the slippery street after the collision. It was actually a white SUV that blended into the snow like some sort of ghost vehicle, but there was no hope of my seeing the license plate. It was too far away, even if the snow hadn't obscured my vision.

"Stop," I yelled. "Damn it, stop." That didn't do any good, either.

The car slid around the corner and disappeared.

CHAPTER TWO

By the time I reached Laura, another car had squealed to a halt. She'd almost been hit for a second time.

The driver jumped out, a cell phone already in his hand, and started waving at the other traffic to stop. Thank God, his car was a shield between her and the other vehicles.

"Laura," I screamed and dropped to my knees beside her.

She was crumpled on the pavement, her left leg at an awkward angle and her eyes closed. She didn't respond.

"Laura," I said more softly.

Still no answer. I wanted to put her head in my lap, but I was afraid to move her. I felt I should do something, maybe CPR. Fortunately, I thought I heard her make a sound, something like a whimper, or I might have tried it.

"We should get her out of the street," the driver yelled as he continued to wave off the oncoming traffic.

"No, we don't dare move her," I yelled

back. "She might have broken bones." In fact, I was sure she had at least one broken bone from the odd angle of her leg.

Damn the driver who'd hit her. People were such fools in bad weather, especially the ones in their jaunty sport utility vehicles. They drove as if they were invincible, all because they had SUVs.

I leaned closer to her, trying to shield her face from the snow. I thought I heard her moan. That had to be a good sign.

Theresa came running out of the cleaners. "I called the police," she said. "They'll be here any minute."

I didn't look up at her until she thrust something at me. It was a blanket that she must have grabbed from the shelf where we kept comforters and folded items for customers.

"You better cover her up so she doesn't go into shock," Theresa said.

I threw the blanket over Laura and felt Theresa put something else over my shoulders.

"You need something, too, or you'll freeze to death," Theresa said.

Laura groaned again.

"It'll be okay, Laura." I hoped she could hear me. "The ambulance should be here any minute. We already called, and it's on the way." I kept up a running monologue, thinking that might keep her from slipping back into unconsciousness.

I was relieved when I heard her try to speak.

"It's going to be all right, Laura. Just hold on."

"My leg hurts." She moaned and tried to move.

"Just stay quiet. The paramedics are on the way, and they'll know what to do. They'll get you to a hospital, and I'll come with them."

I heard sirens in the distance. Thank God. The dark blanket that covered her was almost white with snow. I reached down to pull it over her feet, then pulled off the blanket Theresa had thrown over my shoulders and tried to use it as a tent over Laura's face. I would have preferred to use the second blanket as a pillow for her head, but I knew I shouldn't do that, either.

"Hold on," I said. "The ambulance is almost here. I can see its lights."

In the dark, the snow had the same effect on the flashing lights as a screen over a camera lens. It deflected the image and gave the lights a starburst quality. The rescue vehicle pulled in beside us at an angle on the street. Two police cars were close behind, and their occupants got out to take over traffic control from the man who'd stopped just after the accident.

"Thanks," I yelled to the driver as he returned to his car. I didn't even know his name, although the police went over to interview him. I learned later that he wasn't able to give them any more of a description of the hit-and-run vehicle than I was.

"I think she has a broken leg," I said, and the paramedics confirmed it.

They checked her out, and I heard one of them say he was going to immobilize her neck before they put her on a long board and started an IV. They put splints on either side of her leg, wrapped it in gauze, and carefully lifted her on a gurney for the trip to the hospital.

Meanwhile I'd told a policeman her name. Theresa, who was hovering over me, ran back inside the cleaners to get her address. The policeman didn't ask me for the name of her next of kin. I liked to think that meant she wasn't that seriously injured. It also relieved my mind because her next of kin was my stepfather, Herb.

Laura's parents had been killed in a car accident when she was young. Her mother and the aunt who'd brought her up had been Herb's sisters. Since the aunt had died two years ago, Herb was her closest relative.

I knew I should call him in Phoenix, but then he and my mother would be up here in the bat of one of Mom's false eyelashes. I convinced myself to wait until I knew how Laura really was.

"May I ride in the ambulance with her?" I asked the paramedic when the policeman finished talking to me. "I'm her — uh — cousin."

"It would be better for you if you took your own car, ma'am. Then you'd have a way to get home."

"Okay, where are you taking her?"

"Denver Health."

I knew where it was. It used to be called Denver General, but the name was changed several years ago.

I nodded. "I'll get my car and be right behind you."

Theresa retrieved our customers' blankets from the paramedics, and once we were back inside the cleaners, she insisted that I change out of my wet clothes — a yellow blouse and a beige jacket and skirt that were our uniforms at the front counter. Fortunately, I had a pair of jeans and a sweatshirt in my office that I used when I had to work on repairs in the plant. I toweled off my short brown hair, grabbed a down-filled blue jacket off the hook on the office door, and headed out of the plant. Theresa assured me that she would close up for me.

I swore all the way to the hospital. It was the only thing I could think of as a substitute for trying to speed on the icy streets. It would have been crazy to go too fast on a night like this the way the hit-and-run driver had done.

What kind of idiotic driver would fail to stop after he'd hit someone? He must have known he'd hit a pedestrian. Was he driving without a driver's license? Didn't he have any insurance? Was he drunk? What could have possessed him to keep going, otherwise? I was sure he'd heard the impact. Why else would he have accelerated just after he hit Laura, then skidded around the corner and out of sight?

Once I reached the emergency department, I had to go through security as if I were passing through a metal detector at the airport. I rushed into the waiting room, gave my name to the receptionist, and told her I was there about Laura Donnelly. Then I waited. And waited some more. God, I hoped Laura was going to be all right.

My heart sank as the time wore on, but after what seemed like hours, a doctor came out and told me that Laura's broken leg had been set. Otherwise, she had some scrapes and bruises, but it appeared she didn't have any other serious injuries.

"She was lucky," he said, "but we'll be keeping her for observation, just in case there's any internal bleeding."

Sure. How lucky could she get? And somewhere out there in the storm was a hit-and-run driver in no pain at all.

"May I see her?" I asked.

"She's being transferred to a room shortly, but if you want to wait around, you can talk to her. She'll probably be pretty groggy, though, and I doubt if she'll remember much about the accident."

"How long will she be here?"

"At least overnight."

"Not any longer than that? She lives alone. How will she manage?"

"She should be able to handle herself on crutches just fine."

After the doctor left, I went to the cafeteria to have a cup of coffee and something to eat. I dithered the whole time about whether I should call Herb or not. I'd told myself I'd wait until I knew the extent of Laura's injuries. Okay, I knew what they

27

were now. So why was I hesitating? Maybe Laura would even appreciate some help when she got home. Then again, maybe she would find Herb and my mother, Cecilia, more trouble than help. I knew I usually did.

When I returned to the waiting room, a new receptionist was on duty. She told me Laura had been transferred to a room on the fourth floor. The woman pointed toward the elevators, but I needed a road map to find the room. In lieu of that, I tried to follow tape stuck to the floor as if I were traveling the yellow brick road. I gave up a couple of times and collared people in scrub suits for directions.

"Is it all right if I come in?" I asked a nurse when I finally reached Laura's room.

"Just for a few minutes." She was taking Laura's vital signs.

"What happened?" Laura asked, apparently recognizing me. "I feel like I was hit by a two-ton truck."

I was the one who had a hard time recognizing her. She had a scrape on her forehead and the beginning of a black eye. Her leg was in a cast that went from her foot to the top of her thigh. It looked as if it were made of fiberglass.

"You're not that far off base," I said. "It

was an SUV, just after you left the cleaners and started across the street. The police are looking for the driver now."

I sat down beside her bed and broached the subject I'd been fretting about all night. "Look, do you want me to call Herb?"

Laura grabbed my hand and gripped it with a whole lot more strength than I would have expected. "No, please, don't do that yet. Promise me you'll wait. Let me call him myself when I get home. Okay?"

"Sure, I promise."

Not only would I wait, I felt an overwhelming sense of relief. Apparently, Laura had feelings similar to mine when it came to Herb, a hail-fellow-well-met retired used car salesman who went to pieces in an emergency. She also knew his wife, my much-married mother, who thought no woman was complete without a man. If Mom came up here, she would probably be looking for suitable spouses for both of us even as she played her own dramatic version of nursemaid.

That's not to say that I didn't feel a little guilty, too. Mom and her mate would be royally pissed when they found out that I had failed to notify them the moment the accident occurred.

Relief won out over guilt. I was grateful to Laura for getting me off the hook about calling them. When they chewed me out, I could always say it was her decision, not mine. In exchange for giving me such an out, I vowed to make a concerted effort to find the person who had taken Laura's coat. It was the least I could do.

Okay, I could do more than that. After opting out of calling Herb, I decided it was up to me to chauffeur her home from the hospital and become her official caregiver.

"Call me when the doctors release you, and I'll come and get you," I said, but I still felt a little guilty.

As soon as I got to work the next morning, I sought out Mack Rivers, my plant manager, at the dry-cleaning machines and told him what had happened. He's a big black man in his sixties who's my sounding board when things go wrong. He had worked at the cleaners for as long as I could remember, and he's the closest thing I have to a father figure, my own dad having died when I was a baby.

After I got through telling Mack about Laura's accident and the crazy driver who ran her down, I launched into the story of the coat mix-up at the Rendezview restaurant

Saturday night. Mack wanted to see the coat, so I went up to the front of the plant and got it.

He gave a low whistle when he saw it. "That's a damned expensive coat." He fingered the soft cashmere fabric. "I can't imagine that she wouldn't be trying to get it back."

"I know." I showed him the blue tag in the lining of the sleeve. "Laura thinks I should be able to find out where it was cleaned from this lot number and locate the owner that way."

"You have to be kidding," Mack said. "What dry cleaner is going to be willing to go back through his records to find a blue lot number that matches a red coat?"

"That's what I told her, but she's willing to pay a hundred dollars if someone can come up with the owner's name."

"Any other ID in the coat?"

I showed him the envelope, the bottle of aspirin, and the box of matches with a mountain scene on top. "That's it."

"Hey, that coat looks like it'd be warm," someone said from behind my right shoulder. It was Betty, who'd been a bag lady before I gave her a job in the laundry. She had a habit of eavesdropping on conversations that were none of her business, and she'd retained a lot of her old bag-lady ways, such as never buying anything when she could get it for free. "If you don't know who owns it, I'll take it off your hands."

Mack had more patience with her than I did. "No, Betty, I'm sure the owner wants her coat back."

"Well, if you can't find her, I got dibs on it," Betty said.

I took the coat before she could grab it and headed for my office. When I got there, I hung the coat on a hanger and placed it on a hook on the back of my office door before I went up to the front counter to help with the morning rush of customers dropping off and picking up clothes.

I didn't get around to calling any other dry cleaners until late afternoon. By then, I'd taken Laura home from the hospital, gotten her settled in her high-rise apartment, and promised to return that night with dinner.

When I finally began to make the calls, I found I could eliminate most of the cleaners because, like Dyer's Cleaners, they no longer stapled the tags to the clothes. With the ones who did, most of the owners — the ones I could actually talk to — laughed at me when I asked them to go back through their records looking for a red coat. That was even after I told them about Laura's hundred-dollar reward.

Theresa had said she could handle the afternoon traffic at the front counter by herself, so I'd decided to keep making calls until our seven o'clock closing time.

I was just starting to dial another number when someone knocked on my office door.

"Can I come in?" It was Mack.

I looked at my watch. It was already six-thirty. "I thought you left at four o'clock. What are you doing here?"

"Something was nagging at me, so I went home to look through my pile of newspapers," Mack said, coming into the room. "Look at this." He handed me a copy of that morning's *Denver Tribune*.

Mack pointed to an article buried inside the paper. "It says a woman was killed up near that restaurant Saturday night."

I read the two short paragraphs:

A woman, identified as Joy Emerson of Golden, was killed Saturday night in what Colorado State Patrol officers said appeared to be a one-car accident. The car apparently skidded on icy pavement on Vista View Road and rolled down a steep embankment.

Visibility was poor at the time, and the Highway Patrol is looking for witnesses who may have seen the crash.

"So?" I was trying to ignore the eerie feeling I had about the article.

"So isn't it possible the woman was coming from the same restaurant where Laura had been that night?" Mack said. "And maybe she was the one who grabbed Laura's coat by mistake. That would explain why no one has called about having the wrong coat."

I had to agree that it was a possibility, especially since Laura had said she was held up in traffic by an accident that night, but what really scared me was the thought that Joy Emerson might have been the victim of a hit-and-run driver, too.

If so, were the two accidents just a freakish coincidence, or were they somehow connected?

CHAPTER THREE

I knew that Mack and I were making a leap in logic to think that the woman who'd been killed in the accident Saturday night was somehow connected to Laura's coat.

But I knew one way I could find out. My buddy Nat Wilcox works as a police reporter at the *Tribune.* I called and left a message on his voice mail, asking him if he could find out from the Jefferson County coroner what kind of coat Joy Emerson had been wearing when she was killed. I told him about the mix-up and described Laura's coat, including the fact that there'd been a roll of exposed film in the pocket.

"Call me as soon as you find out," I said and hung up.

I could have tried to reach him on his cell phone, but I didn't want to get involved in a long conversation with him right then. Instead, I needed to get over to Laura's apartment and tell her about the newspaper article.

Theresa and I closed up the cleaners as soon as Mack left, and I gave Laura a quick call to see what kind of food she wanted for dinner. I'd noticed a phone beside her bed, but she wasn't answering it. Maybe she was in the bathroom.

Her answering machine came on. "Hey, Laura, it's Mandy," I said to the machine. "Pick up, will you?" Silence. "I'm waiting." More silence. "Okay, I'll check with you later." I could always call her from whatever restaurant I decided to go to for carryout food.

I hung up and changed into a pair of jeans, a sweater, and a corduroy jacket. Then I grabbed my long tan coat — not cashmere, but it was warm — and headed out the back door to my car.

I knew Laura liked Chinese, so I decided to go to the Great Wall, a restaurant that has takeout and is only a few blocks from her apartment.

The roads had turned to ice where the tracks of cars had melted the snow during the day, then frozen over at nightfall. It took me half an hour just to get to the restaurant, which gave me time to let my imagination run wild.

What if the two "accidents" weren't really accidental? What if the real target had been Laura? In fact, what if the poor woman had been run off the road Saturday night because she'd been wearing Laura's coat?

I grabbed a takeout menu as soon as I got to the Great Wall and dialed Laura's number again. I was prepared to read her the items on the menu, but mainly the call was to reassure myself that she was okay. This time her line was busy, which relieved my mind.

I gave up and ordered the kung pao chicken, Szechuan beef, sweet and sour pork, some hot and sour soup, and rice and noodles. As soon as the hostess brought the cartons to me in two big brown paper bags, I paid and headed for Laura's.

The sidewalk outside the restaurant had been cleared during the day, but a freezing mist had begun to fall, making it as treacherous as the streets. It was tricky even to walk to my car, much less keep my balance with the two huge sacks in my arms. I'd bought so much food so Laura would have leftovers for the next night.

I found a parking place near her apartment building and, with a bag of takeout in each arm, made my way very carefully to her front door. As I edged along the sidewalk, I felt like a tightrope walker, afraid at every step that I might lose my balance and fall. I made it through the outer door of her building, took off a glove, and tried to get to the keys Laura had given me earlier in the day. She'd offered them so I could get in and out without her having to limp to the buzzer to admit me to the building and then wait for me at the door of her apartment.

Before I could secure the bags in one arm and reach for the keys inside my shoulder bag, a man wearing a fur hat came out the entrance.

"Terrible night, isn't it?" he asked, looking for all the world like a Cossack prepared to face a winter on the Russian steppes. "Here, let me help you with that." He held the door open with a gloved hand so I could enter the lobby and then went on his way.

I thanked him, even as I wondered about having a top-notch security system if other tenants — or a visitor like myself — would let a stranger inside the building this easily. All the same, I was grateful to the man.

When I got off the elevator on the fourth floor, the hall was completely deserted. It usually was. The building was new and not fully occupied yet.

Laura's apartment was near the end of the hall. By the time I reached it, I'd fumbled around in my purse and managed to extract the keys. I had them in my right hand and was holding the two bags precariously in my left arm.

I knocked first to warn her. "It's Mandy," I yelled and unlocked the door. I used the hand grasping the paper bags in an effort to turn the knob. My hold on the food was getting more tenuous all the time. I was about to lose one or both of the sacks.

I finally set them down and opened the door. I held it open a crack with my hip as I reached down and grabbed the food. I pushed into the room backward; it was only then that I realized the apartment was dark.

"Laura," I called to warn her in case she'd fallen asleep. But that didn't make sense. She'd been on the phone just a few minutes before.

I set down one of the bags and grappled for the light switch. As I did, I somehow managed to push the door closed, shutting out what little light came from the hallway.

"Damn," I muttered, both because of the door and the fact that the switch didn't turn on anything. I tried to think where the closest lamp was to the doorway. It was on a glass-topped end table, I thought.

I reached for the doorknob in an effort to get enough light from the hallway to find the lamp. When I twisted the knob, the door wouldn't open. Maybe there was a dead bolt at the top that had locked as I shut the door — but that couldn't be. I'd only needed one key in the main lock to get inside. So what could be holding it shut?

My heart began banging as if an alarm were going off. What the devil was happening?

I turned toward the door and gave the knob another tug. This time the door started to open, then slammed shut again. That's all it took to make my internal alarm system go into a full-fledged shriek. It wasn't a "what" that was keeping the door shut. It had to be a "who." Someone was in the room with me, and I was sure it wasn't Laura.

Right then the person gave me a giant shove. I went flying into the room backward with the remaining bag of takeout still clutched in my arms. I landed with a thud on the floor. My head slammed into something, probably the end table. The lamp I'd been trying to locate sounded as if it had toppled to the floor beside me. I heard the clink of breaking glass as the lightbulb shattered. The top of the container of hot and sour soup I'd just purchased popped open. Its contents spilled over my coat.

All this happened in a split second while the door swung open. I saw the silhouette of a man run into the hall. I managed to struggle to my feet, swiping some noodles out of my face. They must have spilled from another container in the sack.

By the time I reached the hall, I could see the door to the emergency exit closing. My first impulse was to run after the intruder, but I didn't know what I'd do if I caught him. I'd been no match for him the first time. What made me think I'd be any better if I took a flying leap down the stairwell and managed to tackle him?

Besides, what I needed to do was call the police. No, what I needed to do was find Laura. An attempt had already been made on her life. What if someone had been successful on this second try? I felt as if my insides were being gouged out. I couldn't face the thought of finding her dead or dying.

I slammed the door shut and leaned against it. I didn't know whether I was more afraid of staying in the apartment or going into the deserted hallway where the

41

burglar might be waiting for me. I opted to stay inside and call the police. Now if I could just find another light switch. Since the one at the door hadn't worked, it had probably been connected to the lamp, now broken on the floor.

My eyes began to adjust to a thin stream of light coming from a window at the far end of the living/dining room. There were also bright shooting lights that seemed to be coming from inside my head. They interfered with my vision, but I could see just enough to fumble my way to the hall that led to the bathroom and the two bedrooms.

I finally found the switch. The overhead light in the hallway almost blinded me, but I could see that one of the bedroom doors was closed. I couldn't bear to open it.

"Laura, are you here?" My voice was so hoarse I couldn't even recognize it.

No one answered.

I stared into the gloom of the living room. It was trashed. The table I'd upended was nothing compared to the devastation of the rest of the room.

I ran over to the counter that divided the living room from the kitchen and started to grab for the phone that I knew was there. The receiver was off the hook. No wonder I'd gotten a busy signal when I'd tried to call Laura from the restaurant. The intruder must have removed it from its cradle so I couldn't call back. I knew I wasn't thinking very clearly, but I stopped just in time.

Don't pick up the phone, I said to myself. *There may be fingerprints on it. Use your cell phone. That's what it's for.*

I fumbled in my purse for the phone I'd used only moments before at the restaurant, turned it on, and called 911. I was put through to a police dispatcher.

"Send someone to —" I couldn't remember Laura's address. I turned on the kitchen light and picked up a telephone bill that was on the counter. The letters seemed blurred, but I managed to read off the address. "There's been a burglary, and I can't find the owner of the apartment."

"Stay on the phone," the dispatcher said.

Okay, I could do that and try to find Laura at the same time.

"I'm going to look for the owner now."

"You should stay where you are and wait for the officer," the dispatcher said.

I ignored the warning and covered the mouthpiece. "Laura," I yelled, my voice trembling.

God, please don't let her be dead. I couldn't stand it if the burglar had done something to my already bruised and battered friend. But maybe she'd gone somewhere for the evening. I didn't think so, but I could always hope.

I went to the hallway and switched on the light in the bedroom that she'd converted into an office. It had been torn apart.

I still had my hand over the mouthpiece. "Laura, it's Mandy."

Suddenly I heard a muffled sound. It came from across the hall. I opened the door to the other bedroom and turned on another light. It was all I could do to force myself to look around the room. My gaze stopped at the bed. The sheets and blankets were rumpled as if she'd been sleeping there only moments before.

A wave of nausea swept over me, and I couldn't make myself look under the bed.

"Laura, it's Mandy," I repeated. "Are you here?"

"Mandy?" The voice was full of fear.

"Where are you?"

"Over here." The sound came from the far side of the bed.

I ran over to where Laura was lying, squeezed up against the underside of the bed. She'd somehow managed to slide down to the floor, broken leg and all, and had pulled a blanket with her.

44

By the time I got there, she was trying to untangle herself from the blanket. I decided not to tell her that the intruder would have been sure to discover her eventually, the way he was tearing the place apart.

"Thank God, it's you," she said, and tears began to stream down her face. "Did you scare him away?"

"Yeah," I said, but I didn't tell her the battering I'd taken doing it.

"Can you help me up?"

I wasn't sure, but I put the phone back to my ear. "I found the owner," I said. "She was hiding in the bedroom, and I'm going to put the phone down so I can help her up." I dropped the phone on the bed without waiting for the dispatcher's response. "Maybe it would be better if we waited until the police get here, Laura. They're on their way, and it might take two of us."

"But I feel so stupid down here."

Better stupid than dead, but I reached down to give her a hand.

"You're all wet," she said, "and what's that in your hair?"

I'd forgotten about the spilled food. I brushed a noodle out of my face. Even the back of my head felt wet. I managed to pull her to a sitting position, her cast-covered leg straight out in front of her. When she grabbed my arms and tried to get the rest of the way to her feet, I almost toppled to the floor beside her.

"We're going to wait," I said. "I don't want to break one of your other bones." I also didn't want to pass out on top of her. The blow to the back of my head was sending stabs of pain to my brain.

I was relieved to hear the buzzer go off just then. Good, it was reinforcements. "I'll be right back."

Laura didn't argue. Either she'd seen the futility of trying to get upright with me as leverage or else she was in too much pain from getting to the halfway point.

I shrugged out of my soggy coat and dropped it on the floor before I went to the front door. "Who is it?" I asked as I pushed the intercom.

"It's the police." It sounded like a man. "We're here about a burglary report."

"Just a minute." I buzzed him in and waited until he took the elevator up to the fourth floor.

When a knock sounded on the door, I looked through the peephole. I wasn't taking any chances. "Can you show me some identification?"

I could see a distorted fish-eye image of a blond officer as he held up his ID. Satisfied, I let him inside.

"I'm Officer Bradley," he said, "and this is Officer Chavez." He pointed to his dark-haired partner.

Chavez was looking around at the destruction. "You really got hit, didn't you?" I decided he was talking about the apartment, not my head, and I nodded, trying to ignore the little jabs of pain it cost me. "Why don't you tell us exactly what happened?"

"It's not my apartment," I said. "The person who lives here hid on the floor in her bedroom, and the first thing we need to do is help get her up."

"I better call an ambulance," Bradley said.

That's all Laura would need, a whole bevy of paramedics to get her to her feet. "No, she has a broken leg —"

Before I could finish explaining, he was on his radio starting to summon help.

"I mean she's already in a cast."

He signed off, which reminded me about the dispatcher. I grabbed the phone as soon as we entered the bedroom. "The police are here. I'm hanging up now." I pushed the END button on the phone and dropped it in the pocket of my corduroy jacket.

Laura, peeking over the side of the bed, assured him she didn't need an ambulance. "Please, could you just help my friend get me up?"

Together the cops and I finally got Laura on her feet.

"Are you sure you're okay?" Bradley asked.

"No, I'm not okay," she said. "I already have a broken leg, and whoever broke in here scared the hell out of me. I felt so totally helpless —"

"I'm sorry," Chavez said.

Laura must have realized how she sounded. "Oh, look, I apologize. I'm still so scared and shaky."

I retrieved her crutches from the other side of the bed and handed them to her before she toppled over. Then the four of us went into the living room, which was pungent with the smell of the hot and sour soup. Laura let out a gasp when she saw the devastation.

Bradley sniffed the air. "What's that smell?"

"It's Chinese takeout," I said and started to help the men pick up the cushions from the sofa so Laura could sit down.

"What do you think the burglar was after?" Bradley asked as Laura lowered herself onto the sofa.

She looked as if she might cry again as she glanced around the room. "I have no idea."

I didn't, either, but I was convinced that the hit-and-run accident plus the burglary didn't add up to a coincidence. No way.

"Tell us everything that happened," Bradley continued.

"Well, I'd fallen asleep," Laura said. "I didn't hear anyone at the door, but then the phone rang, and I heard noises coming from the living room. I could see a light coming from under my bedroom door, and I knew I hadn't left it on. It had been light outside when I fell asleep."

"So what did you do?"

"I was afraid to answer the phone and let the person know I was here. I waited for a few minutes and tried to call 911, but the line was dead, so I eased myself down on the floor and tried to hide. There was so much noise coming from the living room that I guess the person didn't hear me."

"So the burglar only searched the living room."

I motioned toward the second bedroom. "He went through her office, too."

"Oh, God." Laura started to struggle to her feet. "Did he tear it apart, too?"

"Yes," I said, careful not to move my head too much.

She fell back on the sofa and put her hands to her face, covering her eyes.

Just then my cell phone rang.

"Is it okay if I answer it?" I asked, looking at Bradley. "It might be an emergency at work." As if one emergency in a day weren't bad enough.

"Okay, go ahead," he said. He turned back to Laura. "So what made the person leave?"

I moved to the dining area. "Hello," I said into the phone.

"Mandy, how're you doing?" I recognized the voice. It was Herb. My stepfather. Laura's uncle. "I've been trying to reach Laura, and her line is always busy. Do you know what's going on with her?"

Well, yes, I did, but she'd made me promise not to tell him about her broken leg. I'd applauded her decision at the time because the last thing I wanted was for Herb and my mother to come up to Denver right now.

"Uh — no," I said, "I don't know what to tell you."

"What's the matter, Mandy? You sound funny."

I wasn't even aware that I was touching

the bump on the back of my head as I tried to think of what to say. My hair felt wet and matted; it must be the soup.

In the background, I heard Bradley ask, "Did something scare the burglar away?"

"Mandy got here and probably saved my life," Laura said.

I tried to clamp my hand over the phone so Herb wouldn't hear her, but when I did, I saw that my hand was covered with blood.

Chavez saw it, too, and rushed toward me.

"Isn't that Laura?" Herb asked. "What'd she say?"

I uncovered the mouthpiece. "Look, I'll have to call you back later." I shut off the phone, ringer and all, before Herb had a chance to respond. He wouldn't be calling me back tonight.

"What happened?" Chavez asked. "Let me take a look at that."

I tried to fend him off. "It's nothing, really." I went over to a straight-backed chair in Laura's dining alcove and leaned on it like a seasick sailor hanging over the rail. "I'll be fine."

But I didn't feel fine. I felt as if a tidal wave had hit me and was rocking the deck under my feet.

51

Chavez must have been checking out the back of my head. "That's a nasty cut," he said. "You need to have it looked at."

Laura was trying to get up from the sofa to inspect the wound.

"Will you please sit down, Laura? I'll be okay. Just give me a minute."

"I'll call the paramedics," Bradley said.

I tried to stop him. That's when I fainted dead away.

CHAPTER FOUR

When I came to, I was on the floor. The cops were floating above me like angels behind a thin layer of clouds.

I couldn't have been out for more than a few seconds. As I started to get up, I could see that Laura was still struggling to get off of the couch.

"Just stay where you are," Chavez said, looking at me.

Okay, but just until the weather cleared.

"We've called for an ambulance," he added.

Before I knew it, the doorbell rang, and a couple of paramedics came into the room.

"Look, I'll be okay. This isn't necessary." I tried to get up again, but one of the men restrained me.

Would anyone believe me if I tried to explain what I thought had made me faint? It wasn't the cut on the head or even the unexpected sight of blood.

I was sure the reason I had passed out was the sound of Herb's voice on the phone and the knowledge that Mom was waiting in the wings. What a wimp I was. I should never have given them my cell phone number.

The paramedics quickly immobilized my neck and put me on a gurney.

"Can you tell us how you got the cut on your head?" one of the men asked.

"Of course I can." What did he think — that I'd gone into shock and couldn't remember the attack? "I was loaded down with Chinese takeout, and when I let myself in here, someone pushed me from behind the door. I went flying to the floor. When I tried to get up, it was as if I were in one of those haunted houses where they use wet noodles to make people think they're touching intestines."

Now I had the rapt attention of the paramedics, the cops, and Laura, who'd finally managed to hobble over to where I was. They were all staring down at me as if I must surely be hallucinating about Halloween, haunted houses, and internal body parts.

Laura looked as if she might cry. "Oh, Mandy, I'm so sorry." She must have thought I'd lost all touch with reality.

"It was because the soup and noodles had spilled out all over me," I said. It was probably a pathetic explanation, but I was desperate for people, especially Laura, to realize I didn't have some serious brain injury that had sent me into another dimension. I decided the best thing to do was to quit blathering on about wet noodles and stick to the subject.

"Anyway," I said, now back on track, "I saw what looked like a man rush out from behind the door and into the hall. I started after him, but he'd already disappeared down the stairwell by the time I got to the door. I decided it was more important to call the police and see if Laura was all right."

Personally, I thought I'd passed the test for total recall by giving a coherent account of what had happened.

"Didn't you even know you'd been hurt?" Chavez asked.

"I heard a crack when I hit something, if that's what you mean, but I hardly felt it." *Stop right there,* I warned myself. Maybe I could still talk them out of taking me to the hospital if I didn't tell them about the stars I'd seen shooting around the room like some kind of intergalactic laser light show.

The paramedics were already wheeling me out to the hallway by then. Laura was limping along beside them on her crutches, still looking worried.

"Dead-bolt the door, Laura, and put on the chain," I said. "I'll be back as soon as I can."

Laura tried to smile. "Yes, Mom." That was an unkind cut, worse even than the one on the back of my head. After all, she knew my mother.

Maybe I was even showing a latent hereditary predisposition to faint the way my mother did. No, I refused to believe that. Mom went into a swoon at the slightest provocation. She fancied herself the epitome of the fragile southern belle, although she'd been born right here in Colorado. Under her superfeminine facade, though, she was Superwoman. And she had the ability to make Laura's life, not to mention mine, a living hell if she and Herb came up here from Phoenix right now.

I mulled over that possibility as the paramedics carted me off in an ambulance, but I had the feeling there was something more important that I should be thinking about — something I should have told Laura and the police officers. What was it? I gave a mental shrug, which was the only kind I was capable of. Now that I didn't have to put up such a brave front, I decided just to let the headache from hell consume me. It had cut off the circuitry in my brain, and I couldn't recall what I'd wanted to remember.

I knew enough to worry about Laura's safety, though. Maybe I should call Nat to babysit Laura, but he's a skinny five-foot-eight. I wasn't sure how much help he would really be.

So how about Travis Kincaid? He was a six-foot-tall private eye I'd become reacquainted with several months before, but I didn't know if he hired out as a bodyguard. There'd been a lot of sexual chemistry — okay, call it tension — between us, and I'd half expected him to call me later on. He hadn't. For all I knew, there was a similar chemistry between Travis and a whole bevy of women, and I wasn't sure I wanted to expose Laura to that.

My reaction startled me, especially in my present vulnerable state. Was I really worried about Laura — or Travis? Was I exhibiting some irrational jealousy about introducing my friend to the guy who'd intrigued yet unnerved me back in high school? Dear God, I must be out of my mind. I refused to believe that I'd ever had a thing for Travis. After all, if we'd had such a category back in school, he would have been the guy voted "most likely to go into a life of crime," at least according to my fellow classmate Nat.

This was way too complicated for me to grapple with right now. Besides, I had to put my scattered thoughts on hold when I was wheeled into the emergency room.

A doctor asked me how many fingers he was holding up. There were either two or three. I couldn't tell for sure, but I decided to give it a shot.

"Two," I said.

"Good," he said. "We have to make sure you don't have a closed head injury."

He asked me some more questions, and I guess I passed the test. I didn't tell him about the internal body parts, however.

"We're going to inject the wound with an anesthetic to contract the vessels and stop the bleeding," he said. "And your hair's so thick and matted that we're going to have to shave a little around the site."

"Don't worry," a nurse said. "You should be able to tease the rest of your hair over the bare spot so it won't even show."

Frankly, that was the least of my worries right now. I tried again to remember what I'd wanted to tell the cops. Maybe I did have brain damage, although it was a little hard to tell. My head began to feel as if it had gone to sleep way ahead of the rest of my body, thanks to the topical deadening agent the doctor applied to it before he put in the sutures.

Once he was through, he instructed me to keep the wound dry for twenty-four hours, gave me a prescription for antibiotics, told me to come back in ten days to get the stitches out, and said I could go home.

I thought I'd blown it for a moment when the doctor asked me if I had someone who could drive me there.

"I was planning to take a taxi," I said.

"You need to have a friend spend the night with you."

"Oh, I'm going to have the cabdriver take me to a friend's place."

The doctor gave me an appraising look, as if I might be lying, but finally said okay. I was glad I hadn't told him that my friend was even more incapacitated than I was.

"Where's your coat?" the nurse asked as I prepared to leave.

A coat? That was it. I'd never told Laura or the officers about the woman who'd plunged down a mountainside in an accident on her way back to Denver and how that could explain why no one had called the restaurant about the coat mix-up. Besides, if the woman had been wearing Laura's coat, it could mean that the two accidents and now the break-in were somehow connected.

"Where's your coat?" the nurse repeated.

Oh, yes, *my* coat. I told her I didn't have it.

I remembered that I'd shed it in Laura's apartment because of all the Chinese takeout that had spilled on it. I didn't have the keys to her apartment, either. They probably landed on the floor amid the hot and sour soup and noodles when I fell. Fortunately, I had my purse and enough money to call a cab. Someone must have put the purse on the gurney so I'd have ID and my insurance card when I got to the hospital.

The taxi didn't have a heater. Just my luck. Without a coat, I felt as if I'd turned into a chunk of ice by the time I finally reached Laura's building and paid off the driver. Tiny icicles seemed to be stabbing at my brain, but I decided that was from the anesthesia. It was not unlike the way my jaw always felt after I'd had a Novocain injection at the dentist's office.

I shivered as I leaned on Laura's buzzer in the entrance of the building. It took a good five minutes before I heard her voice. Security or no, I wished the guy who'd let me into the building earlier would come along right then. I was about to develop hypothermia.

My teeth chattered when Laura finally answered. "It's M-m-mandy. Let me in."

She was waiting for me at her apartment door when I arrived at the fourth floor. I heard her unlock the dead bolt and remove the chain. She'd followed "Mom's" advice, after all. It just wouldn't have been my mother's advice. Mom would have said Laura needed a man to protect her from all the dangers of modern life.

"Thank God, you're here." Laura balanced precariously on her crutches. "I've been too upset to go to sleep."

I didn't blame her, and being able to give her moral support made me feel a little better. I wasn't sure what other kind of help I could give her, though, being one of the walking wounded myself.

Laura was eyeing me closely. "What'd they do to you? You don't look so good."

"They patched me up, and I'll be fine."

"Well, I'm glad you're here. I've been trying to call you at the hospital because there's something I need to tell you."

I had a moment of optimism before my hopes were smashed. "What? Did they catch the burglar?"

"No such luck. I have bad news."

61

"God, what else can go wrong?"

"Uh — well, Uncle Herbert called me, and I had to tell him what happened to you."

"You what?" I started to yell, but it felt as if the top of my head were being attacked by a snowblower.

Laura looked embarrassed. "Your mom freaked out."

No, I thought, *what Mom did was go into one of her swoons.* She would never do anything so unladylike as freak out.

"I didn't mention about my broken leg, but I'm afraid they may decide to come up here to lend you a hand."

Damn. Laura had failed to cover for me — and after I'd been so careful to shield her from the onslaught of our overzealous relatives. I thought about never speaking to her again, but of course I had to tell her about that other accident.

"I'm really sorry," Laura said. "I know neither one of us wants them to come up here right now, but Herb knew something was wrong when you answered your cell phone. Besides, he heard me in the background. He wanted to know what in blue blazes was going on."

I knew the "blue blazes" was Herb's term, not Laura's, but damn it, she could have figured out some creative lie. She was even more of a wimp than I was.

"Okay," I said, even though it wasn't okay. "Mind if I come in?"

"Oh, no, sorry." Laura limped aside to let me enter.

The smell of soy sauce assailed me once I stepped over the threshold, but I noticed someone had put away the food that hadn't spilled and cleaned up the mess on the rug. All that was left was a big damp stain, and I told Laura to be careful so she didn't slip on it with her crutches. As for me, the smell made me nauseous, and it was all I could do to make it to the couch.

"I'm surprised they released you," Laura said.

"Well, they did." I sounded defensive, but I was still irritated at her.

"But you didn't need to come back here to stay with me."

"Yes, I did, and besides, I remembered something I needed to tell you."

"And you couldn't have done that on the phone?"

I glared at her. "I could have if I'd thought about it. Now do you want to hear what I have to say or not?"

Laura eased herself into the overstuffed chair that matched her beige sofa. "Yes, of course I want to hear it." She was getting testy herself.

I laid out the story of the woman who'd been killed in an accident near the restaurant Saturday night. In my present condition, I couldn't remember her name; I was doing well to recall the story. My theory sounded pretty far-fetched, even to me, as I told Laura about it.

"I'm wondering if that's the accident that held you up when you were trying to get home," I said. "And it occurred to me that maybe the driver of that car is the person who took your coat. That would explain why no one has called the restaurant about it."

Laura's face grew pale, at least the part that wasn't black and blue from her accident. "Do you think she was killed in a hit-and-run by the same person who hit me?" she asked when I finished.

That was exactly what I was thinking, but I shrugged. "I don't know. The newspaper said the State Patrol thought it was a one-car accident, but they're looking for witnesses."

"Oh, God, what if there was a connection —" Laura's voice shook, but suddenly she pounded a crutch on the floor. "What if there was something in her coat that someone wanted?"

"You mean like an empty envelope, a box of matches, or a bottle of aspirin?" I asked.

"No, I mean like something hidden in the lining or sewn in the shoulder pad?" Laura looked as if she were about to bounce out of her chair, but the crutches held her back. "Mandy, we need to check out every inch of the coat as soon as possible."

The thought of driving to the cleaners in the middle of the night to get the coat was beyond my capabilities, and besides, I was still miffed at the way Laura had handled the call from Herb. "No, the first thing *you* need to do is call the police officer who was here and tell him about the coat. I already asked a friend of mine at the *Tribune* to check with the coroner's office about it, but the cop could probably find out faster."

Laura nodded her head. "I hadn't thought of that."

"There's another possibility. Assuming the woman was wearing your coat, what if she was targeted because someone mistook her for you?" As soon as the words were out of my mouth, I was sorry I'd said them.

Laura looked as if she'd been hit by

another SUV. "No, it has to be something about her coat."

I thought I had an argument for why it wasn't the coat, but for the life of me, I couldn't think what it was. My mind felt as if it had turned to icy slush now that I was beginning to warm up.

"Besides, why would anyone want to target me?" she asked.

"I don't know. What were you doing up at the restaurant?"

"I was on a photo shoot, taking pictures for a brochure the owners want to have printed."

A flashbulb went off in my head.

I leaned forward. "What if you took a picture of something or someone you weren't supposed to see?"

CHAPTER FIVE

Everything seemed to come into sharper focus once I knew about the film. It seemed like a better explanation for why someone had broken into Laura's apartment tonight than the coat.

The big question was: If the burglar had been looking for the film, did he find it?

My first impulse was that he wouldn't have continued to tear the place apart if he'd found it. But then again, maybe he'd found it and was getting ready to leave just as I arrived.

Laura looked stunned at the idea that the film could hold a clue to what had been happening, but finally she agreed. "I suppose that's a possibility, isn't it? The policemen and I checked in my office. None of my photo equipment was gone, but the cameras had all been opened."

Damn. "So the burglar got the film?"

"No, I never leave film in my cameras when I've finished a roll."

"Okay." I dreaded getting up right then,

but with some mental coaxing, I figured I could do it. "Tell me where you put the film, and I'll try to find it."

"It isn't here," Laura said.

"You mean you've already looked for it?"

"No, I mean it isn't *here*. It's in the lab I've been using for my processing. I dropped it off in their mail slot Saturday night, but it wasn't supposed to be ready until today."

I felt relief, then another surge of fear for Laura. If the intruder had actually found the film, it might have protected her from any further attacks. Since he hadn't found it, she was still in danger. On the other hand, she might be in danger either way. Someone had come after her even before he came looking for the film, so maybe it was the coat after all. Still, I wasn't ready to give up on the photo angle.

"Did anything strange happen while you were taking pictures at the restaurant?" I asked.

Laura shook her head. "Not really. I took shots of some of the diners, and I had them sign releases, giving me permission to use their pictures in the brochure."

I perked up at that, although perking up was a relative term in my present condition.

"You mean you have the names of some of the diners?"

Laura nodded.

"You need to turn them over to the police in case one of the customers noticed something suspicious. We need to keep a list of the names, too."

"They're somewhere in that mess in my office, but I haven't —" She stopped in midsentence. "Come to think of it, there was one guy at the restaurant who went ballistic because he thought he and the woman he was with might have been in one of the shots."

"Were they?"

"I don't think so, but I made a note to myself not to use that photo if they were. I took another shot just in case I accidentally had them in the background."

"So was there anything else that happened?"

"Well, there were two people beyond an archway at the front of the dining room when I was taking a time exposure before the restaurant opened. I yelled at them, and they got out of the way."

"That doesn't sound suspicious."

Laura shuddered. "But what if they were afraid I'd caught them on film?"

"Did you?"

"I don't know. I'll have to wait until I see the slides."

"What did they look like? Were they men or women?"

"I didn't pay that much attention, but I'm sure they were men. I was at the other end of the dining room, and all I knew was that they were about to ruin my shot."

I gave her time to think about any other strange things that might have happened that night. Instead she got up from the overstuffed chair, using its arms as leverage to get to her feet.

"What are you doing?" I hoped she wasn't planning to start another search for the photo releases in the piles of debris in her office. She couldn't get down on the floor to sort through things, and I wasn't about to bend down right then. I was quite certain my head would explode if I did.

Laura gained control of her crutches and started toward the kitchen. "I'm going to call Officer Bradley to see if he can find out if the woman who was killed was wearing my coat."

I nodded my head. Even that movement cost me. "Good. That's the first thing we need to know. Then I'll go to the lab and get the film in the morning so we can check it out."

Laura stopped and balanced on her good foot like a long-legged crane. "And don't forget, we need to check out the lining of the red coat."

We, of course, meant me, and I needed to get some rest, what with all the jobs I had lined up for morning. There was still one task I had to do tonight, however.

"Do you know what happened to my cell phone?" I asked.

Laura had started for the kitchen counter. She stopped at the dining room table and glanced around. "You must have dropped it when you fainted, but I don't see it."

I didn't feel like looking for it tonight, so I waited while Laura left a message for Officer Bradley, then forced myself up to use her phone. "I need to call Mom and stop her from coming to Denver," I explained.

Laura gave me a pleading look. "I wouldn't blame you if you told her and Herb about me, but I really wish you wouldn't."

My irritation returned. Oh, sure, Laura could blab to them about me, but now I was supposed to be the good guy. Well, we would see about that.

I called my mother, and I'm sure I would have been tempted to rat on Laura if anyone had answered the phone in Phoenix. However, it seemed like a petty thing to do on the answering machine. I tried Mom's number several times, and the machine kept picking up.

When the machine came on for the fourth time, I tried yelling into the phone to force Mom to answer it. Of course, she always wore earplugs when she slept, but surely Herb would answer if she didn't. "Mom, this is Mandy. Please pick up. I need to talk to you." I paused for a few seconds. "Mom, I'm waiting. Herb, are you there? Answer the phone, will you?" I finally gave up. "Look, Mom, I'm okay. It was just a scratch. No need for you to come up here. Call me as soon as you get this message so I can explain." I cut off the connection and started back to the living room.

Laura had already returned to the over-stuffed chair. "Why don't you call your cell phone number?" she asked. "When it starts ringing, we can track it down."

"That won't work. I turned off the ringer as soon I got through talking to Herb." I sat down on the sofa again. "By the way, did you happen to tell him that I was injured during a break-in here in your apartment?"

Laura bit her lower lip and stared down

at the cast on her leg. "Well, no. I guess I implied that you slipped out on the street. I started babbling on about how bad the weather was and that the sidewalks were like ice rinks."

I had thought as much. I gritted my teeth, but I probably would have thrown a temper tantrum right then if I'd had the stamina. As it was, I didn't even have the energy to flounce as I lowered myself into a prone position on the sofa. "If you don't mind, I'm going to sack out here for what's left of the night. I don't think your intruder will risk coming back right now. You might as well go to bed."

Laura shook her head. "No way. I'm going to stay right here and check on you every two hours in case you have a concussion. That's what they did with me in the hospital. It's the least I can do."

Ha. The least she could have done was to have been mum with Mom.

I gritted my teeth some more. "Suit yourself." I grabbed an afghan from the back of the sofa, pulled it over me, and shut my eyes.

Unfortunately, Laura was true to her word. Every couple of hours, she struggled over to the sofa and awakened me, checking to see if my pupils were dilated.

I felt a little guilty about all the work she was going to, but she's the one who didn't think she needed any help from Uncle Herb. At one point, she even brought me some pain pills for my still-throbbing head.

"Thanks, Mom," I said, repeating what she'd said to me as I was being carted away to the hospital. Somehow it made me feel a little better, headache and all, even though I knew for a fact that my mother wouldn't actually wait on me if she came to Denver. She'd stay in a hotel and create chaos from afar.

I made it through the night without any noticeable increase in the dimension of my pupils, which isn't to say that I didn't feel like hell the next morning. I'm sure Laura didn't feel too great, either.

All the same, she insisted that I have some breakfast on the theory that it would make me feel better. The idea made my stomach queasy, but I finally agreed to eat some dry toast.

While we were waiting for it to pop up from the toaster, I called Mack and told him I'd be late getting to the cleaners. It was already eight o'clock, but fortunately, it was his week to open up. Then I asked Laura how to get to the photo lab where she'd left her film.

"Why don't I go with you?" Laura suggested. "The lab doesn't open until ten o'clock, so maybe we can take a look at the coat first. I still think that has to be the reason for everything that's happened."

The last thing I needed was for Laura to go with me and break her other leg on the icy streets. "No, you stay here and wait for the policeman to call. If he doesn't, then call and talk to someone else."

She agreed reluctantly. "And I hate to ask you this, but could you drop by my studio on the way back from the lab? I dropped off a notebook there, and it has the names of the people in the photographs — just in case I can't find the releases here in my office."

She wrote down the addresses for both the lab and her studio and handed them to me along with my cell phone and the keys she'd given me the day before. "The police officer must have put your phone on a dining room chair. The keys were on the floor." She pointed out the key to the studio and explained where she'd left the notebook.

"I had a receipt for the film," she continued, "but with that mess in my office, there's no hope of finding it. It was paper-clipped to the photo releases, and it's not on my desk where I left it, so I'll write a note to Wally Sadler, the owner, asking him to give you the film. They're color slides, by the way, and you don't need to pay for them. I have an account there."

While she composed the note, I collected my coat, now stained and smelling of hot and sour soup and soy sauce. If ever a garment needed to be dry-cleaned, this was it.

I took the note and told her to dead-bolt the door behind me. I decided not to mention the uneasy feeling I had about the receipt. So it had been on her desk in plain sight, huh? No doubt with the name of the photo lab prominently displayed.

With an hour and a half to kill before the photo lab opened, I headed for the cleaners. The parking lot behind the plant had been cleared of snow, but the pavement was still icy from the frozen mist that had fallen during the night.

I wished I had a hat or a hood of some sort, not only because it was still cold, maybe ten degrees, but also to cover my patched-up head. That's what I got for rushing off to Laura's in such a hurry last night. A knit hat might even have cushioned the blow when I met up with the corner of her end table.

I looked in the rearview mirror of my car and attempted to fluff up my hair to hide the scalping I'd taken at the hospital. My hair wouldn't fluff, and when I tried to tease it, the way the nurse had suggested, the joke was on me. Every follicle began to hurt. Damn. A bald spot and a bad hair day besides. I finally decided to give up all attempts at pouffing and try to sneak through the plant to my office without anyone noticing me.

Unfortunately, I had to pass the cleaning department, where Mack held forth at the dry-cleaning machines. Best to sidle past him, I decided, always facing toward him until I could slip around the corner and out of sight. In that way, I hoped to avoid a loud eruption of fatherly concern that all the employees would hear. Later, I could call him into my office, shut the door, and tell him what had happened.

"Hi, sorry I'm late. Is everything under control?" I started edging by him in a semicircle, keeping my eyes squarely on his face.

I don't even know why I tried to fool him.

He was on me like static electricity on nylon. "What the hell is going on?"

"What do you mean?"

"You didn't say anything about being in an accident when you called me a while ago."

I swear the man has ESP. "I didn't say anything because I'm fine."

"That's not what your mother said."

Oh, my God. I looked around the plant to see where she was lurking. That's when he saw the bare spot.

"Not hurt, huh? What the devil do you call that?"

When I looked back, he was pointing to my head, but I wasn't even thinking about trying to hide the wound anymore. "Where — where is she?"

"Don't panic. She called just after you did this morning and said she'd be up here as soon as she could."

Another voice came from just behind me. "Who's 'she,' and what in bloody hell happened to your head, boss lady?"

I didn't have to look around to know who was talking. It was Betty, and unfortunately, my efforts at taking her off the streets and giving her a job were only partially successful. She still had a habit of poking into things that were none of her concern.

Mack looked over my shoulder. "Mandy's mother is on her way here to Denver."

"Not if I can help it," I said, heading for my office and the telephone.

"Save yourself the trouble," Mack said. "She isn't home. She said she caught a flight out of Phoenix last night, but the plane couldn't get into DIA, so it was diverted to Dallas."

I felt like going into another Mom-induced swoon. Like mother, like daughter.

Betty let out a snort. "You mean old Cece is goin' to visit you, boss lady. Wooeee."

"Cece" was Betty's name for Mom, and it irritated my mother almost as much as everything else about the former bag lady. The irritation was mutual, and yet they were sisters under the skin. If Mom was the Wicked Witch of the Southwest, then her counterpart in Colorado must surely be Betty. Together they'd created major problems when they'd tried to help me the last time they'd been together.

"Mom's not going to be here long, Betty, so don't start thinking up any harebrained schemes."

"Speaking of hair —"

"Just get back to work."

"But what happened to your head?"

"It was icy outside last night. I fell. Okay?" I was angry at myself for implying, as Laura had the previous night, that the weather had somehow contributed to my accident. Besides that, I began to itch, as I always do when I fib.

"Yeah, sure." Betty guffawed.

"Back to work, Betty."

She turned and stomped off, which didn't mean she wouldn't be skulking and trying to eavesdrop when I explained to Mack what had really happened.

I asked him to join me in the office. I tossed my food-stained coat on the sofa, shut the door as soon he got there, and spoke in hushed tones. I was sure Betty couldn't hear us, no matter how hard she tried.

"The first thing you need to know is that this doesn't have anything to do with me," I said. "I went to Laura's apartment last night to tell her about the article you showed me."

I decided it wouldn't hurt to make him feel partially responsible for my being there. Then I filled him in about opening her door and being attacked by a burglar who had ransacked her place.

"Laura thinks the burglary has something to do with that coat she brought in here," I said. "She's convinced something is hidden away in the lining, and I wondered

80

if you would help me check it out."

Mack just shook his head. "I don't like this. I don't like it at all."

I had already started to the back of the door, where I'd left the mysterious red coat. "What do you mean?"

"You getting involved in something like this."

I stopped. "What about Laura?"

"She needs to move out of that apartment until the police find out what's going on."

"I agree, and that's what I'm going to suggest as soon as I check the coat. Are you going to help me or not?"

Mack sighed. "Of course I am."

As soon as I retrieved the coat, I joined Mack at a mark-in table at the back of the plant where we checked in our route work. I removed the items from the pocket, and we turned the coat inside out since the lining wasn't sewn down at the hem. There was nothing there or anywhere else in or on the coat. Not unless there was a microdot hidden somewhere that couldn't be seen with the naked eye.

I put the coat back on its hanger and replaced the pocket's contents. "I guess I'll just keep the coat here for the time being," I said. "Laura was so sure it was what the burglar was looking for at her apartment."

That's when I realized what was wrong with her theory. If someone had wanted the coat, why didn't he go for Laura when she was on her way to the cleaners to drop it off — not after she left? What's more, if the person had been looking for the coat when he broke into her apartment, wouldn't he have checked the closet in her bedroom first? Instead, he'd been looking for something small, the way he'd ripped through drawers and torn her office upside down. Thank God for that; otherwise, he'd have been sure to find Laura.

I was gratified that my mind had started to function. For a while last night, I'd thought it might never work again.

Of course, by the same token, if the burglar wanted the film, why did he bother to run Laura down? Now that the fog was clearing from my brain, I even had an answer for that. Maybe the person was afraid that she had not only recorded something she was not supposed to see but would realize it when she examined the film. Why not knock her out of commission first? Perhaps that's why he'd been so careless about making noise during the burglary. He'd been sure she was either dead or safely tucked away in the hospital.

"Go home and get some rest before Cecilia hits town. I can handle things here for a while," Mack said.

"That sounds like a good idea." I returned the coat to my office and grabbed a jacket for myself.

Luckily, I hadn't mentioned the film to Mack. If he'd known, he probably would have wanted to go with me to retrieve it.

This way, he nodded his approval when I went out the back door. I still had time to kill before the lab opened, so I stopped at a drugstore to get my prescription for antibiotics filled.

Once that was taken care of, I headed for the lab. It was just off Eighth Avenue near Broadway heading into downtown Denver.

"I'm looking for Wally Sadler," I said as soon as I entered the lab.

"That's me," said a tall, balding man with rimless glasses.

I handed him Laura's note.

"Let's hope it's here," he said. "The police just left. Someone broke into the lab during the night, but damned if I can find anything missing."

I had an uneasy feeling that the missing item could be Laura's color slides.

CHAPTER SIX

I was convinced that Sadler would come back empty-handed when he went to a file cabinet behind the counter. So much for dire predictions.

He returned with an envelope. "Here it is," he said, removing a couple of small boxes from inside. "Want to take a look at the slides?"

I nodded, still dumbfounded that he'd located Laura's order. I'd been so sure that the pictures were what the burglar had been looking for. Sadler took me over to a slanted countertop, almost like a drafting table, and turned on a switch to light its glass surface from underneath.

Carefully, he removed one of the slides by its cardboard frame and laid it on the glass. I couldn't tell much about the photo in its tiny format, but it looked like a shot of a restaurant. Maybe it really was one of Laura's slides. Then again, maybe it wasn't.

I glanced up at Sadler, remembering the receipt that had disappeared from Laura's desk. "When you finish processing an order, do you file it according to the numbers on the envelopes?"

"No, we just file the film under the name if it's a regular customer," Sadler said.

The intruder had to have known Laura's name when he broke into her apartment the previous night. That meant my idea that the lab's burglary had something to do with her film must have been way off base. I placed the slide back in its box, returned the boxes to the envelope, and turned the envelope over. On the front, a clerk had written GOLDEN MOMENTS PHOTOGRAPHY.

"I'm sorry, I think you've given me the wrong order," I said. "This isn't for Laura Donnelly."

The man pointed at the name. "Oh, it's for Laura, all right. That's what she decided to call her photo studio."

Laura had failed to mention the name, and that could explain a lot of things. The intruder here at the lab could have been the person who broke into her apartment, after all. Once he found the receipt and came here, he hadn't found the film because it hadn't been filed under the numbers on the receipt or under her name.

I thanked the owner, tucked the envelope into my purse, and left the lab. When I closed the door, I got this eerie feeling that someone was watching the entrance. I didn't see anyone, so maybe it was just my head injury and a lack of sleep that were making me skittish.

Besides, assuming that the burglar had stolen the receipt, why hadn't he simply shown up here this morning with the slip in hand and given it to Wally? The only reason I could think of was that he didn't want to risk being identified, especially after he'd already broken into the place. Either that or I'd beaten him to the punch. On the other hand, what if the burglar figured the easiest way to get the film was to lie in wait for Laura to show up and claim it?

Luckily, she hadn't tried. I thought I was safe because no one knew my connection to the film — unless I'd been seen leaving Laura's apartment. Still, I looked both ways as I crossed the sidewalk and got into my car.

I made a couple of passes around the block looking for someone hunkered down in another vehicle. Actually, I was looking for a white SUV like the one that had slammed into Laura outside the cleaners. I didn't see one, but I noticed a dark blue pickup on my tail as I headed back on

Speer Boulevard toward Laura's photo studio. I wondered if someone had been watching the photo lab and become suspicious of my drive-bys. If the pickup was following me, I didn't want to lead the driver to Laura's studio, her apartment, or even Dyer's Cleaners.

I made a quick decision and swung north on Downing toward my apartment in Capitol Hill. I decided I had a better chance of losing someone in my own neighborhood, and besides, I needed to feed my cat. Spot wasn't used to my being away overnight.

The blue truck turned north, too, but I managed to put several cars between us by the time I turned left on Thirteenth, a one-way street heading toward downtown. I could still see the truck in the distance, but I took a quick turn onto a side street, circled the block, and whipped into a parking place in the next street over from my apartment. When I finally decided I'd lost the truck, I grabbed my purse with the slides inside and made my way through a neighboring yard to the back door of my building.

In comparison to Laura's fancy high-rise, the Victorian house that I called home looked a little shabby. I lived in a third-floor studio apartment. Unfortunately, the place was a walk-up or I would have invited Laura to spend a few days with me while we tried to figure out why someone was out to get her. That's when I had a brilliant idea that might be an answer to my prayers. When Mom showed up, she would check into a hotel; Laura could stay with her, which would hopefully solve both my problems.

By the time I negotiated the two flights of stairs, I began to wonder if I, too, should find a first-floor place to bunk or go with Mom and Laura to a hotel. My head was pounding as I let myself into my apartment, but I chose to think it was from the thought of hanging out with Mom, not climbing all those steps.

I needed to change clothes and check my answering machine to see if Nat had called. It should be easy enough for him to find out from the coroner's office about the woman who'd died in a car crash the night of Laura's photo shoot. If she'd been wearing Laura's coat, at least it would explain why the owner of the coat Laura had worn home that night had never called the restaurant.

My first priority, however, was to feed Spot, the cat my Uncle Chet had named for the spots we were famous for removing from clothes. I'd inherited the cat, along with the cleaners, when my uncle died, but Spot still didn't appreciate the fact that I'd taken him in.

He greeted me with thinly veiled disdain, tempered only by the fact that he was hungry this morning. He actually brushed against my legs as if he'd missed me. I knew better. What he missed was my twenty-four-hour-a-day cat-catering service. I re-filled his food dishes and gave him water, then checked the answering machine.

Nat hadn't called, but my mother had. Many times. Her messages were like an on-going saga of her movement toward Denver. She'd called from her home in Phoenix, from the Phoenix airport, in the air over Albuquerque, from Dallas, where she'd been diverted for the night, and fi-nally from the Dallas airport this morning, where she was waiting for a flight to Denver. No call that she was airborne again or had landed at DIA. At least not yet.

I gave a sigh of relief as I went to take a shower, being careful to avoid getting my head wet, per the doctor's instructions. It felt good to finally shed the jeans, sweater, and corduroy jacket, still tainted with the smell of the hot and sour soup.

Once I'd put on a fresh uniform for work, I took a Tylenol and the antibiotic, put on my down-filled jacket, and told Spot I'd see him later — God and my mother willing. I looked both ways when I got to my car. No suspicious trucks there or along the route to Laura's studio.

I'd never been to Golden Moments Photography before. It was in a cluster of shops south of Cherry Creek Mall and just off University Avenue, but I had trouble finding the studio. It didn't have a sign above the entryway yet. I finally saw the address. The studio was squeezed in between a neighborhood bar and a candle shop.

Even though I didn't see any suspicious cars on the block, I still took precautions. I parked in the next block west on a residential street and walked back to the studio. I tried to be casual about it, as if I were going someplace else, but when I approached Golden Moments, I sprinted for the front door. Unfortunately, my mad dash didn't accomplish much. I had to spend several minutes outside the studio, jiggling the key in the lock before I could get the door open.

I locked the door behind me and glanced

around the front end of the studio. It wasn't unlike the call office at Dyer's Cleaners. There was a counter where Laura could greet walk-in customers, and there were samples of her work on the walls. I stopped to admire some of the portraits she had taken. She was very good.

One was of an old woman with every wrinkle deeply etched into her face. It was the kind of face I would like to paint, but I wondered if the average customer would demand that the wrinkles be retouched to remove the signs of aging that gave the portrait its character.

Just in case someone had been following me, I didn't turn on the front lights. I went behind the counter and into a hallway that Laura had told me led to her studio and a darkroom that the previous owner had set up years earlier. Laura had been pleased with the darkroom because she wanted to start doing some of her own black-and-white work. She said she was even thinking of offering classes to camera buffs since black-and-white photography was coming back into vogue.

I opened the door to the darkroom. It was like a black hole. Worse yet, it was a flashback to the previous night. I fumbled for a light switch. I couldn't find one. I panicked. It was as if I expected the same person who'd pushed me in Laura's apartment to reach out of the darkness and shove me to the floor again.

Get a grip, I told myself. *No one else is in here. Just find the light switch. Everything will be okay.* It didn't help.

I kept feeling along the wall. I couldn't find the switch. It wasn't until I went behind the door that I finally discovered it. Who had been dumb enough to put a light switch behind a door?

As soon as the light came on, I slammed the door shut and threw the bolt across it. I leaned against the wall and tried to get control of my breathing. *Well, what did you expect, dummy?* I asked myself. *It's a darkroom, after all.* When I calmed down, I looked around the room. A desk with a phone on it, a computer, printer, and scanner, and a filing cabinet were to the right behind the door, and a long counter was along the wall to my left.

There was an enlarger at one end of the counter, two sinks, and then the trays used for developing the prints. Underneath the counter was a shelf with jugs of developing fluids — all those pesky chemicals that give dry cleaners fits when customers get them on their clothes.

I saw the notebook under the counter, next to a big jar marked DEVELOPER. I flipped through it to make sure it held her notes from the Rendezview. I found a reference to the restaurant and a list of names, but I didn't take time to decipher them. Her handwriting left a lot to be desired. I added the notebook to the envelope of slides in my purse, turned off the lights, and left the darkroom. I was still shaking from my experience with déjà vu. Maybe the blue truck had been a figment of my imagination, too.

Before I ventured outside, I looked up and down the street. Nothing suspicious. But it wasn't until I was in my car that I finally calmed down. I wasn't about to tell anyone about the blue truck or my meltdown in the darkroom.

When I reached the entryway of Laura's apartment building, I had her keys ready so I could let myself in the main door and then into her apartment.

"It's Mandy," I yelled at her door to give her warning, but I drew back when I entered the living room.

Oh, my God. I'd stepped into another black hole. It couldn't be happening again. I was about to make a run for it, go for help for my poor beleaguered friend. Only something didn't make sense. An intense beam of light was aimed in my direction as if someone were about to give me the third degree.

"Did you find anything in the coat? Did you get the film?" Laura's voice came from deep inside the room.

"What on earth's going on?" I was afraid I'd be hit over the head by whoever was trying to force her to give up either the coat or the film.

"Just a minute. I'll get the light," Laura said.

I half expected to see her sitting with her back to me, being interrogated by the same man who'd terrorized us the previous night. To my untrained ears, some devilish instrument of torture was making a whirring chainsaw sound in the background.

A table lamp came on, and, instead, Laura sat facing me. She was running a projector, set up on the table beside her. The sound was probably a fan on the machine.

"Geez. Give me a scare, why don't you?" I stomped into the room and saw a large movie screen. It faced her windows, now covered by thick drapes to shut out the light.

"Sorry," Laura said. "I wanted to have

everything ready so we could take a look at the slides as soon as you got here. You got them, didn't you?"

I nodded. She didn't even seem relieved, but apparently she'd had more faith in my getting the slides than I'd had. Of course, she didn't know that Wally Sadler's photo lab had just been burglarized, and I really had to figure out a way to safeguard her against a further attack. She looked so vulnerable sitting there with her broken leg extended out in front of her.

"First, though, tell me about the coat," she said. "Was there anything hidden in the lining? Did your friend find out if the woman who died was wearing my coat?"

I shook my head. "No, there was nothing in the coat, and no, I haven't heard from Nat. What about you? Did Officer Bradley return your call?"

"Not yet, and I decided not to call again until we had a chance to look at the slides."

That sounded like a good idea, and I crossed in front of the screen. My image projected on it as if I were ten feet tall and about to ski down a steep mountainside in some death-defying feat of derring-do.

Laura swept her hand toward the screen. "I was just killing time by checking on some slides I took a few weeks ago when I asked you to go skiing with me. I'm hoping to sell them to a ski magazine."

Taking a quick look, I saw a sheer drop-off from a ski run that was being projected on the screen. I was glad I hadn't gone with Laura. And to think she'd survived a trip like that, only to break her leg leaving the cleaners.

I couldn't avoid seeing my larger-than-life shadow on the screen as well. I really needed to lose weight, or at the very least start wearing less bulky clothes. I shed my jacket, but I didn't chance taking another look at my silhouette sans heavy outerwear. I slipped out of the spotlight and handed her the slides, along with the notebook, before I sat down on the couch.

"I was so sure we'd find something in the coat," Laura said as she pulled a tray off the projector. "It'll just take a minute to load the new slides in another carousel."

I gathered she was referring to the thing I'd called a tray. Frankly, I hadn't seen a slide projector in years. I thought they went out of style when the video camera came along. Never mind that digital cameras were now making her expensive 35-millimeter equipment obsolete.

"How come you still take color slides?" I asked.

"I'm a photographic purist," she said. "Besides, a lot of magazines still require transparencies because they reproduce better."

"I hate to tell you this," I said, "but your friend's photo lab was burglarized last night."

Laura's hands began to shake as she loaded slides in the slots on the carousel. "Oh, God, do you think it had something to do with my pictures?"

Why try to make things sound better than they really were? "Probably," I said.

"But how?"

"The burglar must have grabbed the receipt from the top of your desk, and that told him where the film was."

Laura had stopped working on the slides. "So why didn't he take the film when he got there?"

"I guess it was your lucky day — or maybe a Golden Moment. That's how your friend Wally filed the work, under the name of your studio."

"I can't believe this is happening. The burglar obviously got the photo releases, too." Laura took a few deep breaths and began to assemble the slides again.

I had more bad news for her. "Mom's on her way to Denver as we speak."

She stopped again. "I'm so sorry, Mandy."

I shrugged. "That's okay. She'll take one look at you, forget all about me, and get Herb to come up here to give you a helping hand." At least, I could always hope.

Laura shuddered. "I suppose I deserve that." She completed loading the carousel, slipped it onto the projector, and turned off the lamp. "I thought I'd start with the first roll of film I took."

The slides were overall views of the interior. Laura explained that she'd arrived at the restaurant early to take the shots before the customers started arriving.

The first picture was of the dining area. It had dark woodwork, wine-colored drapes that looked like velvet, matching fabric on the seats of ornately carved chairs, and an Oriental rug in shades of wine and blue on the floor. It reminded me of pictures I'd seen of Old West bordellos.

"I was afraid of that," Laura said. "That photo is too dark. I didn't give the walls enough exposure."

She flipped to the second shot. The walls were brighter now, and I could make out the brocade-type design of the wallpaper. Everything was perfect except for the eerie images at the far end of the room.

The wispy silhouettes of two men could be seen just beyond an archway. One was shorter than the other, and I could see right through them to the light-colored wall beyond as if they were only foggy apparitions.

"They look like ghosts," I said.

"That's the time exposure I was telling you about," Laura said. "The shot would have been great if those two guys hadn't gotten in the way." She shook her head in disgust. "I'd set up my tripod and was using a slow film and a small f-stop on the camera for three minutes. The men must have shown up in the archway at the front of the restaurant just after I opened the shutter to begin the exposure."

"That's spooky," I said.

Laura nodded. "A person can actually walk through a time exposure and not show up at all if he keeps moving all the time. In fact, that's what I was doing, wanding a light on the walls so that the wallpaper would show up."

"So what about the men?"

"They must have been standing in the archway for a few seconds before I noticed them out of the corner of my eye. When I yelled at them, they got out of the way, but they'd apparently been standing there long enough to make an impression on the film. Once they left, the camera recorded the wall behind them. That's why they look transparent."

I tensed. "But they don't know that you didn't get a picture of them."

"No, I suppose not."

I got up and moved to the screen to take a better look at the images. They still looked like fog monsters with no distinguishing characteristics.

"Could you identify them if you saw either one of them again?" I asked.

"No way. I didn't dare stop what I was doing or I'd have shown up in the picture, too. When I got to the archway, they were gone."

I stared at the see-through figures. Up close, I could detect a faint movement, like a puff of fog, as one man handed something to the other one.

I suddenly felt very cold, as if the ghostly images had reached out icy fingers into the room.

What if the men were after Laura because they thought she could identify them, especially if she'd caught a drug deal or some other shady transaction on film?

CHAPTER SEVEN

I stepped back from the tendrils of smoke that seemed to extend into the room as I studied the images on the screen. That's when I noticed something else.

"What's that?" I peered at the picture from a point midway between the screen and the sofa. "There's a chair just in front of where the men are standing. It looks almost like a double image."

Laura nodded. "I see it. I guess I could have hit the chair accidentally when I walked around to the back of the room. Apparently, it was in one position for half the time exposure and in a slightly different position for the other half."

"But look at this." I went back to the screen and pointed to a spot on the seat of the chair. "It looks like a dark clump of something on the chair, maybe someone's scarf, but it isn't there after the chair was moved."

Before Laura had a chance to answer, a buzzer squawked, and I jumped back as if it had come out of the screen.

"It's someone downstairs on the intercom," Laura said.

I calmed down. "Want me to get it?"

Laura switched on the table lamp. "Sure, but I wasn't expecting anyone. If it's for someone else in the building, don't let the person in."

She didn't have to warn me about that. I was sure we were both probably thinking of how easily the intruder had gained access to the building the previous night.

I depressed the button near the door and talked into a speaker on the wall. "Who is it?"

"Laura, it's your Aunt Cecilia."

Oh, damn. My mother. I wasn't ready for her yet. I seriously thought of answering as if I were speaking a foreign language, then cutting off the connection. Instead, I let up on the button and turned to Laura. "What do you want me to do?"

She was huddled down in her chair as if she wanted to hide. "I suppose you have to let her in."

Okay, this could work. When Mom found out about Laura's broken leg, it might take some of the pressure off of me. Besides, I was hoping Laura could go with Mom to a hotel where she'd be safe until we figured out what was going on.

"I'll buzz you in," I said and pushed the button to unlock the front door. Fleetingly I thought that there was still time to escape by the stairs and leave Laura to deal with Mom by herself.

"Amanda, is that you?" Mom's voice crackled over the intercom before I had a chance. "I've been looking all over for —"

Fleeing was no longer an option. She'd ID'd me, and as usual, she'd called me by my given name. I always thought "Amanda" summoned up the idea of someone in ruffles and fluffy clothes — more like my mother than me.

"Grab the door, Mom," I said and turned off the intercom.

Laura shut off the projector and turned on the light by the chair. "What am I going to do now?"

I didn't say what I was thinking — that Laura should have thought of that before she went blabbing to Herb about my head wound.

Within minutes, Mom was upstairs.

"Oh, my poor Amanda," she said when I opened the door for her. "Herb couldn't come because he's playing in a golf tournament, but I'm here to help." She gave me a hug and blew me an air kiss so as not to disturb her carefully applied makeup.

Mom always liked to make an entrance, and today was no exception. She stomped some imaginary snow off her high-heeled boots and pulled up the collar on her politically incorrect full-length mink coat.

"Brrr," she said. "I always forget how cold it is here in Colorado." This despite the fact that she'd been born and bred here and didn't leave until she married Herb twelve years ago.

I'd figured she would show up either in the mink, remnant of an earlier marriage, or in some flimsy and equally inappropriate attire that was suitable only for the warmer weather in Phoenix.

She glanced over at Laura, who had snatched the afghan off the back of the couch and was trying to hide the cast on her broken leg.

"Hello, dear." Mom did a double take. "Oh, you poor child." She rushed over to the couch, flinging off her fur coat to reveal a pink wool suit underneath.

"What on earth happened to you?" she asked. "Did you fall on an icy pavement, too?"

I thought a nod from Laura would have sufficed. After all, she'd insinuated that my accident had happened outside. Hers actually had occurred in the out-of-doors.

Instead Laura collapsed as if a rug had been pulled out from under her crutches. "Oh, Aunt Cecilia," she said. "I'm so sorry I didn't tell Uncle Herb about it last night. I've felt so guilty ever since."

That's something I hadn't counted on — her having a guilty conscience about the whole thing.

Before I knew what was happening, she started to spill the whole story to Mom, everything from the coat mix-up at the restaurant and her hit-and-run accident outside the cleaners to the break-in and the intruder who'd pushed me into the end table the night before.

"Would you like a cup of coffee?" I asked at one point, hoping Laura would glance over at me so I could give her the evil eye. She didn't have to go into every excruciating detail, did she? "How about some lunch?" I was thinking of the Chinese food, the part that hadn't spilled on the floor the night before.

By then, Mom was sitting across from Laura, patting her hand. Laura seemed to be eating up the attention. They both ignored me.

"We were just going over the color slides I took that night at the restaurant," Laura said. "We're trying to figure out what the burglar was looking for, and we think there might be a clue in the photos."

"Let's see them," Mom said. "I'm good at finding clues. Aren't I, Amanda?"

Laura gave me a quizzical look, but I wasn't about to go into Mom's so-called help when my ex-husband's fiancée had been murdered. The only thing she'd accomplished was to send me off on a wild goose chase that had complicated everything.

"Some tea would be nice," Mom said, "and then maybe you could go get us some sandwiches from that deli down the street."

So she had been listening, after all, but going for takeout wasn't what I had in mind.

"I was thinking of heating up some Chinese food from last night."

Mom pursed her lips in a little pout. She never liked leftovers.

"That would be great," Laura said.

When Mom didn't say anything, I started to the kitchen, but that's when she noticed the wound on the back of my head. "Oh, dear, I completely forgot about your injury. Does it hurt?" She didn't give me a chance to answer. "I'll have to find you a good beautician who can figure out a hairstyle that will cover up that awful bald spot on your head."

I ought to have known that Mom's idea of help would be cosmetic in nature. I was grateful to escape to the kitchen, where, leftovers or not, I intended to heat up the kung pao chicken, the Szechuan beef, and the sweet and sour pork in Laura's microwave. Never mind the fact that I was back in the role of waiting on Mom, not the other way round. After all, I had only myself to blame for that. I'd volunteered.

Nonetheless, I slammed the cartons around, but they didn't have the satisfying clang of pots that I could have banged. I wondered if I was jealous that Laura was getting most of the attention from my mother. Oh, God, that couldn't be it. *Just be grateful that Laura is taking the spotlight away from me,* I told myself, *and that Mom is the solution to where to stash Laura for a while.*

Laura had turned off the light in the living room, and I could hear the muffled sound of their voices over the whir of the projector and the microwave.

I took turns heating up the various dishes in the microwave, and while I waited, I rummaged around in a cupboard until I found some tea. Then I put bags in a couple of mugs while I boiled some water. That ought to make Mom happy. She was always upset with me because I didn't have any tea at my apartment.

"Your mother thinks that thing that disappeared from the chair in the time exposure must be a cat," Laura yelled at me over the noise from the projector.

Oh, sure, blame it on a cat. Mom had never liked cats, especially Spot, although she claimed it was because she was allergic. That's why she would never stay with me while she was in town, which was one of the best reasons I could think of for keeping Spot, surly though he was.

I poured the last dregs of the morning coffee from Laura's pot into another mug and downed half of it while I spooned the food onto three plates. When I finished, I carried two plates into the living room, where Mom and Laura were still staring at the double image of the chair.

"Well, if it is a cat, maybe I spooked it when I yelled at the men," Laura said, reaching up to turn on the lamp again. "It must have jumped down with such force that it moved the chair to a slightly different position for the rest of the time exposure."

Mom gave a delicate little shudder. "Oooh, who would want to eat in a restaurant where there was a cat?"

I set her plate in front of her with unnecessary force. "Maybe it's a mouser that keeps the place from being overrun with rodents."

She gave me a dirty look. "Even more reason not to eat there." She paused. "Perhaps someone should go back to the restaurant and see if the owner really has a cat."

Laura and I both shook our heads. I was still doing it as I returned to the kitchen for the tea. When I finally settled down on the couch with my own food, Mom was still expounding on her cat theory. God forbid she should go running off to the restaurant to check it out.

"Look," I said, "if the place does have a cat, what would it matter unless one of the guys got cat hairs on his clothes and we could match them to the cat's DNA?" That settled, I continued, "Why don't we look at the rest of the slides before we turn them over to the police so they can handle it?"

Laura pulled off the carousel and inserted another one. "These next slides are of the diners."

The first photo was of a candlelit table where a balding man and a thin brunette woman with arms entwined were drinking a champagne toast to each other.

"Ohhh, aren't they adorable?" Mom said.

Laura referred to the notebook I'd brought from her studio. "Their name is Cosgrove, and it was their anniversary," Laura said. "I really like the way they only have eyes for each other."

I figured Laura was looking at the slide with a photographer's eye, but I knew Mom was not.

"When are you going to find some young man to take care of you?" she asked. "Are you dating anyone, Laura?"

"Well, no. I haven't found anyone I like, but I really haven't been in Denver long." Oh, good. Laura sounded defensive. She was getting the cross-examination that was usually directed at me, and she quickly moved to another slide. It was of a man and woman who were just being served a lobster dinner.

"Whoops," Laura said. "I *did* get that guy in the background. You know, Mandy, the one I was telling you about who didn't want his picture taken." She flipped to another slide.

"Go back," I said.

She returned to the previous picture. I

stared at the image of the man and his dinner companion who were sitting at a table in the left rear corner of the shot. He had a thin face with a sharp chin and a thick head of carefully coiffed gray hair. The woman beside him had slicked-back black hair and looked as if she'd tried to cover her face with the menu, but it hadn't been in time.

I studied the slide for a moment. "I'm sure I've seen the man before. I just can't place him." I wondered if he was someone I'd met personally, maybe even a customer, or if he was merely a talking head I'd seen on TV.

"The man threatened to sue me if I used his picture," Laura explained to Mom.

"Maybe the guy's name will come to me later," I said. Or drive me crazy in the meantime. I told Laura she could move on to the next pictures.

We were treated to a series of slides of people watching as a server tossed a Caesar salad at the table, set fire to a dish of cherries jubilee, and held a dessert tray for the customers to choose from.

The images made me hungry, and I scarfed down my Chinese takeout. The slides didn't have the same effect on Mom. She picked at her food, obviously unhappy that all I'd had to do was reheat leftovers, not run out to a restaurant to buy something.

Laura flipped to a slide of an attractive blond woman with a pixie haircut. She was by herself at a table with a briefcase beside her.

"Oh, the poor thing," Mom said.

Of course my mother would feel that way. She would never think of eating at a restaurant by herself.

"The woman who dined alone," she said sadly. It was as if she were giving the picture a title, making it the tragic equivalent of Edvard Munch's *Scream*, where a horrified face looks out on all the pain in the world.

"She looks happy to me," I said, thinking of all the times I'd had dinner alone at Tico Taco's, the Mexican restaurant near the cleaners. Sometimes it beat eating with other people.

"Oh, that's a woman who lives here in the building," Laura said. "Her name's Carol Jennings, and I just took the picture so I could make a copy for her. She's the one who turned me on to the job up there, but we hadn't expected to run into each other that night."

"Surely she wasn't planning to eat alone," Mom said. "She must have been waiting for her date."

"Actually, she said she had a business meeting, but the person never showed up," Laura said.

Whoa. That sounded as if it were worth pursuing, but I'd just taken a bite of the kung pao chicken. I had to swallow before I spoke. "So what was the appointment about?"

Laura shrugged. "I don't know. She waited a long time, and just before she left, she said she'd been hoping to make some money that night, but the whole thing had probably been too good to be true."

That sounded suspicious, too, especially because the woman lived in Laura's building. Here I'd been thinking that the burglar had to gain entry to the building through the locked entrance. What if it had been someone already inside? This Carol person, for example.

"You're sure she didn't say anything else?"

"I didn't know it would be important," Laura said. "I was busy taking pictures, and besides, it was none of my business."

Geez, these true artist types had no curiosity at all. They were too focused on their work. I guess that's why I'll never be a successful painter. I let too many other things interfere, the present situation being an example.

Laura moved to the next slide.

"Oh, now, that's nice," Mom said, "but it's too bad the man has a frown on his face."

The woman in the slide, a plump redhead, wore a big smile as she raised what looked like milk in a toast to her companion. He was a sandy-haired man with a square face and a receding hairline, and he was definitely scowling.

"Well, that won't work." Laura didn't even sound upset this time as she ran her finger down the names in her notebook. "The man said his name was Tom Jones, and even though he okayed my taking the picture, he sure doesn't look pleased about it. In fact, he looks as if he's just swallowed a lemon."

And he'd expected Laura to swallow a whole lot more than a lemon, I decided. "Tom Jones" sounded like a phony name to me. He was definitely not the singer or the fictional hero of the novel by the same name.

"But the woman looks so happy, almost glowing," Mom said.

"She does, doesn't she?" Laura said. "And that's odd that you should mention it. She said her name was Joy — Joy Emerson."

I jolted to attention. "Oh, my God," I said. "That was the name of the woman who was killed in the one-car accident I was telling you about."

CHAPTER EIGHT

Laura looked stunned. Mom merely looked confused, and why wouldn't she? Neither Laura nor I had told her about the one-car crash near the restaurant the night of the coat mix-up. I wished I hadn't blurted it out now.

"Oh, God," Laura said. "You mean my photo was the last picture taken of Joy before she died. She even begged me to send her a copy of it because she said she wanted to remember her and Tom's special evening." Laura looked as if she might cry.

"The poor, poor woman," Mom said. "What exactly happened?"

I tried to deflect her curiosity. "We don't really know."

Laura ignored me and proceeded to tell Mom about the woman who had plummeted off the highway the night of her photo shoot.

Even though I would have preferred to question Laura without Mom around, I finally gave in to the inevitable. Mom wasn't about to leave at this point. "Did you get the woman's address?"

"Actually, I gave her mine," Laura said.

I didn't blurt out what I was thinking this time, but if Laura gave out her address, that could explain how a burglar would have known where she lived.

"Do you remember anything else about the woman?"

Laura nodded. "As a matter of fact, I do. I made a note not to use her photo in the brochure because later she started drinking margaritas like they were water. By the end of the evening, she'd had way too much to drink. She and Tom got in some sort of fight, and she went storming out of the restaurant."

If the woman was drunk, that might also explain why she'd grabbed Laura's tan car coat instead of the long red one as she left the restaurant. In fact, that was the only reasonable explanation I could think of for a mix-up between two coats that didn't look anything alike.

Laura was saying the same thing when I tuned back in. "— And maybe she grabbed the first coat on the rack, even though it didn't look anything like hers."

"Or maybe she had a similar coat at home and forgot what she wore that night," Mom added, always the authority

116

on having a large and varied wardrobe.

"Did Tom Jones —" The name sounded phony even as I said it. "Did he try to stop her when she left?"

"No," Laura said. "In fact, that's around the time I was talking to Carol from here in the building about how she'd been stood up that night. Tom was at the next table, and by the time he went after her, Carol had already left."

Apparently, Joy and Tom had come to the restaurant in separate cars. Maybe he'd waited until she took off and then ran her off the road. After the fact, he could have decided that Laura's film could link him to the crime. Tom Jones suddenly went to the top of the charts as my number one suspect, but it still didn't explain about the coat.

"He returned to the table after a few minutes and ordered another drink," Laura continued.

Okay, that meant he probably hadn't followed her, but that didn't change my opinion of him. Maybe he'd been the man paying off someone to kill her in that earlier photo.

I got up. "I'm going to call Nat and see if he found out anything from the coroner."

"Oh, you're still friends with Nat," Mom

said. She knew darned well I was, but she'd always disliked him, even though we'd been friends since junior high.

"I'm absolutely sure now that the woman took my coat," Laura said.

I grabbed my cell phone, went to the kitchen, and started down through Nat's many phone numbers. This time I got lucky on the first try.

"Nat Wilcox here," he said in the business voice he uses only when he's at his desk at the *Tribune* office.

I didn't bother to give my name. "Did you get my message? And did you find out if the woman who died in that accident Friday night was wearing a tan car coat with a lot of pockets?"

"Oh, hi-ho, Mandy," he said, ignoring my questions but slipping easily into the cliché-riddled speech he reserved for friends. "I haven't had time to check. Besides, aren't you going to say 'pretty please,' or at least get down on bended knee?"

"I'm not trying to propose, Nat."

"Ah, come on, Man. I need someone to beg. I've been depressed lately. I haven't had a date since that cheerleader dumped me for a computer nerd."

Sometimes I could understand why

Mom felt the way she did about him, but if he'd just quit falling for beautiful blondes who were taller than his skinny five-foot-eight, he'd be all right.

"Look, this is important," I said.

"How important can it be to find out if a dead woman has a coat that belongs to someone you know? Your friend surely doesn't want it back."

"If you must know, I think maybe the woman was killed and that her death is connected to a break-in at my friend's apartment." I probably shouldn't have said that, but frankly, it was deliberate. I knew that the one way to get some action out of Nat, always the police reporter, was to mention the possibility of a crime.

Sure enough, Nat perked up. "Okay, what's the story, and I'll check it out."

"I'll tell you once you find out about the coat. While you're at it, maybe you could see if they've determined a cause of death."

"Okay, will do, but you gotta give me the whole story. All the facts, ma'am. Is that a deal?"

"Fine." I crossed my fingers just in case I decided to give him information only on a need-to-know basis. "Call me back on my cell phone."

We hung up, and I went back into the living room. Now came the tough part. "While I'm making calls," I said to Mom, "I better get a reservation for you at a hotel."

I held my breath, afraid that Mom might actually suggest staying at my place. That's what she'd done on her last trip; she said she'd found some medicine that might keep her from having an allergic reaction to Spot. Fortunately, I'd talked her out of it.

"That would be nice, dear," Mom said this time.

I gave a sigh of relief. A brief one. I knew Laura was going to have a fit at the other half of my plan. Unless, of course, she didn't have the guts to do it in front of Mom. "While I'm at it, I was wondering if Laura could stay with you until we get to the bottom of this break-in."

Laura glowered at me, but by the time Mom turned to her, she'd managed to wipe the if-looks-could-kill expression off her face.

"Of course, Laura," Mom said, all smiles. "I don't like to stay in those big, impersonal hotels all by myself, and this way Mandy won't have to stay with me."

Laura tried to protest. "Oh, I couldn't

120

impose that way, Aunt Cecilia."

Mom cast her objections aside with a flourish of her hand. "Nonsense, Laura, it'll be fun, and I really think you need to get out of this apartment for a while. The burglar might come back."

Laura didn't offer any further resistance, but she gave me another dirty look as I went back in the kitchen.

I got them a room with two double beds at the Adam's Mark hotel downtown. The reservation clerk said the room would be ready at two o'clock. Since it was only noon, I'd have to stick around for a couple more hours before I escorted them to the hotel. I wanted to make sure they were safely tucked away before I went back to work.

"All done," I said as I came back to the living room. "Check-in time's at two."

Laura didn't say anything, and I got the distinct impression she was pouting.

"Aren't you going to ask Mandy if she'll do it?" Mom asked, looking over at Laura. When Laura still didn't respond, Mom turned back to me. "Laura wondered if you would go upstairs and see if Carol Jennings could come down here and take a look at the slides. We think maybe she overheard what Joy and her boyfriend were arguing about."

"Good idea." I was glad to get out of the apartment now that the atmosphere had turned as icy as the out-of-doors.

Laura finally decided to speak. "It's apartment 710. I'd call her, but I don't know her phone number."

"Why don't you call the police while I'm gone and tell them what we've learned?" I asked.

Laura nodded her head, and I took my cell phone with me and started to leave. However, when I opened the door, a middle-aged man with thinning hair and rimless glasses was standing on the other side of the threshold, ready to knock. We both jumped.

"I'm Harvey Winslow, the manager," the man said. "Is Laura here?"

I stepped aside to let him enter, and Laura made introductions.

Apparently, he was feeling guilty about a burglar getting into the building. "I'm sending someone up to clean your rug this afternoon."

I stayed around only long enough to hear Laura thank him and tell him she'd be staying someplace else for the next few days. When I got on the elevator, I noticed that Winslow had posted a message about the break-in the previous night. It was a warning about letting strangers into the building when residents were going in or out the main door.

No one else was on the elevator, and when I got off on the seventh floor, the hallway was empty, too. Carol's apartment was right across the hall. I knocked on the door, but there was no answer. I tried again, but after three attempts, I was about to give up. Just then, the elevator doors opened and a man got off. I jumped.

"Something I can do for you?" he asked.

How about asking me out on a date? I thought, giving myself a mental slap for sounding as desperate as Nat. The man looked vaguely familiar, but I couldn't place him. I could understand why I couldn't place the man in Laura's slide, but how could I forget someone who looked like this guy? He was drop-dead gorgeous — six feet tall, wavy brown hair, and a 120-watt smile that seemed to light up the hallway.

"I was looking for Carol Jennings," I said. "Do you know when she'll be home, by any chance?"

He shook his head. "Sorry, she's a flight attendant, and she's away a lot."

"Okay, thanks." I'd let the elevator door close as I wallowed in the glow of his smile.

I went over to push the button.

"Are you new here in the building?"

I turned back to him, still trying to figure out where I'd seen him before. "No, why?"

He was looking at me with eyes so blue that I suspected they must be the result of contact lenses. "Didn't I see you coming into the building last night with a bunch of groceries?"

Of course, now I remembered. He'd been the guy who'd held the door for me, but I hadn't noticed how good-looking he was because he'd been bundled up against the cold. Besides, I'd been so busy juggling bags of Chinese takeout that I was surprised I'd noticed him at all.

"Yes, that was me," I said.

"Good thing I came along when I did. You looked so helpless trying to wrestle all those groceries and get into the building at the same time."

He lost points with me by calling me helpless, but he gave me another light-up-your-world smile. "I'm Alex Waring, by the way."

"Mandy Dyer," I said. "I was just bringing dinner to a friend last night."

"So Carol's your friend," he said, but it sounded a lot like a question. "Then you must know her a whole lot better than I do."

I couldn't decide whether to correct him or not, but I suddenly realized he was looking at me suspiciously. Maybe he'd read the sign in the elevator and was wondering if he'd let a burglar into the building the night before. He might even be wondering how I'd gotten in today since Carol wasn't home.

"Actually, I was visiting someone else in the building," I said, "and my friend wanted me to see if I could find Carol."

He was definitely looking skeptical now, probably thinking I'd planned to rip off Carol's apartment as well, and I was getting more nervous by the second. "I guess I'll just write her a note and leave it under the door." Bad idea, of course, because I didn't have a pen or paper, only a cell phone. "Whoops," I said, making a production out of going through the pockets of my uniform. "I don't seem to have any scratch paper, so I guess I'll just wait and check with her later."

"If you want something to write on, I can help you." He motioned for me to follow him to an apartment at the end of the hallway.

I hesitated until I realized he couldn't

have been Laura's burglar; he'd been leaving the building seconds before I surprised the intruder. He had more reason to be suspicious of me than I did of him. Lord, I hoped he wasn't planning to get me to his apartment and call the cops.

He inserted a key, opened the door, and invited me inside. I declined.

He looked puzzled. "All right, then, I'll go to the den and get you some paper. I'll be back in a minute."

From the door, I could see that his living room was twice the size of Laura's. I would have expected it to be decorated with lots of leather sofas and a big-screen TV. Instead, it looked as if it should be in a museum.

The antique chairs had high backs, silk cushions, and spindly legs and looked as if they'd be uncomfortable to sit on. The sofa wasn't much better. I decided he must be either gay or married and had let his wife run amok with the decorating.

I wondered what his den looked like, since he had a whole wall full of books and a rolltop desk that I could see in the living room. Most of the books were huge leather-bound volumes that resembled law books.

As quickly as I'd been attracted to him, I mentally backed off. No matter how handsome he was, I didn't need to get interested in another lawyer. I'd been married to one, Larry the Law Student, as I'd called him, and he'd dropped me as soon as he passed the bar.

I stared at the books, wondering if they really were law books. They were definitely a set, all dark green. If not law books, what? Really weird possibilities flitted through my mind: Maybe the tomes hid porno movies or were bound volumes of his memoirs.

Just then, he came out of the den. "Here you go." He handed me a sheet of stationery and a beautiful fountain pen. No tacky ballpoints for him. He even provided me with a legal pad so I'd have something to write on. Oh, yeah, he had to be a lawyer.

I put my cell phone in my skirt pocket and started to write. The pen flowed smoothly, but I had trouble deciding what to say. "Carol — Please come to Laura Donnelly's apartment —" That wasn't going to work. Laura wasn't going to be there in a couple of hours. Maybe I should tell her to call the hotel, but I didn't know the number. Okay, what about giving her my cell phone number, even though we didn't know each other? As I started to write, the cell phone in my pocket began to ring.

Just my luck. "Excuse me," I said to Alex. "I better answer this."

He nodded. "Of course." He moved back a discreet distance and started going through the mail that was lying on a small table by his door.

I got out the cell phone and said hello.

Nat didn't bother to return the greeting. "What did you say that woman's name was, Mandy?"

I didn't want to have this conversation in front of a person who, God forbid, might be a lawyer. "I already gave it to you when I called yesterday."

"Joy Emerson. Right?"

"Yes, that's it."

"Why did you think she was killed?"

I frowned, but Alex was the only one who could see me. "I can't go into that right now."

"You said you'd tell me if I found out the information."

"Not right now." I gladly would have strangled Nat if he'd been here. "Just tell me what you found out."

"Okay, but first tell me again what your friend's coat looked like — the one you thought the dead woman might accidentally have picked up at the restaurant."

I couldn't stand this. All the questions required more than a yes or no answer. If Alex wasn't suspicious of me before, he probably was now.

"Hold on a minute." I looked over at Alex, who had glanced up but now appeared to be going through his mail again. "I really have to go. I'll finish the note down in my friend's apartment. Thanks for the paper." I took a few steps into the apartment, thrust the legal pad at him, and scooted back out the door, shutting it behind me.

I slipped into the stairwell that was only a few steps away from Alex's apartment and leaned against the door.

"Now, what did you ask, Nat?"

He ignored me. "Who were you talking to?"

"Never mind." By then, I'd remembered Nat's original question. "I already told you my friend's coat was a tan wool car coat with a lot of pockets and a roll of exposed film in one of them."

"Sorry, that's not the coat Joy Emerson was wearing. She had on a full-length black leather coat. The coroner said the autopsy isn't completed yet, but it looks like drunk driving. Her blood alcohol level was over the top."

I couldn't believe what I was hearing. I'd been so sure we were on to something when we saw Joy's picture on Laura's color slide. Now I knew that Joy didn't have Laura's coat, and she probably wasn't the victim of a hit-and-run driver, either.

CHAPTER NINE

"Did you hear me?" Nat asked at my stunned silence.

"Yes, I heard you."

"Okay, it's payback time. What made you think the woman had been killed, and why did you think she had your friend's coat?"

I started down the stairs toward Laura's apartment.

"Are you still there?" Nat asked.

I didn't answer. I was too busy trying to compute what I'd learned.

"Come on, Mandy. It's time to ante up with your part of the bargain."

I finally sat down on the steps just before I reached the sixth floor. I guess there wasn't anything to be gained by keeping the information from him, but out of habit I insisted on our standard agreement. "First, you have to agree that what I say is off the record. Okay?"

"Sure." Nat probably figured it was no big deal to make the promise since he couldn't see any byline material in the information.

Once we'd reached an accord, I laid out the whole story about the coat mix-up at the restaurant, Laura's hit-and-run accident, and the break-ins at her apartment and the photo lab. Nat had never met Laura, but I'd told him about her.

"Apparently someone is after the slides Laura took at the restaurant," I said, "and when we saw the picture she'd taken of a woman named Joy, everything seemed to fall into place. The woman had been drinking, according to Laura, and went storming out of the restaurant after a fight with her boyfriend. I thought maybe the boyfriend hired someone to run her car off the road and is after Laura and her film because they could identify him."

I wondered if Nat had decided this might be newsworthy, after all. He seemed to perk up. "So this is really about the pictures, not the coat."

"Yes, except if she was drunk, we thought it could explain why she might have grabbed the wrong coat on her way out." I had started walking down the steps again and was almost to the fifth-floor landing.

"So what's on the other slides?"

I sat down again and began to describe them, starting with the one of the blurred images of two men it was impossible to identify. "They look like fog monsters," I said.

Just then, I heard a noise somewhere above or below me. I stopped talking, but I couldn't hear anything. The sound had to have been my imagination. Still, I was getting nervous.

After all, the burglar had disappeared into this same stairwell the previous night. Common sense told me he wasn't still here, not unless he'd come back. I held my breath, and this time I thought I heard someone else's breathing. I couldn't see either ahead of or behind me because of the bend in the stairs, but the cement steps and drab gray walls of the stairwell began to press in on me. I had to get out of there.

"What the hell's going on?" Nat asked.

"Just a minute." My voice echoed up and down the hollow shaft. I hadn't noticed it before, but now I realized that anyone in the stairwell would have been able to hear everything I said. It was like an echo chamber.

I pushed into the fifth-floor hallway, carpeted and wallpapered in soft shades of blue in sharp contrast to the starkness of the stairwell. Someone was just entering an apartment at the far end of the hall. I gave a sigh of relief. Maybe that was what I'd heard. Not someone in the stairwell but here in the hall. Only thing was that my own footsteps as I headed toward the elevator were cushioned by the carpeting and didn't make a sound.

"Anyway," I said, whispering now, "there's one slide that shows a man in the background who didn't want his picture taken. He looks familiar, but I can't place him." That gave me an idea. "Maybe you'd recognize him if you could take a look at the picture."

"You'll owe me one." Nat was always eager to add up points so I'd be in his debt, but I could tell he was hooked by now.

"Forget it. I'll figure out who the guy is by myself."

"Hold on. I didn't say no. I haven't taken my lunch hour yet. Where are you? I'll come and take a look."

I gave him Laura's address.

"I'll be there ASAP." Only Nat could make his good-bye sound like an office memo.

If he wanted to talk in initials, I could do it, too. "Okay, but don't forget this is FYI only."

He hung up, and I hit the elevator button to take me down to Laura's apartment. The doors slid open immediately, and I got on and pushed four. It was only one floor down, but I had no desire to take the stairs again.

When I arrived at Laura's place, Mom let me in. I told them what I'd learned about Joy. "She wasn't wearing your coat, and her blood alcohol level was over the legal limit."

"Where'd you get that pen?" Mom asked.

Her question took me by surprise. I looked down at my hand, and sure enough, I still had Alex Waring's pen. I'd forgotten all about it, as well as the note I'd been trying to write when I left his place.

"Carol wasn't home," I said, "and a neighbor loaned me his pen to write her a note." I needed to return it to him right away, or he'd think I was a thief as well as a burglar.

Mom grabbed the pen. "My goodness. This is a Montblanc pen. They're very expensive."

Too bad. Why couldn't he have given me a ballpoint with advertising on it so I wouldn't have needed to get it back to him? I wadded up the unfinished note and threw it in a wastebasket.

Laura was still sitting in the chair by the projector. "I can't believe that Joy didn't have

135

my coat." She ran her hands through her curly blond hair in a gesture of frustration.

"Look, I better take the pen back to its owner," I said. If I could get it away from Mom, that is.

She was looking at it as if she wanted to keep it when the doorbell rang. Nat must have flown to get here this fast — and finagled himself into the building besides.

Mom went over to answer the door. "Well, hello," she said with admiration in her voice. I knew it wasn't Nat.

"Excuse me, I'm Alex Waring, and I'm looking for a Mandy Dyer. She took my pen."

Mom pouffed up her enhanced blond hair as she stepped aside to let him into the room. "That would be my daughter, but she really isn't a kleptomaniac. Just absent-minded."

Thanks, Mom. At least she hadn't worked it into the conversation that I was unattached and looking for a man.

Alex seemed as reluctant to come inside as I'd been at his place, but Mom batted her false eyelashes at him and insisted. "Please, do come in." She introduced herself. "Of course, you know my daughter. She's the owner of Dyer's Cleaners, but I guess you could already tell that by the logo on her uniform." I could see she disapproved. "And this is my niece, Laura Donnelly."

Laura struggled to get up.

"Please don't bother," Alex said. "I was sorry to hear about your break-in last night."

How did he know it was her apartment that had been broken into? For that matter, how had he known where to find me?

He glanced in my direction. "I realized you'd taken my pen just after you left, but you seemed to have vanished into thin air by the time I got out in the hall."

Let him think it was magic. I wasn't about to explain about my quick getaway into the stairwell, and for a moment I wondered if he could have been the one listening at the top of the stairs.

"Luckily," he continued, "the manager knew where I could find you."

I stiffened because the manager had apparently blabbed to him about the break-in, too. The security in this building left a lot to be desired, but I guess it wasn't Alex's fault. "I'm sorry about the pen," I said. "I didn't realize I had it until I got down here, and I was just getting ready to return it." I went over to my mother and pried it out of her hand as she gave Alex an appraising look.

I wasn't sure which she was more interested in, the pen or the man. She was probably sizing him up as a potential husband for either Laura or me.

Alex smiled at me as he took the pen. "I knew it was just an oversight."

Like hell he did. If he had, he wouldn't have called the manager so fast.

He went over to Laura. "I'm sorry about your string of bad luck. The manager said you'd also been in an accident and broken your leg. If there's anything I can do for you, please let me know."

"Thanks, but —" Laura said.

"That's really sweet of you, and I'm sure Laura appreciates the offer," Mom interrupted, apparently deciding that Alex might be a more suitable suitor for Laura than for me, since they lived in the same building. "I'm staying with my niece for a few days, and we might just take you up on that offer."

Oh, dear God, don't tell me that Mom's going to change her mind about going to a hotel. I wanted Laura out of here for a while. I wished I could signal to the middle-aged matchmaker that I'd decided Alex was either gay or married.

Mom was unaware of my rambling thoughts. "If it isn't too much trouble, perhaps I'll ask your wife to get us a few things when she goes to the supermarket sometime."

I wanted to pull out my hair — what hadn't been shaved off at the hospital — at her obvious attempt to find out his marital status.

Alex gave her his 120-watt smile, but I could tell he was on to her. "I'm afraid I'm not married, but I'll be glad to pick up a few things for you when I go shopping."

Mom looked smug. Now, how was she going to find out if he was gay?

Just then the buzzer sounded. I went over and spoke into the intercom.

"Mandy, it's me. Let me in."

I buzzed Nat inside, even though I hadn't gotten around to telling Laura and Mom that he was coming. Laura looked puzzled, but Mom didn't seem to care. She was telling Alex how much she admired his pen.

I moved around them so as not to interrupt their conversation. "It's my friend Nat," I said to Laura. I really wished I could explain why I'd invited him here, but I didn't want to do it in front of Alex.

"I have a whole collection of pens," Alex said. "Maybe you'd like to see them sometime."

Laura's doorbell sounded again before

Mom had a chance to accept the offer, and she turned to answer it.

"Oh, it's you," she said, which pretty well summed up how she felt about Nat.

He didn't look much different than he had when we were in junior high. He was skinny and still wore his hair long because he thought it made him look a little like John Lennon. At the moment, it made him look as if he'd had as bad a hair day as I had. Dark spikes of hair were standing up all over his head where he'd just yanked off his motorcycle helmet, and his round granny glasses were steamed up now that he'd come in out of the cold.

He tried to rub off the condensation with his hand. "Hey, Mom Cecilia," he said. "Is that you? How you been?" He'd always liked to torment her, and I could see her cringe at the thought that he might consider her a mother figure.

He charged on into the room, and I introduced him to Laura and Alex. Obviously, he still couldn't see well. He took off his glasses and cleaned them on the tail of the plaid polyester shirt he was wearing under his black leather jacket. "So where's the picture you wanted me to see?"

"In a minute," I said. "Laura's neighbor was just leaving."

Mom frowned at me for being so blunt about rushing Alex out of the apartment. Well, if Mom could be obvious about finding out his marital status, I could be the same about seeing that he left. I didn't want a stranger here, even one as good-looking as Alex, when we looked at the slides.

"I'm glad to have met all of you," he said as I came over and escorted him to the door.

"Sorry about the pen," I said.

"It was a pleasure to meet you, Alex, and I'm sure we'll be seeing you again," Mom said as I shut the door behind him.

"What happened to you?" Nat asked as I came back into the room. He'd apparently noticed the bare spot on the back of my head once he got his glasses cleaned.

"I'll tell you later." It was the one part of Laura's break-in I hadn't told him about.

By then, Nat had sat down across from Laura on her beige sofa and, now that he could see, was giving her the once-over. "Wow, that's quite a bruise you have on your forehead," he said. "I hope it doesn't —"

I interrupted, explaining that I thought Nat might be able to identify the man who hadn't wanted his picture taken.

"So you're Herb's niece," Nat said.

141

Laura nodded as she waited for us to sit down. Mom flounced off to a seat at Laura's dining room table — as far away from Nat as possible. I joined him on the sofa.

"Okay, you can turn off the lights now," I said.

Nat ignored me. "Mandy's told me a little about you. So you're a photographer, huh?"

What was with him? He was usually the one who was in such a rush.

"I know you're on your lunch hour, so we better get started," I said.

Nat didn't even bother to look at me. "How long have you been a photographer?"

Laura gave him her best smile, and I wondered if she was just being polite or if she was flattered by his interest. "Ever since I was in high school."

"Where was that?"

"In Minnesota."

"I should have known," Nat said. "You look Scandinavian."

Oh, good grief. I suddenly realized what this was all about and why I should never have introduced them. The reason he wasn't his usual impatient self was that he had a thing for tall, leggy blondes, although how he could tell that she was tall and leggy was beyond me. After all, she was sitting down with her broken leg resting on a footstool in front of her.

"Can we get on with it, Nat?" I asked. "I have to get Mom and Laura over to the hotel and then go to work."

Nat remained totally oblivious to anything I had to say. "I'd like to see your portfolio sometime."

"Sure," she said.

I groaned at Nat's obvious come-on, and Mom gave an irritated little sniff from the back of the room. "Yes, we do need to get going, Nathaniel." It was obvious that she'd picked up on Nat's interest in Laura, and she didn't approve.

Laura looked puzzled that we were both in such a rush, especially since Mom and I seldom agreed on anything. She quickly turned off the light and started the projector.

When she came to the slide that showed the man who hadn't wanted his picture taken, Nat got up and moved to the screen, his interest in Laura put on hold for the moment. He peered over his granny glasses at the slide with the man and woman in the background.

"Hot diddledy dog," he said in one of his fractured phrases that drove me crazy.

143

"Well," I said, "are you going to tell us who the man is?"

"Sure, he's Charlie Ambrose, the state senator, and there have been rumors that he's thinking of running for a U.S. Senate seat this fall." He poked a finger at Charlie's female companion, who was trying to hide her face behind a menu. "If that isn't his wife, then he's in a world of hurt, politically speaking, when this gets out."

CHAPTER TEN

"That could be it," Laura said. "If the man in the slide is running for office and running around on his wife besides, he certainly wouldn't want his picture taken."

Nat had come back to the sofa and was casting adoring looks at her. "There's one way I can find out for you. I'll go talk to him."

I jumped into the conversation. "No, Nat, absolutely not. Laura already called the police. Didn't you, Laura?"

"I thought I'd wait until we got to the hotel," Laura said.

Nat was unperturbed by the fact that the police were involved. When he was on the scent of a story, he was like a tenacious Chihuahua. "Yeah, but you know they aren't going to get serious about a simple burglary."

I didn't know anything of the kind. "What about two burglaries and a hit-and-run accident?"

Nat shrugged, a concession that I might have a point. "It still wouldn't hurt to check the morgue —" He looked over at Laura. "That's what we call the newspaper library, even though everything's on computer now. No more pulling clips."

Well, that's what Nat called it. He still lived in the past where reporters wore trench coats and stuck press passes in their hats. He probably would have adopted a similar outfit, except it didn't fit his other image as a macho motorcycle man.

"Maybe I can find a picture of him and his wife in our files at work," he continued. "If the senator's wife doesn't look like the woman in the photo, then we can confront him about it."

I got up from the sofa. "I think you're forgetting one thing, Nat. You agreed that this whole conversation would be off the record."

He didn't even glance my way. "I'm not doing it for the story. I'm doing it to help Laura."

Oh, yuck.

Laura gave him another smile as Mom announced from the back of the room, "If we're going to go to the hotel, we better get started —" She paused. "Although maybe we should just stay here."

I was sure she was thinking of the proximity to the handsome Alex if they stayed in the apartment.

146

"I vote to stay here," Laura said.

I stomped my foot, which is probably what I should have done with Nat. "No, you need to go someplace else for a few days."

Mom must have realized that staying would mean sleeping on Laura's sofa. "You're probably right, Amanda."

Laura's smile faded, but I broke out in a grin. How often had Mom ever said I was right?

"What about the other slides?" Nat asked. "Let's take a look at them."

Maybe it was just to delay the inevitable trip to the hotel, but Laura kept the lights off and flipped through the rest of the slides as she explained what they were. Nat seemed to hang on her every word, but I didn't like the fact that he was taking notes.

"Hmmm, I wonder who that Tom Jones guy really is," he said when Laura got to the slide of Joy and her date. "Want me to see if I can track him down, too, Laura?"

"That would be great," she said.

I never should have brought Nat in on this. His everlasting quest for the big scoop, combined with his obvious infatuation with Laura, could have disastrous consequences. Not only did he make a real pest of himself when he was "in love," but once he was on the trail of a story, he tended to forget all the etiquette of dating, such as sticking around to pick up the tab for dinner and giving his companion a ride home. Later he would wonder why the woman said she never wanted to see him again in her lifetime.

"I'll get right on it," he said, "and I'll call you tonight."

Mom had listened to enough. She got up from the dining room table and drew open the curtains at the big window behind her. "I'll help you pack, Laura."

Laura shut off the projector and started to struggle to her feet. Nat jumped up like a jack-in-the-box to help her.

"Thanks," she said as she balanced on one long, slender leg while he handed her the crutches.

Nat's gaze moved from her legs up to her eyes, a couple of inches above his own. "Where you gonna be staying?"

"The Adam's Mark," Laura said, although I could see Mom shaking her head in the background. Nope, Nat's puppy-dog adoration definitely wasn't lost on her.

"Better yet," Nat said. "I'll stop by tonight and tell you what I find out." He started to leave, albeit a bit reluctantly, and

I followed him into the hallway.

"You are not to go see Senator Ambrose," I whispered. "Do you understand?"

He nodded. As if that would dissuade him when he was in pursuit of a story. "I bet that Laura's a real looker when she isn't all black and blue," he whispered back. "She may be just the woman to help me get over the cheerleader. Why didn't you introduce me to her a long time ago?"

He'd answered his own question, and when things didn't work out between him and Laura, I'd be in a really awkward position. Up until now, all his failed romances had been with women I didn't know.

When I came back into the room, Mom still seemed willing to help Laura pack. I wrote out the note to Carol that I'd been trying to write earlier. This time I used a pen and piece of paper from my purse. I listed Laura's home number and all of my numbers, including my cell phone, and asked her to call us as soon as possible. I didn't know the hotel number, but it was probably just as well to keep Laura's whereabouts secret for now.

"I'm going to go leave a note for your friend Carol to call us when she comes home," I said.

"Do you think we still need to talk to her?" Laura asked.

I nodded. "Absolutely. She was at the restaurant alone. She might have had a chance to observe something that you were too busy to notice."

I left and took the elevator up to the seventh floor. When the door slid open, I was surprised to see Alex at Carol's door. He seemed even more startled to see me, and he slipped something into his jacket pocket.

"You must be wondering what I'm doing here," he said.

Well, yes, I was, but I didn't admit it.

"I thought I heard someone in Carol's apartment when I came down to your friend's place," he said, "and I was going to tell her that Laura wanted to see her."

I wondered why he hadn't mentioned this earlier.

"Unfortunately," he said, "it sounded as if someone was having an argument, so I wanted to wait until things calmed down. I'm afraid she and her boyfriend have a bad habit of fighting all the time."

That was interesting. "So is anyone home now?"

"There doesn't seem to be." He stepped back from the door. "I was going to write her a note." He extracted his recently re-claimed pen from his pocket and pointed it at the piece of paper in my hand. "But I see you've already written one."

I wasn't about to take his word for it that no one was home. I moved over to the door and knocked. I banged on the door and even leaned my ear against it to see if I could hear any noise inside. Nothing. If Carol and her boyfriend had been there, they were gone now. I settled for slipping my note under the door.

"Sorry they got away," Alex said as he turned to head down the hallway to his apartment.

And what about him? He'd seemed almost guilty about something. Could he be Carol's combative boyfriend, even though he'd said he scarcely knew her, and could they have been the ones listening at the door to the stairs? I couldn't help but remember how Laura had said Carol was hoping to make a lot of money when she met someone at the restaurant. That meant she had either information or merchandise to sell. She was a flight attendant. What if she'd brought illegal drugs into the country?

What if the person she'd been waiting for was one of the two blurred images in that time exposure at the restaurant? The man wouldn't have wanted to show up once he knew Laura was taking photographs that night.

I realized I was going off on a flight of fancy, but why not? Nothing else made sense. When I got back to Laura's place, she and Mom were still packing.

"How well do you know Carol Jennings?" I asked as I stood in the bedroom door and watched them.

Laura glanced over at me from where she was seated on the bed, giving Mom instructions on what she wanted to take. "Not very well at all. We met one day down in the exercise room, and when I told her I was a photographer, she mentioned the possibility of a job taking photos for a brochure at the restaurant. It had just been remodeled."

"So she must have known the owner," I said, wondering what the owner knew about her. Maybe I should put that on my to-do list if and when I found out Carol had anything to do with what had been happening.

"Did you ever meet her boyfriend?" I continued.

"No, why?"

I shrugged. "I was just curious. Alex said they argued a lot."

When I couldn't think of anything else to ask, I suggested that I gather up the slides in the living room and put them in the boxes so Laura could turn them over to the police. By the time I'd finished, Mom and Laura were ready to leave.

Although the side streets were still icy, the main roads had gotten better, thanks to all the traffic. I drove my Hyundai, and Mom followed me in her big rented Buick to the hotel's underground parking garage. Once there, I found a cart to haul their luggage up to the registration counter. Laura had insisted on bringing her cameras with her, and Mom had enough suitcases for a six-month stay, which made me uneasy.

As soon as I found out their room number and turned them over to a bellhop, I reminded Laura to call the police about the slides and left.

It was after three o'clock when I got back to work. Mack was just unloading one of the cleaning machines.

"So did Cecilia find you?" he asked.

Before I could answer, Betty ran up to join us. "Wooee," she said. "That mom of yours is a real corker, ain't she, boss lady?"

I hated it when I agreed with Betty.

"She came in here this mornin' lookin'

like a big old brown bear."

When she'd met my mother the previous summer, Betty had said Mom's floral-patterned chiffon dress looked like a garden with too much fertilizer on it. I wasn't sure which remark was more unflattering.

"She was all gussied up in a mangy old fur coat," Betty continued, "that looked like she was about to go into hibernation for the winter. You oughta seen her."

"I already did, Betty, and I thought she looked very nice." I had to defend my mother, after all.

The ex-bag lady chuckled. "You'da thought she didn't even remember me, the way she got all bent out of shape when I asked if she'd done any more jail time lately."

I could see why Mom had been offended. She probably didn't want to be reminded of her last outing with Betty any more than I did. In an effort to dig up some clues in the death of my ex-husband's fiancée, Mom had wound up getting arrested. That was one of the many reasons why I didn't want her help now or in the foreseeable future.

Mack didn't say anything, but I was sure he was trying to suppress a chuckle as he kept unloading clothes.

"Tell her we oughta get together while she's here and *do lunch*." With that, Betty gave a guffaw and left.

"I have to go up front for a minute," I said to Mack, "but will you stop by my office before you leave?"

I headed down the main aisle through the pressing equipment and lines of clothes to the call office, where Theresa gave me my messages. I glanced through them. Despite all my inquiries to other dry cleaners, no one had called back about the red coat. The only messages were from people with cleaning problems and a note from Ann Marie, who works the counter, that said a customer named Owen Jeffries had come in to complain that we'd lost his "lucky shirt." It was white, no less, like ninety-nine percent of the items that went through our shirt laundry, so this was going to be fun.

I checked the computer. Jeffries had wanted his shirts returned on hangers with the rest of his cleaning.

"I'll be back at four-thirty to help you here at the counter," I said to Theresa.

En route to my office, I checked the orphan-garment rail in case the lucky shirt might have lost its ticket. I also checked the processed shirts waiting to be bagged. No lucky shirt.

I asked Angelina, who assembles the orders for pickup, if she'd start a search of the conveyor in case the shirt had accidentally been placed in another customer's order, then continued back to where Betty was getting ready to go home. I motioned for Toni, who runs our shirt press, to join us. "I was wondering if maybe you have a shirt back here that you've set aside to be rewashed," I said. They both shrugged, so I gave them the information about the shirt and told them to check around the laundry department anyway.

"How you gonna tell one white shirt from another one?" Betty asked.

"Yeah, it's like looking for a needle in a haystack," Toni said.

Betty snorted. "More like looking for a needle in a box of needles, if you ask me. I figure I could find a needle in a haystack if I looked long enough." She probably could, since she'd dug through trash looking for God knows what in her former life as a bag lady.

"Okay, thanks," I said and returned to my office.

I closed the door and took the items out of the pocket of the red coat. I was still thinking about Carol, who'd hoped to make a lot of money that night in the restaurant.

What if the coat had belonged to her and those pills in the aspirin bottle were a sample of some new and illegal designer drug she was peddling?

Once I removed the cap, I grabbed a tissue from the top of my desk and poured a few of the pills on it. Damn. They really were aspirin. It said so on each tablet. I poured out the whole bottle and started going through the pills one by one. They were all the same.

When I was almost through, someone knocked on my door. "Just a minute," I yelled as I tried to scoop the pills back into the bottle.

"It's just me."

Fortunately, I recognized Mack's voice. "Come on in."

He opened the door and gave me a curious look. "What the heck are you doing?"

"Checking the pills in this bottle of aspirin in case they might be illegal drugs or something."

"And are they?"

"No, they're just aspirin." So he wouldn't think I was nuts, I explained about the color slides I'd picked up that morning and the picture of Carol Jennings, the woman who'd dined alone. I concluded with my theory, now somewhat weakened, that she might have been at the restaurant to make a drug deal of some kind.

"What was in the other pictures?" Mack asked.

I told him about the rest of the slides and how Nat had identified the man who didn't want his photograph taken as a well-known local politician, Charlie Ambrose.

Mack shook his head. "I don't like this. I don't like this at all. It reminds me of *Rear Window.*"

"What?" I got up and returned the envelope, the matches, and the bottle of aspirin to the pocket of the red coat. "Why does everything have to remind you of a movie?"

Just because Mack belonged to an amateur theatrical group and was an avid movie buff was no excuse.

"You remember the old Alfred Hitchcock film, don't you?" he asked, ignoring my complaint. "Jimmy Stewart had a broken leg just like Laura does, and he had nothing better to do than stare out his window all day. He began to suspect that a neighbor across the courtyard had killed his wife, and before long he had poor Grace Kelly sneaking into the man's apartment to get the goods on the husband."

"So?" I said.

"That sounds just like what Laura is doing to you, having you run all over town to pick up the color slides."

"It was my idea."

There was no stopping Mack when he got off on his protective-parent kick. "Sure it was, and pretty soon you'll be off checking all the alibis of the people in those pictures."

"No, I won't. Laura is staying at a hotel with Mom, and she's going to turn the slides over to the police."

"Good. Go home and get some sleep and stay out of trouble." Mack put the emphasis on the last part of the sentence. "I'll see you tomorrow."

I returned a few of the phone calls to customers with cleaning problems. By then, it was four-thirty, and I went back to the call office. Theresa and I were kept busy until shortly before seven. When the last customer left, I went around the corner of the counter, locked the door, and turned the sign in the window to CLOSED.

"Have a good night," I said as Theresa left.

I returned behind the counter and started to wheel a laundry cart, filled with bags of drop-off orders, through the door to the mark-in station. Suddenly there was a banging on the door. I finished wheeling the cart into the plant area before I returned to the call office. I was prepared to shake my head and tell a last-minute customer that we were closed for the night. However, if the customer looked particularly desperate, I'd been known to open up again.

In this case, I didn't have to make that decision. Nat's nose was pressed against the door, and he was waving his hands over his head as if he were a lost skier trying to signal a low-flying aircraft about his position.

"What do you want?" I asked with more than a bit of irritation when I went over and unlocked the door.

"I'm glad I caught you, Man." The shortening of my name just added to my aggravation, and I was afraid of where this was going. "I found a photo of Senator Ambrose and his wife in our files. She didn't look anything like the woman in Laura's slide, so I've set up an appointment to go talk to the senator at eight-thirty tonight. Want to go with me to see what he has to say?"

CHAPTER ELEVEN

I opened the door and yanked Nat inside the cleaners. "You louse, I told you not to set up an appointment with the senator," I yelled.

"But I figured out a way to talk to Ambrose without making him suspicious." Nat drew back from me as if I might do him serious bodily harm.

Actually, I'd been thinking of grabbing him by the scruff of his neck and shaking some sense into him. "And just how do you propose to do that?"

He grinned. "Well, for starters, I thought you could come with me so I wouldn't get carried away and say something I shouldn't."

I was so angry I was sure I was trembling. "That doesn't tell me anything."

"Okay, here's the plan. Senator Ambrose has introduced a law to crack down on DUIs. His plan is to up the penalty on bar owners if they knowingly let a customer leave their establishments and get behind the wheel when he's under the influence." Nat looked as if he expected me to praise him for his brilliance. "So I've set up this interview to discuss the idea."

"Just what will that prove?"

"Well, after we've talked awhile, I'll ease into a question about this accident up on the Vista View Road last Saturday night. I'll say I learned the driver had been drinking at a restaurant called the Rendezview up there. Then we can watch and see what his reaction is."

"And if it's a blank stare, what then?"

He shrugged. "I'll play it by ear. See where the conversation goes. That's the skill of a trained journalist, Mandy."

I'd been right about Nat. Once he knew the photo was of a public figure, he couldn't let it alone. Damn. And he was so arrogant about it besides. Did he actually expect Ambrose to break down and confess to all manner of heinous crimes?

"So do you want to go or not?" he asked.

No, I didn't want to go, but yes, I would. The one thing worse than not going was letting Nat go by himself. He might blow the whole thing if I wasn't with him.

"All right, I'll go, but I'm going to give careful consideration to terminating our friendship when this is over," I said.

"I knew you couldn't resist." Nat gave me a satisfied look, not unlike Spot's when the cat manages to sneak out of my apartment and make me go chasing after him.

"But I'm not going on your motorcycle," I said.

"I figured you'd say that, so I went by my place and got my car." He fumbled around in a pocket of his fleece-lined jeans jacket. "While I was there, I picked up a camera so you can make like a photographer." He handed it to me.

It was one of those cheap point-and-shoot cameras. "Don't you think he'll get suspicious of this?"

"Naw, he'll be too interested in getting up on his soapbox and talking about his proposed law. You know how politicians are."

Too bad we couldn't go by the hotel so I could get a real camera from Laura. I rejected the idea as quickly as I thought about it because I wouldn't know how to operate a fancy camera, anyway. With a point-and-shoot, I could always fake it, especially since we were never planning to develop the film.

"You better change clothes so we can get a move on," Nat said.

I looked down at my tan skirt and yellow blouse with the Dyer's Cleaners logo embroidered on the pocket. Nope, it wouldn't do to wear what I had on. The senator might wonder at a dry cleaner who moonlighted as a photographer.

Nat came back with me through the plant and waited outside my office door while I changed into a pair of gray slacks and a blue turtleneck sweater, which fortunately I'd just had cleaned. Since the snow had almost disappeared from the streets and sidewalks around the plant, I decided not to bother wearing boots, but I did grab my blue down-filled jacket as I left.

When I came out of the office, Nat made the comment that I was probably overdressed. That was only in comparison to his jeans, wash-and-wear plaid shirt, the jeans jacket, and high-tops.

I put on my jacket, locked up the cleaners, and followed him outside to his car. Nat's old VW Beetle wasn't a lot more comfortable than riding on the back of his motorcycle, but at least it was warmer. Or so I thought. Nat informed me that the heater wasn't working. I, for one, tried to keep the amenities in my equally old and rusted Hyundai in working order.

Nat drove south on University, merging onto southbound Interstate 25 just before we reached the Denver University campus. When we passed the Park Meadows Mall, he caught C-470, a divided highway that swings around the edges of Denver's suburbs.

The snow and wind that had blown

through Denver Monday night had moved on east and were now creating havoc in the Midwest. All that was left as we headed west on 470 was a bitter cold that gave the landscape a still-life look, as if it were a Currier and Ives print, although I wasn't sure if any of them had been night scenes.

Nat turned south off the highway into a high-density development of condos and town houses and began to drive down a residential street. I assumed we were nearing our destination.

"Aren't we going to be early?" I asked.

Nat shrugged. "I have to make a quick stop on the way."

I felt my anger index rising. "You didn't say anything about doing that."

"We're just about there. It won't take a sec."

"Please tell me this doesn't have anything to do with Laura's film."

"Can't say. It's a surprise."

My irritation had reached the boiling point. "Look, you better tell me what this is about or —" I stopped because what the devil was I going to do? I was a captive in Nat's car, and I had only myself to blame.

Nat slipped into the driveway of a two-story town house that was attached to its neighbor on the north. "Good, someone's home," he said.

"Damn it, you better tell me what's going on or I'm going to screw up your relationship with Laura." There, I'd thought of something I could do.

He doused the lights and turned to me. "Okay, if you must know, I thought we'd pay a surprise visit to Tom Jones."

I couldn't believe what I was hearing. "You mean the guy with Joy Emerson in the restaurant? We didn't even think it was his real name, so how can you be sure?"

"He won some sort of contest for being the top salesman in his insurance company not long ago, and his picture was in the paper. It's him, all right." With that, Nat jumped out of the car and started to the door. It was around the corner from the attached garage and up some steps.

"You can't just barge in on this guy and start asking questions," I said, following him but hoping to dissuade him.

He was already ringing the doorbell. "Sure I can. I'm a reporter."

A man answered the door.

"Are you Tom Jones?" Nat asked.

The other man nodded, and I could tell he was definitely the guy in the picture. He had the same thinning sandy-colored hair and square jawline.

"I'm Nat Wilcox from the *Tribune*, and I'd like to ask you a few questions about Joy Emerson and what happened last Saturday night."

Tom didn't invite us in. Instead he came outside and closed the door behind him. He didn't say anything. He just stood there in jeans and a T-shirt as the cold air whipped around us.

"I understand that you were with her up at the Rendezview restaurant that night," Nat said.

Tom looked from Nat to me as if I might be the photographer whom he'd been foolish enough to let take his picture that evening.

Finally he nodded, but it was such a small movement I could hardly tell. "So what's this all about?" he asked.

"We think she may have been run off the road that night, and we're looking into it."

"No, it couldn't be." Suddenly Tom's body came alive. He started shaking his head so hard that it looked as if it might fall off his shoulders. "She had too much to drink, and she shouldn't have been driving."

"If you knew she was drunk, why didn't you try to stop her or at least go after her?"

All Tom's resources melted away. His shoulders slumped. He dropped his head. It was as if he were suffering a meltdown before our eyes. "I thought she'd come back inside. I waited a while, and I finally went to look for her."

"So you're saying she was gone by then?" Nat asked.

"N-n-no," Tom said. "Her car was still in the parking lot, but just as I got to the porch, she took off. I knew I could never catch her."

"So what did you do?" Nat asked.

"I went back inside and had another drink. Ask anybody who was there."

That was the same thing Laura had said, but I was thinking of the white SUV that had run Laura down and the dark blue truck that might have been following me. I couldn't keep out of the conversation. "Did you see another car take off after her out of the parking lot, by any chance?"

He glanced at me in surprise, and he seemed to regain some of his composure. "Yeah, come to think of it, there was a little yellow-looking sports car that roared out of the lot just behind her."

A yellow car. Not a dark truck or a white SUV. I almost wished I hadn't asked.

Apparently, Nat wished I hadn't, either. He gave me a dirty look as if he were willing me to shut up. I did.

"Why did she get up and rush out of the

restaurant?" Nat asked.

"We had a little tiff. She wanted to go to Las Vegas, and I didn't. That's all."

I had a feeling there was more to the story than that, but Nat's next question surprised me.

"What kind of coat was she wearing when she got there?"

Tom looked as puzzled as I was. "I don't know. We came in separate cars. I was already at the restaurant when she arrived."

Despite my best intentions, I interrupted again. "What kind of car did she drive?"

"A red Toyota. Why?"

"Yellow paint ought to show up on a red car if someone ran her off the road."

Nat frowned at me again. "Is there anything else you can think of?"

Tom shook his head.

"Well, I'd go to the police if I were you, and if you think of anything else about that night, give me a call." Nat handed a business card to Tom and turned to leave.

I followed, and when I looked back, Tom Jones was still standing in the doorway staring off into space.

I waited until we were back in the car. "So what did that accomplish?"

Nat started the engine. "It shook him up. Sometimes you have to rattle a few chains to get things moving."

"And why the question about the coat? You already told me the coroner said she was wearing a black leather coat."

"I'm working on a theory," he said, but he didn't share it with me. Instead, he waited until he pulled out on the street. "Did you notice how he came out on the porch and wouldn't invite us in? He's obviously married."

"We don't know that for sure."

"As long as we're criticizing each other," he said, "why the hell did you have to ask such a leading question?"

"What do you mean?"

"Leading — as in 'Did you see anyone follow her out of the parking lot?' You should have asked him if he saw anything or anyone suspicious in the parking lot. Naturally, he's going to say he saw another car when you prompt him that way."

"Well, excuse me. I'm a dry cleaner, for criminy sakes, not a highly trained re-porter." I cringed at the word "criminy." Now I was using one of Nat's outdated ex-pressions, besides. "But maybe he really did see a yellow car for all we know."

"Oh, yeah, and a yellow submarine, too," Nat said.

CHAPTER TWELVE

"Now that we're through with your little side trip, do you mind telling me where Senator Ambrose lives?" I asked.

"Not far. Up in the foothills out in Jefferson County."

Oh, great, there was sure to be snow as we got into the mountains, and me without any boots.

Nat made his way back to 470 and started west again while I sat and swore at myself for not asking sooner. The farther we went, the more irritated I got. He should have volunteered the information whether I asked or not.

I stared out the side window and pouted. The snow that had been plowed off the pavement was piled along the road and had turned into an ugly brownish-gray mass. My mind was beginning to feel the same way, both from all the confusing facts and from the exhaust that was leaking into the car.

Steam was forming on the windshield, and it began to obscure the view. Nat's view. With his thick granny glasses, he was never that good a night driver under the best of circumstances.

I shivered and gritted my teeth. "Damn it, will you roll down the window?"

"I didn't want you to complain about freezing to death," Nat said.

"Better to freeze than to be asphyxiated or have you run into a tree because you can't see the road."

Nat rolled down the driver's side window as I scooted down into my jacket like a turtle withdrawing into its shell. I'd already retracted into the mental shell that was my brain.

The condensation on the windshield began to clear, but ice dripped from my voice as I finally asked if we were taking any more side trips.

Nat shook his head, and I guess he took my question to mean I was over being mad. "Hey, I'm sorry I blew up about the yellow car," he said. "Actually, it wasn't a bad question, and we need to discuss how we're going to approach the interview with Charlie Ambrose before we get there."

"What's to discuss? You're the one with the plan. I'm just along for the ride."

"And to judge Ambrose's reaction and

take a few candid shots of the senator at leisure," Nat said.

"Yeah, right."

"But if you think of anything that might get him to talk, jump right in."

I didn't even bother to answer.

"Together I'm sure we'll come up with something."

Now it was a "we" thing. But God forbid that I should ask any more leading questions.

He pulled off the divided highway when we got to Morrison and started to follow Bear Creek Road into the foothills. More snow had fallen closer to the mountains, and the pavement still had icy patches on it, unlike the more-traveled C-470.

Nat leaned toward the windshield and squinted at the road ahead. "You're going to have to help me with the signs."

"You mean you don't even know how to get to his house?" I couldn't believe it. I felt like he was asking me to direct us toward our own execution. A state senator must surely have a lot of power, and if he found out what we were up to, he could get Nat fired from his job at the very least. I didn't know what he could do to a dry cleaner, but a lawsuit came to mind.

Nat motioned to the glove compartment.

"There's a flashlight in there and a map with an *X* for where the guy lives. Read the directions to me."

Rather than get lost, I did as directed. Paper-clipped to the map was a slip of paper with directions that the senator must have given to Nat. "Okay, we're looking for Pine Tree Road," I said, a second too late. "I think that was it. You just passed it."

Nat backed up the car and headed off to the right on a gravel road that hadn't been plowed. "You'd think a senator would have enough clout that the county would keep his road open," he grumbled.

"He probably has four-wheel drive and doesn't care," I said, "unlike some people who are foolish enough to come up here in the middle of the night in a car with tires with no tread." We would probably get stuck and freeze to death overnight, thus avoiding a lawsuit for slander.

"When you come to a bunch of mail-boxes, turn right," I continued. "According to the map, his house is at the end of the road."

We eventually found the mailboxes, and Nat managed the turn. The VW bumped and slid its way up the hill until we came to a dead end beside a Jeep Cherokee. At least it wasn't a dark blue truck, a white

174

SUV, or a yellow sports car. Then again, who knew what was inside the two-car garage in front of us?

A huge house loomed above us with its lights blazing out from floor-to-ceiling windows. The structure was a modified but hardly modest A-frame. Behind the triangular structure, the house spread out to either side at the rear of the building.

We'd gone as far as we could go in the car, and we had to walk the rest of the way. Nat, oblivious to the snow, got out and started up the hill. I followed, still mad that he hadn't told me we were going on an Arctic expedition so that I could have changed out of my flimsy shoes. Actually, the house wasn't that far from the Rendezview, which would mean Senator Ambrose wouldn't have had to go very far for his clandestine meeting with the unknown female.

We climbed a set of stairs up to the big double doors. Nat rang the doorbell while I stomped the snow off my shoes.

A man with a thin face and carefully coiffed gray hair opened the door. No disputing the fact that this was the guy in Laura's color slide.

"Nat Wilcox, I presume," the man said. "Come right on in."

Nat introduced me to Ambrose as his photographer, Mandy Macabee. The senator shook my hand with such a firm grip that it gave a whole new meaning to the term "glad-hander."

He escorted us into a living room. It took up the whole A-frame part of the house. The ceiling soared up to the rafters, although there were stairs at the back that led to a balcony that overlooked the room and probably gave access to the bedrooms beyond.

"Won't you have a seat?" He motioned to a sofa and some overstuffed chairs that made a semicircle around a fireplace with several logs blazing in it. "Unfortunately, I'm batching this week, but I can offer you some coffee."

Nat shook his head. I'd have liked something hot to drink after my bone-chilling ride, but I settled for squeezing between a glass-topped coffee table and the sofa to take the closest seat to the fire.

"As I said on the phone," Nat started, "I'm interested in doing an article on your proposed legislation . . ." He went on talking about the bill, and I tuned out as I tried to get warm. "Why don't you take a few pictures, Mandy?"

I jumped at the mention of my name.

Fortunately, I'd remembered to bring the camera, and I dragged it out of my pocket. I wished I'd used the flashlight while we were in the car to figure out how it worked.

"We're interested in getting a few candid shots of you as we talk," Nat said, as if that explained the cheap point-and-shoot.

Luckily, Ambrose ignored me completely as he started to expound on his pet project. I tried to study the camera to see if I could figure out how to take a flash picture. I finally thought to open the lens cover. It made a little whooshing sound, and I could see the word AUTO on it. I assumed that meant automatic, so I looked over at Nat and the senator.

Nat was frowning at me as if to say he wished I'd make some pretense of taking pictures. I could say the same for him and his interview technique since he didn't seem to be taking notes.

The senator droned on, but I took a picture, anyway. The flash went off, and I was pleased with myself. Ambrose jumped and then went on with his pontificating.

I kept taking photos from time to time, but after the first shot he didn't flinch anymore. Not until I heard Nat mention something about the woman who'd been killed Saturday night on a mountain road leading from a restaurant called the Rendezview.

In the viewfinder of the camera, I could see the senator stiffen, but he gave Nat the blank look that I'd predicted back at the cleaners. I took a picture, and he glared at me.

Nat began to explain how the authorities thought the accident was the result of drunk driving, based on the level of alcohol in the woman's system. He said she'd been seen drinking at the Rendezview. Had the senator ever been there?

Through the viewfinder, I could see Ambrose put on a stony-faced mask. He shook his head.

"You've never heard of it?" Nat asked.

"What was the name again?"

"The Rendezview."

"I may have heard of it."

"But you've never been there?"

"I don't remember."

Nat didn't respond. Now was the time for his journalistic skills to kick in. Or how about some creative ad-libbing? Say something, Nat. Anything.

The silence was deafening. My skin prickled as the seconds ticked off. I couldn't stand it, even from behind the protective shield of the point-and-shoot. I started moving the camera around so I wouldn't have to look at Nat or Ambrose. Praying that Nat would ask a follow-up question, I stared down through the viewfinder at the coffee table. The main thing on it was a giant ceramic ashtray with some matchbooks and matchboxes in it. I moved on to a copy of *TV Guide* and did a double take.

Oh, my God. I couldn't believe what I was seeing. I moved in closer, still looking through the viewfinder. One of the boxes of matches had a silhouette of the mountains on it. I'd seen those same matches before — in the pocket of the red coat. They were from the Rendezview.

I moved the camera down from my face and blurted, "You have too been at the Rendezview."

Ambrose looked over at me in surprise, and his mouth tightened.

Before I had a chance to explain about the matches, Nat jumped in. "We know you were at the restaurant Saturday night. We have proof."

Ambrose's face contorted in anger. I retreated behind the camera as he turned to me. "There'll be no more photographs. I want both of you out of here."

Before I could drop the camera, I took another picture accidentally. By then, Nat was on his feet.

"What's the matter?" he asked. "We're just trying to establish if other customers saw the woman before she left that night."

"Out." The senator gestured toward the door as if he were giving a Nazi salute.

Nat started to leave, but I just sat there. Ambrose took a step toward me. "This is about that other photographer up at the restaurant Saturday night, isn't it? Did she sell the pictures to you guys?" He turned toward Nat. "Or was it that woman who was sitting all alone at the next table? Was she one of your flunkies at the paper, sent there to spy on me?"

He had to be referring to Carol, the flight attendant.

"I thought she was acting weird," he continued. "What kind of woman dines alone in a nice restaurant?"

Nat backed up, but Ambrose was in his face. "And I bet you were the scrawny little dark-haired creep outside the window. As soon as she saw you, she got up and made a dash for the exit."

Nat and I did the same thing toward the senator's door.

"It's none of your goddamned business what I was doing there." Ambrose kept yelling as we slipped and slid our way down the hill.

CHAPTER THIRTEEN

I was puffing by the time I got to Nat's car. I'd had to hold myself back so I wouldn't tumble down the steep and icy slope. However, the main reason for my shortness of breath was fear. Ambrose's reaction to what I'd said had scared me badly.

Why had I blurted out that we knew the senator had been at the Rendezview? I must have been out of my mind, and as it had turned out, the worst thing Nat could have done was bring me with him to see the senator. I was the one who was supposed to see that Nat didn't go too far in the interview. What a great help I'd been.

"Let's get out of here," I said after I scrambled into the car. "I'm so sorry for exploding like that."

"What are you talking about, Man?" Nat sounded excited. He put the VW in reverse, and the car skidded around to head downhill. "You were great."

I was stunned at his reaction. "You can't be serious? I only did that because you weren't saying anything. You seemed to have gone into shock."

Nat shrugged as he ground the gears and shifted into first. "Oh, that. I was just giving him the silent treatment. You know, like the cops do when they're trying to get the bad guy to confess. Guilty people can't stand a vacuum in the conversation."

"Well, that must mean I'm guilty of something, because the quiet was driving me up a wall."

Nat shifted gears and put his foot on the accelerator. The VW shot down the hill as if we were on a bobsled run. "So what's the big deal?" He glanced over at me. "Any method that works; that's my philosophy. You went right to the guts of the matter." He squeezed his fist and punched it into the air as if we'd driven a blow to the senator's midsection.

I guess I should have been pleased that Nat was taking this fiasco so lightly, but I felt I needed to clear things up. "I said it because I saw a box of matches from the restaurant on the coffee table, not because of the pictures, but you never gave me a chance to explain."

The car skidded to the right side of the driveway as we reached the gravel road, but it didn't seem to bother Nat a bit. "Who cares? Charlie Ambrose is guilty as hell about something."

"Will you slow down?" I yelled. When Nat regained control of the car, I voiced my biggest fear. "The senator's probably already on the phone with your editor trying to get you fired."

"Au contraire." Nat was absolutely gleeful. "The senator's shaking in his boots right now about what we know and what I'm going to write about him. He's probably already at work on his denial statement."

"A denial of what?"

Nat had scrunched down in the driver's seat, his nose inches from the windshield. "Who knows what he's worried about? But I'm going to find out. Maybe it doesn't have anything to do with the woman who was killed Saturday night, but it could have everything to do with Laura's hit-and-run and the break-in."

Even though Nat was now driving at a reasonable speed, the car slid as he came to the stop sign at Bear Creek Road and made a left turn, then finally pointed itself in the right direction. I vowed not to ride with him again any time soon, either on the back of his motorcycle or in his car.

When I was sufficiently recovered from the trip down the unplowed gravel road, I asked, "And what about the guy the senator noticed outside the window? The description sounded a little like you."

"He must have been a handsome dude, huh?" Nothing could dampen Nat's enthusiasm now that he thought he had the senator in the crosshairs of his carefully aimed pen.

"I think the senator's words were 'a scrawny little dark-haired creep,'" I reminded him.

"Yeah, how about that?"

"I'm assuming the guy wasn't really you."

"Of course not. I'm neither scrawny nor creepy."

Nat was so focused on Senator Ambrose that he wasn't really interested in the guy outside the window, but I couldn't quit thinking about him. I assumed Carol Jennings was the woman who'd dined alone, and if she was, why had the man caused her to jump up and leave? Was the skinny little guy the person she'd been waiting for, maybe her cohort in some shady deal? Had she gone outside to meet him?

"Maybe we should —" I started to say.

"We need to go to the hotel and tell Laura what we found out." Nat's voice overrode mine, and I thought better of my suggestion to have him go with me to try to contact Carol again. In an instant, he had switched over from wearing his reporter's hat to wearing his heart on his sleeve. "I can't stop thinking about her, Man."

"Look, she's not like most of your other girlfriends who spend all their time on their appearance. She doesn't even wear makeup."

"Really," Nat said. "I thought you were the only one like that."

I ignored the crack. "And don't you realize that it could ruin my friendship with at least one of you if it turns out she can't stand you?"

Nat had his head in the clouds about both Laura and the senator. "Never, and besides, I could see it in her eyes. She has the hots for me."

I wasn't willing to go that far. "Even assuming she might like you, she's not the type of woman to put up with your shenanigans." Actually, neither was any of the other women in his long and checkered dating past.

"What shenanigans?" Nat asked.

How could someone be floating on a cloud and have his head buried in the sand at the same time? "Like dumping your dates in the middle of dinner to go chasing off in pursuit of the almighty scoop."

"That's the beauty of it, Man. Laura's a photographer. She can go with me."

There was no talking to Nat when he was like this, so all I said was "Don't call me 'Man.' I hate it."

I did go to the hotel with him because I needed to put in an appearance and I wanted to try to stifle some of his out-of-control ardor for Laura. Besides, maybe if he saw her in a good strong light, he'd notice that I was right about the makeup. Nat tended to go for women who layered the stuff on with a trowel.

Boy, was the trip a mistake. When we got to the hotel room, Mom ushered me through the door with a flourish. "Come in, Amanda." She saw Nat, and her voice lost some of its enthusiasm. "Oh, and you brought Nat. Well, I guess you might as well come in, too. You have to see what I've done to Laura."

Laura sat on a chair near a small table at the back of the room. She was gorgeous now that Mom had applied a pencil to her pale eyebrows and added some shadow and mascara to bring out the blue-green of her eyes. The bruises around her eyes had almost disappeared under Mom's careful hand. The lip gloss, outlined with a pencil around the edges to give Laura's mouth a slightly fuller look, was the perfect shade for her light skin.

Mom stood to Laura's side so we could admire her work while Laura, to her credit, looked downright embarrassed.

"I couldn't stop her, Mandy," Laura said. "I tried, but it didn't do any good."

"Well, we couldn't have you running around with your face all black and blue," Mom said, "especially the next time you see that nice Mr. Waring who seemed so interested in you."

I had a feeling Mom threw that in for Nat's benefit, because as far as I could tell Mom had monopolized the nice Mr. Waring for most of the time he was in Laura's apartment.

I don't think Nat even heard Mom. He seemed dumbstruck by Laura's transformation.

Once again I couldn't stand the silence. "We just stopped by to tell you something we found out," I said. "Nat, tell Laura what it is."

He stood there stupefied. I wanted to kick him or punch him in the ribs so he would come out of his daze.

"Nat."

"Wow," he said, "you're a real knockout."

So much for getting to the point of our visit.

Laura smiled at him. She'd always had a nice smile, and now that Mom had worked her magic, it was downright dazzling.

"Isn't she a work of art?" Mom said.

I could see Laura's face turn red, even under the carefully applied makeup and the light touch of blush on her cheeks.

Mom's zeal knew no bounds. "I do wish you'd let me give you a makeover sometime, Amanda."

"Not now, Mother," I said. "Nat has to take me back to the plant to get my car. So will you get on with it, Nat, and tell Laura what we came here for?"

Nat finally seemed to regain a semblance of consciousness, although his words came out in a slightly higher octave than usual. He laid out the whole story of how he'd discovered that the woman with Senator Ambrose in the photo wasn't his wife and how that had inspired our trip to see the senator. "When Ambrose didn't take the bait at the mention of the Rendezview, we just flat-out told him we knew he'd been there Saturday night."

I was surprised about his use of "we." However, if Nat chose to take even partial credit for what I still thought of as my faux pas, it was fine with me.

He had gone over to Laura and was kneeling beside her chair. For a moment, I thought he might propose. "Anyway," he continued, "the senator had a hissy fit and kicked us out of his house."

Laura gasped.

A hissy fit indeed. I noted that Nat's crush on Laura hadn't improved his slangy way of talking. I, for one, would have called the senator's reaction something a lot scarier.

Mom, suddenly developing a hitherto unknown respect for people in positions of authority, said, "Oh, a state senator surely wouldn't have broken into Laura's apartment." That from a woman who was old enough to remember Watergate and had once broken into a lawyer's office herself.

"I'm going to get to the bottom of this, Laura," Nat said as he grabbed her hand. Oh, surely he wasn't going to kiss it. No. Instead, he said, "I promise," and reluctantly got to his feet.

"The senator said something about seeing a —" I said, but Nat cut me off. I decided he was afraid I would mention that Ambrose had seen "a scrawny little creep" outside the window who looked like Nat.

Give me more credit than that, I thought, as Nat quickly changed the subject. "I also found out there is a *real* Tom Jones who's an insurance guy, and we stopped to see him, too. He says he saw a yellow sports car leaving the parking lot just behind Joy, but he didn't follow them down the hill."

Laura nodded. "That's true. He left for a few minutes and then came back to the table."

"I'm going to keep on this, Laura. I promise." He stopped, then continued as if it were an afterthought. "Hey, maybe we could go out for dinner tomorrow night and I'll bring you up to speed about what I find out." I thought he was going to leave then, but instead he sat down on a chair next to Laura to await her answer.

"That would be fine," Laura said eagerly. It had to be because she was tired of being locked up with Mom, who had immediately turned their overnight stay in the hotel into a let's-make-Laura-over party.

"So how're you holding up?" Nat asked her.

"We need to get going, Nat. You have to take me back to the plant to get my car," I said.

"In a minute." Nat tried to shoo me away with a wave of his hand.

Mom cleared her throat. "I thought maybe tomorrow Laura and I would go back over to her apartment and get some more of her things. I bet that nice Alex Waring would help us get them down to my car."

No wonder Laura thought dinner with Nat would be a reprieve.

"What I want to know," I asked, ignoring the whole Nat-Alex thing, "is if you called the police about the slides."

Laura nodded. "Yes, a police officer came and got them this afternoon."

Nat gave me a dirty look. Undoubtedly, he'd wanted to keep the information about the slides just between the four of us. After all, that's what scoops are all about.

"And just for the record," I continued, "was Carol Jennings the only woman in the restaurant that night who was dining alone?"

Laura considered the question for a moment. "Yes, I'm sure she was. She was sitting at a table right next to the senator."

I finally pried Nat away from Laura so he could take me to fetch my car. He raved the whole way about what a beauty she was. When we got to the cleaners, I jumped out of the VW, glad to be free from his ongoing monologue about her. I'd been afraid Nat would want to have dinner someplace, but fortunately, he didn't. I had other plans.

I jumped into my car and headed over to Laura's apartment building to see if Carol had ever shown up and if she knew anything about the "creep" outside the window. I used Laura's key to get inside the high-rise and rode the elevator to the seventh floor, hoping I wouldn't run into Alex Waring in the hall again.

As soon as I reached Carol's door, I could hear a voice coming from inside. Good, someone was finally home. I rang the bell and waited.

"Just a minute," a female voice yelled.

The door opened a few seconds later. "Carol Jennings?" I asked, but I knew it wasn't. This woman wasn't blond, and she didn't have the pixie haircut of the woman in Laura's photograph.

"No, I'm Sally Babcock, her roommate," the brunette said, closing up a cell phone. "I just got in from Chicago." I wondered if she was a flight attendant like Carol.

"I've been trying to reach her, but she hasn't been home all day," I said.

Her freckled face wrinkled in a frown. "She was on vacation this week, but I don't think she's been here since Saturday."

A cold spike of fear jabbed my spine. "Why do you say that?"

"There was a note slipped under the door from an old boyfriend of hers who said to call him as soon as she got home Saturday night, and there was another note from someone named Mandy."

I stiffened, but I tried not to show my alarm. "That last note was from me."

Sally didn't seem to pick up on my nervousness. She merely looked disgusted. "Geez, I hope she wasn't stupid enough to go off with her ex-boyfriend. He was such a little creep, and she'd kicked him out of here just before I moved in with her."

That word again. "Creep." "Little creep," besides. The same words Senator Ambrose had used about the guy outside the restaurant window.

"It really irritates me that he still has a key to our building," Sally said. "She was supposed to have gotten it back from him."

"Uh — what's his name? Maybe she's staying with him, and I can contact her at his place."

"Lots of luck. His name's Ricky Monroe, but I haven't a clue where he lives. He moved around a lot." She looked back inside the apartment and shook her head. "I bet he was here while I was gone, though, the way she left the place in such a mess."

Either that or Ricky had trashed the place the same way someone — maybe him — had trashed Laura's apartment. After all, if he had a key to the building, he probably had one to the apartment, too.

I decided I needed a whole lot more information, and to get that I'd have to explain my mission. "Do you know Laura Donnelly?"

Sally shook her head.

"Well, Laura's a friend of mine, and she lives downstairs, but right now she has a broken leg, so I'm trying to help her. She ran into Carol at a restaurant called the Rendezview Saturday night, and she wanted to talk to Carol about something that happened there."

"So Carol did keep the appointment," Sally said. "That might explain it."

"Explain what?"

"Oh, she went back east recently to clean out the house of an uncle who'd died. She found a stamp that someone told her might be valuable, and she was going to show it to somebody else that night."

Oh, my God. A stamp. There was a stamp on the envelope in the pocket of the red coat back at the cleaners.

CHAPTER FOURTEEN

I could almost see the stamp. It seemed to get larger, then fade away, as if I were twisting a telephoto lens in my mind. For the life of me, I couldn't make it come into focus enough to see what was on it.

Sally had no way of knowing what I was thinking, although I was sure my eyes had glazed over as I tried to remember what was on the envelope.

"Carol was hoping to sell the stamp Saturday night," Sally said. "Maybe she actually did get some money for it and she's off someplace celebrating."

"Do you know what the stamp looked like?" I asked, trying to sound as if I were making polite conversation.

I guess the question was so polite it seemed totally innocuous to Sally. "Carol could have at least let me know where she was going," she complained, "and she left the place in a mess, besides."

"The stamp?" I asked again.

Sally shrugged. "Oh, it was a stamp of an old airplane. It looked like it was doing a stunt at an air show or something. That's all I remember."

"What do you mean, doing a 'stunt'?"

"It was flying upside down."

I needed to end this conversation and get back to the cleaners to check out the stamp on the envelope. "When Carol gets home, will you be sure to give her my note?"

"Sure," Sally said. "You know, that explains a lot of things. I bet that slimy little creep Ricky was waiting for her when she got home that night, and she's gone somewhere with him."

I was glad the explanation satisfied her. It didn't satisfy me. I was more afraid than ever that something bad had happened to Carol.

"Well, thanks —" I started to leave, but I had another thought. "Does Carol happen to have a picture of Ricky? I think maybe I've seen him around the building."

I was surprised that she didn't question my motives for wanting to see what he looked like. Instead, she went over to a desk, pulled out a photograph, and handed it to me. "I don't know why Carol doesn't get rid of this."

I studied the picture. Ricky Malone was short and wiry looking, but I could see that he had a certain animal magnetism. He had sleepy dark eyes, a curly lock of hair that fell over his forehead, and a permanent pout on his lips.

"No, I guess I haven't seen him after all." I handed the picture back to her. "Do you know where he works, by any chance?"

Sally shook her head. "Wherever it is, it's probably illegal. I think he's had a few run-ins with the law."

This got scarier all the time. "Maybe she has a new boyfriend and she's with him." I was thinking of Alex, who'd been at her door the last time I'd seen him.

"If she does, it's news to me."

I gave up, thanked her for her help, and hurried back to my car. I don't even remember my trip to the cleaners. All I could think about was the stamp. It could be the answer to everything that had happened.

It's a wonder I remembered to turn off the alarm system and reset it when I let myself in the back door of the plant. I hurried to the office, turned on the light, and pulled the envelope out of the pocket of the red coat. I didn't even bother to sit down.

I stared down at the stamp. Damn. No airplane. The stamp was dark, and I had trouble telling what it was. I finally moved over to my desk and turned on a lamp. Still no airplane. It was a commemorative stamp with a farm scene of Ohio on it and the current one-ounce rate. I shoved the envelope in a desk drawer and slammed it shut.

Now what? Maybe I could throw a temper tantrum, although my head was beginning to ache from the bashing I'd taken the previous night. I didn't want to make it worse by stomping and tearing at my hair. No, what I needed to do was talk to someone who would be a voice of reason and help me put my jumbled thoughts in order. I called Mack.

Thank God, I caught him at home. "Have you eaten yet?" I asked.

He was instantly on alert. "What's the matter? It's way past the dinner hour."

I'd lost all track of time. "Oh, I'm sorry. What time is it?"

Mack didn't even bother to answer. I guess he could hear the stress in my voice. "Where are you? I'll meet you at that all-night diner on Colfax."

I tried to backtrack as I glanced at my watch. It was already eleven-thirty. "Never mind. I didn't realize it was so late. I'll pick up something on the way home."

Mack wouldn't hear of it. "I'll be there in twenty minutes."

"Thanks," I said, but he'd already hung up.

He was waiting for me by the time I reached the restaurant. I could see the worry lines in his dark face even before I sat down, and I couldn't help thinking how old he looked. His hair was getting whiter all the time, and I was afraid he'd be retiring soon as plant manager. I didn't know what I'd do without him.

"What the devil's wrong?" he asked.

I wanted to ease his concern, but unfortunately I hadn't thought up a satisfactory story on the drive from the cleaners. "Remember how I told you that Mom was making fun of the woman who dined alone in one of Laura's photographs?" I asked. "Well, frankly, after that, I just couldn't face having dinner by myself."

"That's a crock," Mack said. "Now tell me what's really going on."

The waitress was at our booth before I had a chance to say anything, but it gave me time to realize that I shouldn't have called him in the first place if I wasn't going to level with him. I put in an order for a cheeseburger, French fries, and coffee. Mack said all he wanted was coffee, and the waitress departed.

"Okay, shoot," he said.

I told him about Joy's black leather coat, the visit to Tom Jones, and the ill-fated trip to Senator Ambrose's house. "Nat set up an appointment with the senator on the pretext of questioning him about some proposed legislation."

I saw Mack frown, and I hastened to add, "It wasn't my idea. In fact, I was really irritated when Nat told me about it. He said I'd better go with him to see that he didn't step out of line, but once we got there, I noticed a box of matches from the Rendezview on the coffee table. It was just like the one in the coat, and when the senator denied that he'd ever been to the restaurant, I blurted out that I knew he had."

Mack grimaced, as if he'd known all the time that I would do something rash and irresponsible.

"Before I could explain about the matches, Nat jumped in and said, 'Yeah, we know you were there Saturday night. We've got pictures.' Ambrose jumped up and accused Nat of being the skinny little creep who'd been outside the window that night. He said the woman at the next table must have been a reporter who was spying on him, too, because she got up and left as soon as she saw the man outside."

"I take it the guy wasn't Nat," Mack said.

I shook my head. "But the woman was Laura's neighbor, Carol Jennings." I paused to try to get my thoughts in a more logical order. "So after Nat dropped me off back at the cleaners, I drove over to Laura's apartment building to see if Carol had ever shown up. I'd tried to contact her earlier today, but she wasn't home."

The waitress returned with my burger and our coffees, but I hardly noticed.

"This time her roommate answered the door, and she told me she didn't think Carol had been at the apartment since Saturday night." The same prickly feeling of fear ran through my body that I'd had when I first heard that bit of news. "I have this awful feeling that something has happened to her. Anyway, the roommate said Carol had gone to the restaurant hoping to sell a stamp she'd found among the effects of an uncle who'd just died. However, Laura had talked to her that night, and Carol said the buyer never showed up."

Mack's eyes lit up. "Not the stamp on the envelope?"

No wonder I liked to talk to him. He was always able to see where I was going, even before I got there.

"No, that's the trouble. The stamp was supposed to be of an old airplane, so I rushed back to the cleaners to take a look at the stamp on the envelope. It wasn't an airplane. It was a new stamp with a rural scene of Ohio on it." I finally ran out of breath and stopped talking.

"So now you're back to thinking the burglar was after the roll of film," Mack said.

Actually, I hadn't gotten beyond the disappointment about the stamp.

"It's interesting about the stamp, though," Mack said. "This neighbor of Laura's was trying to sell a stamp, and there was a stamped envelope in the pocket of a coat someone had abandoned at the restaurant, almost as if the person had been trying to hide something."

Maybe Mack wasn't following me as well as I thought. "I told you it wasn't the stamp on the envelope."

"Did the roommate say anything else about the stamp?"

"She said it looked as if it were flying upside down in a maneuver at an air show."

"Upside down, huh?" Mack thought for a moment. "I think I've heard of a stamp that was printed upside down. It's supposed to be quite valuable. Do you think that's what she was referring to?"

"I don't know, but there's something else I haven't told you. The roommate mentioned that Carol's ex-boyfriend is a skinny little creep named Ricky Monroe, and that she hoped Carol hadn't gotten a lot of money for the stamp and gone off someplace to celebrate with the guy."

"But no one showed up to buy the stamp," Mack said, "so presumably she didn't have enough money to go on some expensive trip."

"Exactly. What's really scary is that the senator used the same exact words to describe the guy who appeared outside the window at the restaurant."

"So you're thinking they're the same guy, but if the creep at the restaurant was her ex-boyfriend, he probably wasn't there to buy the stamp."

"Right. From what Carol's roommate said, the ex-boyfriend may have a police record."

"And what was his name again?"

"Ricky Monroe. The roommate even showed me a picture of him, but unfortunately, she had no idea where he lives or what kind of work he does."

My cheeseburger had grown cold while we talked. As I took another bite, I realized that the next logical step was for me to locate Monroe. I needed to call Nat and see if he could track down the ex-boyfriend through his police contacts.

It had helped to talk to Mack. All I needed to do now was get on the phone with the ace reporter and troublemaker. I set about eating my cheeseburger in earnest so that I could get home as fast as possible, but when I glanced up, Mack was giving me a suspicious look. It isn't always a good thing that he can read my mind.

"I don't want you to get any bright ideas about trying to track down this Monroe character and talk to him," Mack said. "Do you hear me?"

My mouth was full, so I nodded, because I had indeed heard him. I decided the nod in no way indicated that I was agreeing to follow his advice. The best thing to do now was change the subject.

I gulped down the last of my burger with a drink of coffee. "I do have one idea that should meet with your approval. Do you remember Cedric Filmore?"

"How could I forget?" He obviously knew Filmore from the years when Mack had helped out at the counter of my uncle's old cleaners in downtown Denver.

"Well, he still comes into the cleaners faithfully once a month, and he used to own a stamp shop, didn't he? Maybe I should talk to him."

"That's a great idea."

To be honest, I didn't even like talking to Filmore about his clothes. He was never satisfied with the amount of starch in his shirt collars or the creases in the pants of his three-piece suits. In fact, if ever a person could be described by a single word, it was Cedric Filmore, and the word was "curmudgeon."

"He *is* a bit of a grouch, though," I said in what was definitely an understatement. He was also as old and gnarled as a bristlecone pine.

"More like a cantankerous old coot," Mack said, "but I bet he knows the stamp business inside out."

"And hopefully upside down," I said.

Mack grimaced, but he remained enthusiastic. I was sure this was partly because he thought it would get my mind off Ricky Monroe. That's exactly what I'd intended, but there was no way it was going to keep me from looking for the skinny little creep.

I polished off the last of the French fries and paid the bill, including Mack's coffee. It was the least I could do after he'd met me in the middle of the night.

We said our good-byes at my Hyundai, but I guess I hadn't fooled Mack with my talk about the stamp dealer. "And I don't want to hear that you're trying to find Ricky Monroe. Give that information to the police," he said.

"Give what information to the police?" I asked. I didn't really have anything except vague descriptions of a stamp I couldn't find and a creepy little guy who might or might not have anything to do with the burglaries and the hit-and-run.

"Just don't go trying to talk to this Monroe character. Agreed?"

Again I nodded.

I was still itching from the fib when I called Nat from my apartment. Surely he could find out something about Monroe that might be worth taking to the cops. If the guy was into illegal activities the way Carol's roommate said, he must have a record.

Only trouble was I couldn't reach Nat at home, at work, or on his cell phone. I left a message and fed Spot, who was acting surly about being left without food for the better part of a day. Then I took a couple of Tylenol, as well as the antibiotic the doctor had prescribed, and climbed into bed. I was asleep within minutes.

In the morning, I took a shower, put on a fresh uniform, and even managed to tease my hair over the wound so that it hardly showed. Mom might not be satisfied with the way I looked, considering the stunning makeover she'd wrought on Laura, but I was feeling pretty good about myself when I left for work.

I pulled into the parking lot at eight-thirty, intent on calling Nat again. Surely I could catch him at the *Trib* this time of day.

Mack wasn't at his usual place in the cleaning department, but when I rounded the corner to my office, I saw him in the lunchroom. He waved at me as he took a sip of coffee, and I couldn't help but feel a twinge of guilt for keeping him up so late the previous night.

A few seconds later, he showed up at my door with a cup of coffee and a doughnut for me. He handed them to me and sat down.

"I want to talk to you before you go off half-cocked about this Ricky Monroe character," he said. "I didn't believe you for a minute when you said you wouldn't go looking for him, so I took matters into my own hands."

"What are you talking about? You didn't locate him, did you?"

"No, but I can act as impulsively as you do sometimes. I went home last night and hired that private investigator, Travis Kincaid, to try to find out about him."

"You did what?" I reeled back from

207

Mack's words as if he'd lobbed a grenade in my direction.

Travis was the guy I'd been thinking about on my ambulance ride to the hospital Tuesday night. He worked for Triple-A Investigations — or maybe he was Triple-A Investigations, for all I knew. I'd gone to the agency last October when I'd wanted to find some information about another shady character. How did I know that the investigator would turn out to be someone I'd known from high school? A bully in grade school, at least according to Nat. The bad boy in high school who used to rumble around on his motorcycle and seldom attended classes. Worse yet, the person I'd stood up when he asked me out in my junior year because, frankly, he scared the hell out of me.

It had been bad enough that I didn't know how to back out of hiring Travis when I found myself face-to-face with him at Triple-A. It was even worse that I'd had to call him to rescue me when I was trapped inside a house that Nat and I had unwisely entered without the owner's permission.

The last person in the world I wanted to see right now was Travis Kincaid. This was definitely not the way to start my day.

CHAPTER FIFTEEN

"How could you hire Travis Kincaid?" I practically spat out his name.

Mack was innocence itself. "What do you mean?"

"I told you I didn't like Travis," I said, fumbling through some papers so I wouldn't have to look at him.

"No, you didn't. All you ever said was that he'd been a bully back in grade school."

Okay, so I'd left out a few things, including Travis's outrageous behavior when I'd hired him last fall. He'd actually had the audacity to grab me and kiss me when, to use his words, he was finally "off the clock." He'd infuriated me, but not being one to let another person have the last word — or kiss, for that matter — I grabbed him as he was turning to leave and showed him what a real kiss was like. I'd regretted my impulsiveness ever since.

Mack interrupted my thoughts. "He seemed like a nice enough fellow to me. I thought the two of you hit it off pretty well."

Good grief, I hoped Mack wasn't trying

to play matchmaker. I had a mother for that. "Just because Stan and I broke up doesn't mean I need a man in my life." I was referring to the homicide detective I'd dated for a while.

"How about a friend?"

I really hated this conversation. "I have enough friends," I said, "although I'm not sure how long you'll be one of them." I started to get up, hoping to signal that this exchange was over.

Mack had the nerve to grin. "You sound just like Audrey Hepburn."

I sat down again, surprised to be compared to the forerunner of all the extrathin actresses of today. "What are you talking about?"

"The way she blew off Cary Grant in the movie *Charade*."

I should have known better than to ask. I'd opened the door to one of Mack's endless movie quotes. He had a million of them.

"Cary asked if he could call her sometime, but she told him, 'I already know an awful lot of people, and until one of them dies, I couldn't possibly meet anyone else.' "

"I don't like the part about dying," I said, thinking about Laura's near miss.

"But I don't need any more friends, either, until I boot one of the ones I already have out of my life." I was on the verge of doing just that with Mack. I settled for trying to boot him out of my office. "We need to get to work now, but I really wish you'd consider unhiring Travis."

"No can do. He's already on the job." Mack still wasn't taking the hint to leave. "Come to think of it, that movie, *Charade*, was about stamps. Audrey's husband is killed, and these three other guys are looking for some money he was supposed to have. No one can find it, but it turns out the husband had invested the money in some valuable stamps, and they were hiding in plain sight on an envelope he had in his possession when he died."

"Sorry, Mack, but the stamp on the envelope in the coat is only worth thirty-seven cents."

Mack ignored me. "One of the stamps in *Charade* was supposed to be an early Swedish stamp, one was Hawaiian, and one was from some country in Eastern Europe."

"That's the dumbest thing I've ever heard," I said. "Somebody would have been sure to notice three stamps from different countries on the same envelope."

Mack smiled. "Well, they never had a close-up of the envelope, or else the audience might have noticed it even if the actors didn't. Besides, you didn't pay any attention to what kind of stamp was on the envelope in the coat, either."

"Okay, you have a point."

Mack got up to leave. "I still think you ought to check with Cedric Filmore to see what you can find out about that stamp Laura's friend was supposed to have."

It had only been a diversionary tactic, but now that Travis was on the case, I couldn't very well call Nat to help me find Monroe. Nat couldn't stand Travis and would have a fit if he found out Travis was looking for the guy, too.

Mack left the room, and I headed through the plant to the front counter. As soon as I arrived, Ann Marie turned to me with relief. "Here's the owner now."

The man she was addressing was on the pudgy side, with a ruddy complexion that indicated he either drank too much or had forgotten his sunscreen the last time he went skiing.

"What can I do for you?" I asked.

"I'm Owen Jeffries," he said. "I wanted to see if you ever found my lucky shirt."

Oh, yes, the lucky shirt. "No, I'm sorry.

212

We're still looking." I punched in his name on our computer. "I'll look for it again today, and if I find it, I'll bring it to your office." I noted that he was on our business route to a real estate office in the neighborhood. "Were there any identifying marks on the shirt besides the fact that it was white?"

He motioned to Ann Marie. "I told this young lady here that it had my monogram embroidered in blue on the pocket. It said *OJ*."

Not a monogram I'd be happy to wear, but one that would help me track down the shirt.

"I promise I'll look for it personally," I said.

O.J. seemed as if he wanted to argue with me, so I quickly added, "If we can't find it, we'll buy you a new shirt and monogram *OJ* on it free of charge."

"No, I want the shirt I brought in," O.J. said. "It's lucky for me."

He left when several other people came into the cleaners. After several cloudy but snow-free days, another storm was predicted for tonight, so apparently a lot of customers had decided to come in early. Unfortunately, Julia, my morning counter manager, had to leave for a doctor's appointment. That left me to work the counter with Ann Marie, the slightly confused young woman who'd taken O.J.'s original complaint.

Ann Marie is twenty-going-on-fourteen, and she still wears her hair in a ponytail. I personally think it is pulled too tight, which may account for her generally ditziness.

"It would have helped if you'd told me that the lucky shirt had a monogram on the pocket," I said.

"Whoops." She chewed her lip. "I forgot."

I didn't get around to looking for the lucky shirt until two o'clock, when Theresa, my afternoon counter manager, and her helper showed up for work. First I checked with the employees I'd asked to look for it the day before.

"I checked through all the shirts that were folded and boxed," Angelina said from where she was bagging the finished garments, "but I can't really check the conveyor because someone is always turning it on to get an order."

She was right, of course, and I decided to delay my own search until after closing time. The trouble was that a customer might already have picked up an order with O.J.'s shirt accidentally tucked away inside. In that case, we'd have to wait until the customer returned it — if he ever did.

At least Betty's prediction that finding the shirt would be like looking for a needle in a box of needles was no longer true. The shirt had a monogram that would make it easier to find.

I began to think of Cedric Filmore again. I returned to the call office and checked his address and phone number on our computer. He was still listed at Filmore's Philately in downtown Denver even though I would have sworn he'd have retired years ago. He must be in his eighties by now.

I told Theresa I'd be back at five o'clock, detoured to my office for my coat, and headed out the back door of the cleaners. When Mack asked me where I was going, I said I was on my way to Tico Taco's to grab a late lunch. I was still irritated at Mack, and I wasn't about to give him the satisfaction of knowing I was going to act on his urgings to visit the stamp dealer.

I parked in a lot on Fourteenth and walked a block to the building that housed Filmore's Philately. It wasn't anything like I would have expected. It was on the second floor, and when I walked in I was struck by the fact that the place looked like a high-priced jewelry store with locked glass cases that held stamps instead of gems.

Filmore always looked as if he were straight out of the Victorian era. He carried a watch in the watch pocket of his pants, and he consulted it frequently as if he had no time for idle chitchat. Somehow I'd expected his place of business to be dark and foreboding with heavy wooden filing cabinets instead of the shiny metal ones that I could see behind the counter.

A young man with close-cropped blond hair looked surprised when I opened the door. "We don't have much walk-in business," he said, getting up from a computer. "What can I do for you?"

"I wondered if I could see Mr. Filmore. I'm Mandy Dyer." When the man seemed to want more explanation than that, I added, "He knows me. I'm his dry cleaner."

He nodded, said a few words into a telephone, and then pushed a button that unlocked the door of a waist-high divider. The security reminded me of being at the police department.

"Please follow me." He led me through another door that he first unlocked, then down a hallway to Filmore's office. It was as modern as the main room with a huge oak desk, a computer, a few comfortable-looking leather chairs, and more metal filing cabinets. I guess I'd been expecting something like Alex Waring's living room with its spindly-legged furniture that a person was afraid to sit on. Go figure.

Filmore was looking through a magnifying glass at some stamps in a huge book on his desk. He glanced up over a pair of half-glasses as we entered the room, and he had the same irritated look on his face that he always wore when he inspected the clothes that he was picking up.

"I'm just finishing up an appraisal, so I don't have much time." He pulled his watch out of its pocket and glanced at it, presumably to see exactly how many minutes he would allot me. "Did you ruin one of my suits?"

"We don't have any of your suits right now," I said. "I have a question about stamps."

I swear his expression changed from irritation to interest in a split second. "Yes, go on." He closed the book and slipped it into a matching dark green case that looked as if it were made of cardboard.

"I wondered if you know anything about a stamp that has an airplane on it. It's supposed to be quite valuable."

"What kind of airplane?" he said.

I shook my head. "I didn't see the stamp, but the person who described the plane said it looked as if it was at an air show because it was flying upside down."

"Oh, my, you don't mean the twenty-four-cent Jenny Invert, do you?" Filmore was definitely interested now. I could tell because he put down the magnifying glass and gave me his full attention.

I shook my head. "I'm not sure."

"Well, if that's what you're referring to, it wasn't flying upside down. It was produced in two separate printings, and it went through the press the wrong way on the second run. The red frame bearing the twenty-four-cent rate was one way and the airplane on a blue background was the other. It's the most famous philatelic error in the world."

I felt as if I'd suddenly gone into a tailspin. "How much would one of them be worth?"

Filmore leaned toward me. "First, tell me, do you know a person who has one?"

"I'm not sure of that, either. The woman and the stamp both seem to have disappeared."

"Oh, dear, that is a shame." He dropped back in his chair. "Then I'm assuming you're here to see if the stamp would be valuable enough for the woman to abscond with it."

I nodded, even though I was thinking more of foul play.

He swiveled his chair to a filing cabinet behind him, searched through a drawer, and removed a newspaper called *Linn's Stamp News*. "Here." He pointed to a picture of four stamps. "This is a block of the Jenny Inverts."

The stamps were of an upside-down airplane, all right. I could see it belly-up under a frame that said U.S. POSTAGE and gave the twenty-four-cent rate.

He tapped a pencil on the paper. "There are six of these blocks, and three of them sold for $2.5 million several years ago. The price for a single stamp in Scott's stamp catalog is listed at $170,000 to $200,000 in mint condition. At the lower end of the quality scale, a single stamp is probably worth $50,000 to $60,000."

I gulped. Surely Carol wouldn't have had something that valuable with her Saturday night.

"The actual stamp is quite small," Filmore said. "Its value comes from the fact that only one hundred of the errors were ever found."

"Are you saying that there might be more?"

Filmore shook his head. "The post office

later said it found and destroyed eight other panes but that no others ever got into circulation."

"So when was this?"

"They were issued on May 13, 1918, to commemorate the first airmail flight in this country. The service was to be launched two days later between Washington, D.C., Philadelphia, and New York, using a fleet of the Jenny biplanes, which were being used to train American and Canadian pilots in World War I."

I could see that Filmore was warming to his subject. He tucked a thumb into the watch pocket of his pants and continued, "Interestingly enough, the pilot who flew the plane from Washington to Philadelphia took off in the wrong direction and landed nose-over-tail upside down in a field in Maryland. If that wasn't life imitating art, I don't know what was."

"About the stamp —" I said.

"Oh, yes, a stamp collector named William T. Robey bought the pane of one hundred stamps on May 14 at a post office in Washington, and he knew immediately that he'd struck gold." Filmore chuckled, something I'd never seen him do before. "The poor clerk who sold it to him said that he didn't notice the error because he'd never seen an actual airplane.

"Robey went back to work, where he told a few people about his find. The word spread quickly. By afternoon postal inspectors were at his office and demanded that he give the stamps back. He refused and set out immediately to sell them. His reasons were twofold: He was afraid the post office might give him more trouble if he kept them, and if more errors showed up, it would decrease the value of his find.

"A dealer in Philadelphia paid him $15,000 for the pane and turned around and sold it immediately for $20,000 to an eccentric millionaire, Col. E. H. R. Green, whose mother had been one of the richest women in the world."

I'd found out what I'd come for, and I started to get up, but Filmore waved me back to my seat. I sat. After all, if I could get on his good side by staying, he might be more pleasant when he came to the cleaners.

"Green's late mother, Hetty, was known as 'the Witch of Wall Street' and 'the world's greatest miser.' In fact, she was so tight that she failed to get medical help for her son when he was young. He lost a leg and had to hobble around on a cork prosthetic for the rest of his life. As a consequence, he would have his chauffeur park on Nassau Street in New York City, and stamp dealers would bring their collections to him so he could make his purchases."

"Obviously, the pane of stamps was eventually broken up," I said, hoping to get him back on the subject of the Jenny.

"Almost immediately. Green had the dealer separate the pane into the blocks, and the rest were broken up into individual stamps, some of which he sold. After he died, his Jennys were disposed of at auction, and to my knowledge, only two of the stamps are unaccounted for at the present time. It would be quite a find if the woman you mentioned actually had one of them. Where did she get it? Do you know?"

It took me a few seconds to realize he'd asked me a question. "I understand she found it in her uncle's effects when she was helping settle his estate, but I don't even know his name."

"Interesting," Filmore said. "So it could be a legitimate Jenny Invert with a traceable provenance or it could be stolen. It could also be a fake."

"A fake error — that sounds redundant," I said.

Filmore actually chuckled again. "Oh, my, yes. In fact, recently a Jenny Invert was offered on eBay, but it was just a reproduction pasted on another stamp. You could see the design of the underlying stamp protruding on either side.

"It was an obvious fake, but some counterfeits are so good that the only way to tell is to use a watermark solution or sophisticated electronic equipment. Even then, it's essential to send such a stamp to a stamp expertizing service to have it authenticated."

"Well, thanks for your time." Again I started to get up, but he wasn't through talking.

"If this woman you mentioned actually absconded with the stamp, it won't be the first time nefarious things have happened to the stamp. Several have been stolen, including one from a permanent display at the New York Public Library."

I was beginning to wonder if he'd ever wind down.

"And there was an interesting lawsuit in which a man sued his brother for return of a Jenny Invert that he said was in an album an elderly neighbor gave him as a boy. He claimed he'd left the album behind when he took off from home as an adult, and even though there was no evidence presented that the stamp existed, a jury awarded him $150,000, plus $32,505 interest." Filmore pointed to the stamp paper he'd shown me earlier. "*Linn's* compared the verdict to 'a murder case without a body.'"

That jerked me to attention. God, I hoped Carol wasn't a murder victim whose body would never be found.

I jumped up from my chair. "I need to get back to work, but I really thank you for the information."

He didn't try to stop me this time. "Please let me know what you find out, and if you locate the woman, tell her I'd be interested in making an offer on the stamp once it's authenticated."

"I will, and thanks again."

As I made my way down the hall to the outer office, I couldn't help thinking of the frailty of human life and the fragility of a piece of paper worth two hundred thousand dollars.

When I got outside, the sky had turned dark. The weather matched my mood, and I needed to keep busy. I even let Theresa go home early, once it started to snow, since we probably wouldn't be overrun with customers.

I was right. It wasn't busy, and as soon as I locked up, I began the search for the missing shirt. It might be lucky for O.J., but it wasn't lucky for me. I was still looking at nine o'clock when the phone rang.

"Dyer's Cleaners," I said when I picked up the receiver.

"Amanda, this is your mother."

"Hi, Mom." I felt a pang of guilt for not talking to her all day. "I was going to call you later."

There was a pause on the line. "Well, I'm not at the hotel."

Why did I have an uneasy feeling all at once? "Where are you?"

She ignored my question. "We were wondering if you could come and get us?"

"Where are you?" I repeated.

"Uh —" I thought for a minute something had happened to the connection. "Well, dear, I didn't want you to find this out until we got back to town, but we decided to have dinner at the restaurant where Laura took the pictures."

"The Rendezview?" I couldn't believe it. "You and Laura are up at the Rendezview? Why, for God's sakes, and what happened to her date with Nat?"

"Oh, she went on the date, all right, and I have to tell you, Amanda, that I don't really approve."

"Who are you with, Mom, if it isn't Laura?"

She sniffed indignantly. "Well, if you must know, I'm with *your* friend Betty."

225

CHAPTER SIXTEEN

"Are you out of your mind?" I shouted into the phone. "Didn't you learn anything after that disastrous trip to Aspen with Betty?"

Mom was in no mood to be reminded of her arrest the time she'd asked the bag lady to accompany her to Aspen. She chose to ignore my question and give her rationale for today's foray to the mountains instead.

"I needed someone to drive my rental car in case it started to snow while we were up here," Mom said, as if it were the most obvious thing in the world that someone from Phoenix would need a chauffeur in winter weather. "Betty said she could drive in the snow. She didn't tell me that she couldn't drive in the dark."

"I suppose she also failed to mention that, to the best of our knowledge, she doesn't have a driver's license."

Mom turned away from the phone. "You don't have a driver's license?"

I could hear Betty in the background. "Well, you didn't ask me that."

Mom spoke into the receiver again. "I

have to tell you, Amanda, that some of your friends leave a lot to be desired."

Oh, sure, now it was my fault.

"So you see, we're in a terrible fix, and we need someone to come and drive us back down the mountain."

Personally, I would have liked to leave them stranded for the foreseeable future, but I sighed heavily to show I was put upon and said, "Okay, I'll need directions."

She gave them to me: up Mount Vernon Canyon on I-70 to Vista View Road. "It's a winding road with a few drop-offs, but you can't miss the restaurant. It sits on an over-look with a view of the whole city. I see now why they call it the Rendezview in-stead of the Rendezvous."

That's not what I wanted to hear — a winding road with drop-offs as seen through a raging snowstorm.

"The restaurant has a neon sign out at the road," Mom continued, "although you might not be able to see it very well if the snow's still coming down as hard as it is now."

I was resigned to attempting the rescue despite my reservations about it. "Okay, but it'll take me a while to get there."

"That's fine, dear. We'll go back in the dining room and have some dessert to top off our meal." At that, I almost reneged because I hadn't had anything to eat since Mack brought me a doughnut that morning. "Oh, yes." She lowered her voice until I could barely hear her. "We found out several interesting things, but I'll tell you about them later. The phone might be bugged." She cut off the connection.

I was muttering to myself as I tried to think of what to do. I obviously couldn't drive up to the restaurant by myself, because then I'd have two cars and only one driver capable of navigating in the storm.

In desperation, I dialed Nat's work number at the *Tribune*. Much as I hated the thought of another wild ride up to the foothills with him, Nat was preferable to Mack, whom I was still mad at.

Nat's phone started ringing, but that's when I remembered he was on a date with Laura.

Before I could hang up, someone answered the phone.

"I'm sorry. This is Mandy Dyer. I was looking for Nat Wilcox."

"Mandy," the man said. "This is Jason Williams."

I'd met Jason at a few parties I'd gone to with Nat when he was between tall blond girlfriends.

"You're not the only one looking for him," Jason said. "We've been calling all over town to try to locate him. It isn't like Nat to have his cell phone turned off, so I'm over here at his desk trying to find his appointment book. You wouldn't have any idea where he is, would you?"

Theoretically, that was a dumb question since I'd just called the paper looking for him, but actually I had remembered where he was.

"What's the problem?" I asked.

"Senator Ambrose wants to talk to him and says no one else will do."

My stomach lurched. I was still reeling from Mom's call, and this new revelation was almost more than I could take. If Ambrose was planning to pull some strings and get Nat fired, it would be on my head. After all, I was the one who'd blurted out that we knew the senator had been at the Rendezview the night of Laura's photo session.

I could have told Jason to try Mom's room at the hotel; Nat might be there later. Instead, I said, "No, I'm sorry, I don't have any idea where he is." It was as if I thought that would protect Nat from losing his job, at least for a little while.

I hung up and considered my options for rescuing Mom and her middle-aged cohort.

I could think of only one other possibility: Call Mack and hope he'd forgotten about my irritation this morning when I learned he'd hired Travis Kincaid to investigate Ricky Monroe.

And I'd been wrong when I'd told Mack that I already had too many friends and thus couldn't accommodate Travis in my inner circle. What I actually needed was a lot more friends who didn't interfere in my life but whom I could call in emergencies.

Having no one who fit the bill, I dialed Mack's number. I'd been afraid he wouldn't be home, but he answered after three rings. I just hoped he would forgive me and help me out of my current predicament.

The thing I like about Mack, though, is that deep down he's a really nice human being. He didn't say anything about our argument when I asked him for the favor and told him about the latest escapade of my mother and Betty.

"What on earth possessed Cecilia and Betty to do something like that?" Mack asked.

"I have no idea about Mom, but Betty probably felt that the whole thing was a hoot, the same way she did when Mom was hauled off to jail that time."

"Well, I guess it doesn't matter," Mack

said. "Do you know where this restaurant is?"

I gave him the directions.

"Okay, I'll be right over to pick you up."

I told him I was still at work but that I'd meet him at my apartment. Before I left the plant, I changed out of my shoes and into boots and put on my heavy down-filled jacket and a matching knit hat that I'd resurrected from my office desk.

The streets were already getting slippery; I didn't even want to think what they would be like up in the foothills. It took me twenty minutes to get home, a trip that usually took only ten. Mack was waiting when I got there. He pulled his truck out of a parking space in front of my building, and I nosed my Hyundai into it. Normally that would have been cause for celebration — getting a parking space just outside my door — but not tonight.

I climbed out of my car and up into his truck. "Thanks for helping me out," I said as I shut the door and pulled on my seat belt. "I wouldn't have called you except I couldn't think of anyone else to ask."

Mack grinned. "See, you really do need more friends, just like Audrey Hepburn did in *Charade*."

Okay, maybe the idea that I already had

too many friends wasn't a good argument for why I didn't want to know Travis Kincaid any better. Maybe I should admit that after we'd shared a kiss that blew me away, he'd never even bothered to call again.

As if he could read my mind, Mack said, "Kincaid called tonight. He says he's on to something about this Ricky Monroe character, but there are a few more details he needs to check. He'll stop by tomorrow morning at the cleaners with a report."

Just what I wanted to hear — after a long night of trying to get Mom and Betty back to Denver, I'd have to try to avoid Travis in the morning.

"At least I won't have to deal with him," I said, hoping Mack would get the hint.

Mack went south on Broadway until he hit Eighth Avenue. It feeds into Sixth Avenue, a mini-freeway that was the closest way to get to I-70 for the trip up to Lookout Mountain. The snow started coming down harder the closer we got to the foothills.

"Don't worry," Mack said. "I have four-wheel drive."

I wasn't worried about that. I was worried about how Mom's rental car would handle on the trip home.

"Maybe I should drive Cecilia's rental

car back, and you can drive my truck," Mack said, again reading my mind.

I rejected that idea. I had a better chance of controlling a car than I did Mack's truck. I changed the subject and spent most of the trip across Sixth Avenue telling him what I'd learned from Cedric Filmore about the upside-down airplane stamp. "You were right. It's called the Jenny Invert, and it could be worth two hundred thousand dollars."

"See, I told you that you ought to talk to Filmore," Mack said.

I nodded in agreement. After all, Mack was my savior tonight, and I couldn't stay mad at him. My feelings toward Travis weren't Mack's problem; they were mine.

While I was at it, I decided to unload on Mack about my fears for Nat. "Senator Ambrose has requested a meeting with him, but Nat doesn't know it yet, and I'm really worried. Why would Ambrose want a meeting unless he has talked the publisher into firing Nat?"

"Or maybe Ambrose wants to come clean," Mack said.

I shook my head. "When has a politician ever wanted to come clean?"

By then, Mack had merged onto I-70, just before the freeway heads uphill. The traffic was light, but the farther we went, the more evidence we found of the problems a snowstorm can create. Several cars were already stuck along the side of the road, and the police were cleaning up an accident on the other side of the median where a semi had jackknifed across the eastbound lanes of traffic.

Ahead of us a dump truck was putting down sand, and several cars were following in its wake in an effort to get traction on the highway. Mack had switched to a lower gear and seemed oblivious to the dangers around him.

I began to look for the turnoff to the restaurant when we neared the top of Lookout Mountain. I could barely see the exit sign through the film of snowflakes, but Mack made the turn as easily as if this were a summer day.

After that, the driving conditions got worse. Sand trucks hadn't gotten here yet, but Mack negotiated the turns and avoided the drop-offs as if he were a long-haul truck driver.

Finally, I saw the blurred image of the neon sign that announced we'd reached the restaurant. Mack pulled off the road to the parking lot.

There was only one car up close to the

building, and it was covered with snow. I assumed it was Mom's rental, since the storm seemed to have chased the other customers away. There were a few vehicles at the back of the lot, presumably employees waiting for us to rescue Mom and Betty so they could go home.

We got out of the truck and struck out for the front door of the restaurant, knocking the snow off our boots before we went inside.

Mom was sitting at a table at the front of the otherwise empty restaurant. She had her back to Betty, and she seemed to be sulking. It didn't bode well for our trip home. "Thank goodness," she said. "I didn't think you were ever going to get here."

"Yeah," Betty said. "The waiter was getting irritated at us for not leaving."

Mom turned around and snapped, "I think what he was mad about was that you ruined the cherries jubilee."

"Well, who in tarnation ever heard of someone settin' fire to food? It was the damnedest thing I ever saw."

Mom sniffed. "That was no reason to pour water on it when he put a match to the brandy."

"Well, what in blue blazes did you expect me to do? Sit here and watch the whole place go up in smoke? You're just lucky I didn't push the pan over and try to stomp out the fire with my feet."

"Hmmph," Mom said and turned back to us.

"Uh —" Mack said, chuckling. "What say we get out of here?"

I was feeling slightly hysterical myself, but as long as we were here, I might as well ask a few questions. I went over to a man with fire in his eyes and cherry-juice stains on his shirt. "I'd like to talk to the owner or manager if one of them is still around."

"I'll get the owner," he said and left.

A minute later, a well-dressed man with thinning gray hair joined us. "I'm André Dumas, the owner," he said with typical French aloofness but only a hint of a French accent.

I introduced myself. "I was wondering if you know Carol Jennings. She was here Saturday night, and I've been trying to locate her."

"Ah, *oui*, she worked here as a hostess for a while when she was laid off at the airlines."

Well, that could explain how she'd known to steer Laura to the photo assignment, and why she might have suggested meeting someone here. "I was wondering

236

if you talked to her that night or if" — how did I put this? — "if you knew the men who were here just after the restaurant opened, possibly to see her."

"I'm sorry," he said. "I spoke to Carol briefly, but otherwise I can't help you. I was very busy that night."

I didn't know what else to ask, so I turned to Mom. "Have you paid your check?"

André looked over at the menopausal mischief-makers with disdain. "We already comped their meal."

I had an uneasy feeling about that, but I decided not to ask for an explanation. "Okay, thanks. We'll get going now, so that you can close up."

The owner turned and left. Mack retrieved Mom's fur coat and Betty's green cloth one from the rack in the entryway where presumably Laura's coat mix-up had happened the previous week.

Mom pointed out what I'd earlier identified as her car, and she suggested that she wait for us inside while we dug it out of the snow. I started to tell her she'd have to help, but Mack shook his head at me.

"Betty, why don't you stay in here, too?" Mack said. "Or maybe we should all go back to town in my truck and get the car later?"

It sounded like a good idea to me, although I didn't relish another trip up here later to retrieve the car.

"No," Mom said. "I really need to get the car back to town so I'll have transportation."

Luckily, Mack had a shovel and a box of sand in the back of his truck. Bless him. Otherwise I don't think we would ever have gotten the car out of its entrapment. He shoveled while I scraped ice and snow off the windows.

Finally, we waved Mom and Betty to join us outside.

"Look," Mack said as he brushed snow off his clothes. "It's coming down pretty hard now, so I'll go first and break a trail for you. Try to follow my tracks."

He climbed in his pickup and circled the parking lot until we got moving. Once we did, he took off.

"You could have at least warmed up the car before we came out," Mom complained from the passenger seat.

"Just be glad I'm here at all," I said.

"That strange truck's still parked back there," Betty said from the backseat.

"Excuse me?" I turned my head to look at the truck she was pointing at. It was covered with snow, too, but the windows had been cleared off. I couldn't help thinking of the truck I thought had followed me Tuesday.

"Yeah, Cece got cold feet about drivin' home when we saw two guys over by the truck."

"You weren't supposed to tell Mandy about that until we got home," Mom said.

Personally, I wished Betty had mentioned it before Mack left.

"The guys were kinda back in the shadows," Betty continued, "but Cece was scared because she said one of them had a really big head."

I glanced over at Mom. "You have to be kidding."

Betty laughed. "Yeah, that's what I said. Any fool could tell the guy had an Afro."

I wondered aloud if the "big head" could have been a tall chef's hat, but Mom and Betty both rejected that idea.

"Well, at least there's no sign of the men now," Mom said with a shrug of her fur-clad shoulders. "They must have left in the car that was parked back there, too."

I hated to tell her that her optimism was premature. As I pulled out of the parking lot, I saw the truck — its lights still off — begin to move as well.

CHAPTER SEVENTEEN

I wondered if my eyes were playing tricks on me. Maybe the truck hadn't really started up as I moved out of the parking lot. I couldn't see it once I made the turn onto the road out to the interstate. The car skidded in the snow, but I didn't care. I was badly spooked. I wanted to put as much distance as I could between Mom's rental and the mystery truck, whether it was moving or not.

"Please slow down, Amanda," Mom said. "If you're going to keep driving like that, maybe I should have ridden back to town with Mack."

I wished all three of us had gone back to town with him. If not that, I wished he had waited until we left instead of blazing a trail for us to follow.

Just then, I thought I saw the renegade truck pull out on the road behind us. The back window of the Buick was beginning to ice over again, so it was hard to tell.

"By the way," Mom said, "the restaurant doesn't have a cat."

"Excuse me?" I was totally distracted by

the truck. We'd turned a corner, and it was gone from view.

"The cat," Mom repeated.

"Yeah, Cece thought there was a cat in one of the pictures the photographer lady took at the restaurant." Betty's voice came from over my right shoulder as she leaned forward from the backseat. She was so close she obstructed my view in the rear-view mirror.

"Damn it, Betty, sit back and put on your seat belt."

For once she did what she was told, and I could see the truck coming around the curve just behind us. It had its lights on now, and they were reflecting like spotlights in my eyes. I adjusted the rearview mirror.

"Where's the defroster for the back window?" I asked. Fortunately, I'd turned on the front one while Mack and I were digging out the car.

"Oh, my, we didn't need it when we came up here," Mom said. "You should stop and find it before we go on."

"Did you know there's a big old car right behind us?" Betty asked.

"I know," I said. "It followed us out of the parking lot."

"Oh, dear." Mom strained to look behind her. "I don't like that at all. What if it's the scary guy with the big head?"

"The Afro," Betty said.

I tried to find the rear window defroster on the dashboard, but it was hopeless. I gave up and stepped on the accelerator, trying to keep the car in the tracks made by Mack's pickup.

"I bet it's one of those demolition derby killer machines," Betty said, "and it's going to plow into us."

The truck had its high beams on now, and I had to duck to keep its lights, distorted by the snow, from blinding me. I had a short reprieve as we went around another curve, and then the lights appeared again, closer this time.

But suddenly they weren't there, and I wondered if the truck had gone off the road. It had been going a whole lot faster than it should have in the snow.

"That stupid driver is out of his mind," Betty said. "He's got his lights off, and he's trying to hit us."

That explained why I couldn't see him. I felt the impact as he hit our car. The rental slid into the other lane before it skidded back to our side of the road. Thankfully, no car was coming from the opposite direction.

"Oh, my God," Mom yelled. "We're all going to die."

For a second, I thought we were going to plow into the rocks on our side of the road. Just in time, I managed to turn the wheel and settle into the ruts that now looked as if they'd been made by several cars coming out of a road that took off up the hillside to the right.

The truck pulled back from us, and as it did, another vehicle careened out from the side road and squeezed between the truck and us.

Mom kept screaming.

"Hey, there's another car back there," Betty said.

I was sure now that this must have been how Joy died, not from drunk driving. But I didn't know how being sober was going to help me once there were two vehicles on our tail. Were the drivers in some sort of conspiracy to run us off the road?

The vehicle from the side road had slowed behind us, and from the little I could tell when I glanced in the side mirror, it was blocking the pursuit of the killer truck. If this new vehicle, wherever it had come from, would stay between the truck and us, I thought there was a chance we could make it out to the interstate, where I could try to flag someone down for help.

My optimism didn't last long. Suddenly I saw a double set of headlights. The crazy driver who'd rammed into us was trying to pass the other vehicle. I would have let him pass if I'd been the innocent person caught in the middle of the chase, but that driver pulled over into the oncoming lane, and the truck from the restaurant dropped back.

A few moments later, the truck made another run to get around the slower vehicle. It must have been riding the edge of the roadway as the driver sped forward, and this time he made it. He started bearing down on us again. I pulled the Buick over as far as I could toward the uphill side of the road, but I felt the impact as his bumper hit the back of our sedan. This time I couldn't control the car. It veered to the outside of the road, and just as I turned the wheel, the truck hit us again and we slammed into an outcropping of rocks on the other side. From somewhere overhead, an avalanche of snow came down and covered the car.

Mom's screams turned into muffled whimpers. Betty was so quiet I thought she must be unconscious.

"Is everyone all right?" I asked shakily.

"What are we going to do now?" Mom

asked finally. "Someone is going to have to dig us out from this."

"Are you crazy, Cece?" Betty said, and I was relieved to hear her voice from the backseat. "If someone digs us out, it'll be the guy who tried to kill us. What we gotta do is lock all the doors and pretend we're dead in here so he'll go away."

Mom apparently hadn't thought of the possibility that our rescuer might be the driver of the truck that had been after us. She began to rock back and forth, crying softly.

"Of course, we'll probably all freeze to death, so it don't much matter either way," Betty said.

If that was her idea of comforting Mom, it didn't work. Mom's sobs became louder, but at least Betty hadn't mentioned that we'd probably be asphyxiated from the fumes if I kept the engine running.

The windshield wipers were now immobilized under a pile of snow, and I debated whether to turn the engine off or not. I finally decided to do it in case the exhaust pipe was covered in snow as well.

Once that was done, I fumbled on the seat between Mom and me. "Where's my purse?" I asked.

She didn't answer, but I finally found it

on the floor at her feet. I dug out my cell phone and tried to put through an emergency call for help. The phone didn't work.

I took off my seat belt and tried the door. The snow was jammed up against it, so I looked back at Betty. She was turned around in the seat and was peering out a tiny spot in the corner of the rear window that wasn't covered in snow. That was a good sign; maybe we weren't completely buried.

"Try your door, will you?" I asked.

"No way. Not me," she said. "I can see the truck back there, and the guy just got out and is heading in this direction. He looks like Bigfoot."

"Ohhh," Mom moaned. "It must be the guy with the big head." She sank down inside her fur coat.

I could hear a digging sound outside my door and some muffled words, but I couldn't make out what they were.

We were trapped like animals in a cage. Finally, I grabbed the can of hairspray I'd been using to try to pouf my hair over the shaved spot on my head. I would zap the guy with it when he opened the door. It wasn't Mace, but it would have to do.

I could still hear the digging and the muffled voice. "Did it sound as if someone said 'Mandy'?" I asked.

Neither of my companions answered.

There it was again. I definitely heard "Mandy."

"Oh, dear Lord, how does he know your name?" Mom asked.

Someone was scraping on the window with a gloved hand. The inside of the window had steamed up, and I tried clearing it away. I could barely see the outline of the person who was making a circular motion with his hand as if he wanted me to roll down the window. No way, mister.

He pressed his face closer to the glass, and I finally recognized him.

"Oh, thank God, Mack," I said, although I wasn't sure he could hear me. He'd obviously been the person in the other vehicle that came barreling out of the side road, and I finally had the sense to open the window.

"I was scared to death when I saw that guy trying to run you off the road," Mack said. "Are you all okay?"

"I think so," I said.

Mom came out of her mink long enough to nod her head, but Betty was more expressive. "I'd like to kill the bastard who done this to us. Where is the creep, anyway?"

"He kept on going down the hill after he ran you off the road," Mack said. "Good job of driving, Mandy, to keep from going off the other side."

Even if our car wasn't in such good shape, I decided to acknowledge Mack's compliment with a nod of my head. After all, we could have plunged down the hill, not into it, and all been killed.

"I bet it was the man with the big head," Mom said.

Betty wouldn't let it go. "The Afro," she said again.

"Let's get you out of here," Mack said. "No sense trying to dig the car out. You can ride back to town with me, like you probably should have done in the first place."

First, Mack had to clear away the snow from the doors so we could get out of the car and transfer to his pickup. Fortunately, it had a narrow backseat. Betty and I climbed in the back while Mom took the seat beside Mack.

"So what made you wait for us at a side road?" I asked when he started the car.

"I made a mistake," he said. "I thought I saw someone in the other truck back in the parking lot, and I should have done something right then."

Mom peeked out of her collar to glance over at him. "Really, you saw someone in the truck?"

Mack shook his head, apparently not in response to her question but because he regretted leaving ahead of us. "I figured I was just being paranoid, and I didn't want to upset you. But the more I thought about it, the more I thought something was weird. I pulled off the road, and when I saw the guy coming hell-bent on your tail, I tried to cut him off so you could get away." He glanced back at me. "I'm sorry he got by me, Mandy."

"Don't apologize," I said. "Who knows what would have happened if you hadn't waited for us?"

"I know what would have happened," Betty said. "The guy woulda come back and killed us all."

Mom gave a delicate little shudder. "Thank you, Mack, for saving our lives."

Mack nodded as he kept his eyes on the road. At least the snow was tapering off so it wasn't so hard to see ahead of us now.

I tried my cell phone again, and this time I got through to an emergency number at the State Patrol office. I told the dispatcher about the hit-and-run truck and the abandoned rental at the side of the road.

I covered the mouthpiece on the phone. "What color was the truck, Mack? It had snow on it when I saw it."

"It was a dark color," he said. "That's all I could tell, and it didn't have a license plate on the back."

I wondered if I should tell the dispatcher that a similar truck might have followed me earlier in the week. I finally decided against it and shut off the phone. "Do you want to call the rental company now or later?" I asked Mom.

"Later," she said.

"You do have insurance on the car, don't you?"

She nodded. "Of course I do, Amanda." I guess she thought it was a dumb question to ask the wife of a retired used-car dealer.

I decided to ask her a few questions that weren't so dumb. "What the devil possessed you to come up here in the first place, and why'd you bring Betty along?"

My companion in the backseat seemed to take offense at the second part of the question. "Because we're a good team, ain't we, Cece?"

I could see Mom cringe, and she looked back at Betty accusingly. "I already told you, she said she could drive if it started to snow."

"You didn't say nothin' about no night drivin'," Betty said.

Mom ignored her. "For another, I thought Betty could create a diversion while I looked in the reservation book to see who had been at the restaurant last Saturday night."

"And I did a bang-up job, didn't I, Cece?" Betty said. "I raised all kinds of a ruckus when I found a hair in my soup. Of course, it was one of mine, but the waiter didn't know that. They gave us our meals free."

It was my turn to cringe.

"Unfortunately," Mom said, "all they had was a sheet of paper with tonight's reservations on it, not a reservation book like a really fine restaurant would have."

"But at least they didn't have a cat, huh, Cece?" Betty pointed to her head of short-cropped gray hair. "I told that owner guy I thought it looked like a cat hair, and he swore they didn't have a cat."

I don't know why I felt that I had to play devil's advocate right then. "How do you know the owner wasn't lying?"

Mom glanced over her shoulder. "I know he wasn't because I quit taking my allergy pills yesterday. You know how I always sneezed around Spot until I got those pills.

Well, I didn't sneeze at all in the restaurant." She turned to Mack as he reached the entrance to I-70. "So you see, Mack, it was worthwhile for us to come up here, even if you had to come and get us. Now we know for sure it wasn't a cat in that photo of the restaurant."

I thought I could see Mack's jaw tighten in irritation, but he didn't say anything as he merged onto the interstate. Fortunately, now that the snow was ending, the sand trucks were out in force. I liked to think it made Mack's job easier, although the occasional vehicle off to the side of the road was a reminder of how bad it had been earlier. I kept thinking about the truck that had pursued us. I was hoping I'd see one that matched that description in a ditch, but I didn't.

"What did the men in the parking lot look like?" Mack asked as we started the drop into Denver. "I mean besides their head size and hairstyle."

"Well, the man with the big head was tall, and the other one was short and thin-looking," Mom said.

"He was scrawny, if you ask me," Betty said. "I could have taken that little one on with one hand tied behind my back."

"What I don't understand," I said, "is all

the cars — a dark truck, the white SUV that hit Laura, and then the yellow sports car that was seen leaving the parking lot just behind Joy Emerson."

"Oh, my goodness," Mom said. "I didn't know about a sports car. Maybe those awful men are renting cars and then taking them back to the rental agencies all banged up."

"Seems to me more like there's a whole gang of folks out to get you guys," Betty said.

CHAPTER EIGHTEEN

All the way home, I kept replaying what had just happened. Why had Mom and Betty suddenly become the focus of what had been going on with Laura? How did the guy with the big head and his scrawny partner even know the connection between them? Was it because of something Mom and Betty had seen or simply because they'd been nosing around?

I posed some of these questions to Mack once we dropped Mom off at the hotel and Betty at her apartment. We still hadn't come up with any answers by the time Mack double-parked in front of my place.

I thanked him for his maximum-effort job that night. "I don't know what I'd do without you, Mack, and since I've kept you up so late two nights in a row, I'll open up tomorrow morning."

He wouldn't hear of it. "Try to stay out of trouble," he said and drove away.

As soon as I got to my apartment, I fed Spot, slipped on pajamas, and flopped down on the sofa. I didn't even bother to convert it into a bed.

But I tossed and turned all night, worrying about Mom and Betty, Carol's disappearance, the stamp she was supposed to have, and Senator Ambrose's request to see Nat. Spot must have sensed my agitation. The cat actually slept at the foot of the sofa. It was as if he were trying to comfort me by lying on my feet, and no matter how much I kicked and flung myself about, he was willing to ride out the storm.

By the time I got to work the next morning, I felt battered and bruised by the night's activities and aftermath. I spent the first few hours at the front counter, but as soon as business slowed down, I headed to the back of the plant.

"Boy, that was one wild night, wasn't it?" Betty said as I passed the laundry.

I nodded and kept going. When I reached my office, I called Carol Jennings and crossed my fingers that she would finally be home. I got her roommate, Sally, out of bed.

"No, she still hasn't shown up," Sally said, and I heard her yawn. "But I'll give her your message when she does."

We hung up, and I tried to decide what to do next — begin searching the conveyor for O.J.'s lucky shirt or take Mom's suggestion, long shot that it was, and call rental-car places to see if any of their customers had returned cars with scratched bumpers and dented fenders.

Just as I made a decision and grabbed the Yellow Pages, Travis Kincaid showed up at my door. With all the other things that had been going on, I'd completely forgotten that Mack had said he would be stopping by today.

To be honest, Travis looked as unhappy to be here as I was to see him. I could tell because of the jagged white scar that ran from the left corner of his mouth up toward his ear. According to Nat, the scar had been the result of some gang fight he'd gotten into back in junior high when he'd been a bully extraordinaire. The scar only enhanced his reputation as the bad guy in school.

It seemed to show up when he was irritated more than when he was doing the irritating. Unfortunately, it did nothing to detract from his dark, rakish good looks or his piercing brown eyes that looked as if they could see inside your soul.

Get a grip, I told myself. *Don't let this guy get to you the way he usually does. Say something.*

Travis broke the silence first. "Mack asked me to come in here so I could give you the report on Ricky Monroe."

So where was Mack? Much as I appreciated what he'd done for me the night before, I was still put out that he'd hired Travis. He should have listened to what Travis had to say and relayed the information to me, not directed the private investigator to my office.

Besides, I'd had everything under control before Mack had gotten into the act. I'd been planning to have Nat help me find Ricky Monroe. Mack was the one who thought Monroe sounded too dangerous for me to go looking for.

What was really dangerous was for me to be around Travis. I always seemed to embarrass myself when I was near him, and I didn't want to do that this time.

I was tempted to yell for Mack to get in my office right now, but I decided I might as well get the whole thing over with. "Okay, have a seat and give me the report."

Travis took the chair opposite me. The jagged white scar still stood out on his face. "I'll wait until Mack gets here. He said he'd be in as soon as he started one of the machines."

Oh, great. Now what did we talk about? Travis seemed in no mood to start a conversation, and the silence stretched out between us like a long, lonely road. I sat and stared at the silvery thread of a scar on his face.

"Where'd you get that scar?" I blurted out before I even realized I'd spoken.

Travis seemed surprised but amused by the question. I wondered what he'd expected me to say. Surely not something about our last meeting and that sizzling kiss I'd given him, which apparently was sizzling only to me.

"Oh, this." He shrugged and traced the scar with his index finger. "If you must know, I got it when I racked up my bicycle in junior high and smashed into a broken beer bottle with my face."

"I heard you got it in a knife fight," I said. In fact, Nat had told me that Travis had been so mean back then that he'd taken on a whole gang single-handedly.

"Yeah, I heard that rumor, too, and I sure wasn't about to deny it," Travis said. "People gave me a wide berth after that, and it kept me out of trouble."

Okay, so maybe he hadn't been the bully Nat always described. That didn't mean he hadn't become an arrogant teenager who intimidated people with his macho image.

"As a matter of fact, that's why I tried to help you when you took a header off your bike back in school," he said.

I wished he wouldn't bring that up. It had been a humiliating experience for me.

"It was Nat's bike," I said.

"Oh, yeah. Anyway, I thought you might be hurt, but you didn't seem to appreciate my help."

Well, no, how could I? He'd had Lucy Carmichael, known as "Loose Lucy" to the guys in school, practically glued to his back when he came along on his Harley and found me sprawled in a ditch at the side of the road.

Mack came into the room just then. "So did you tell Mandy what you found out?" he said to Travis as he closed the door and took the other chair across from me.

"No, we were reminiscing about the good old days back in high school," Travis said.

I'm sure I looked appalled. On the other hand, Mack looked smug, as if he'd been sure we'd get along if we were in the same room long enough.

Fat chance. Not while I remembered how I'd had to walk the bike all the way home with Travis and Lucy following behind me for a while, then zooming ahead and waiting for me. I was never sure whether Travis did this to aggravate his girlfriend or to show off for her.

"Okay, let's hear the report," I said. "I have to get back to work." I had to fight the impulse to drum my fingers on the desk to show how really busy I was.

I heard a tapping sound anyway, and it took me a few seconds to realize it wasn't my fingers but someone banging at the door. Talk about bad timing. Before I could say anything, Nat opened the door and rushed in. Things were quickly going from bad to impossible. I was sure Nat was here to tell me he'd been fired.

"What the hell's going on?" he asked, looking from Travis to me.

Ordinarily, I'd have been mad at him for charging into the room, but under the circumstances, I tried to be kind. "We're having a meeting, but it should only take a few minutes. Why don't you —"

I'd started to say "wait outside." Before I had a chance, Nat went over and plopped down on the couch at the side of the room as if we'd all been waiting for him to show up to get the meeting started.

"Okay," he said. "I have something to tell you, but I guess it can wait."

This wouldn't do. I got up and motioned him to the door. "You can tell me outside." To Mack and Travis, I said, "I'll be back in a minute."

Nat frowned at me, but he followed me out of the office. The moment the door was closed, he hissed, "So what is Travis Kincaid doing here?"

Despite my good intentions, his accusatory tone annoyed me. "It really isn't any of your concern."

"Don't tell me you hired that lowlife again?"

"No, as a matter of fact, Mack did. Now, what do you want?"

Nat had a one-track mind when it came to Travis. "So what exactly is he doing for Mack?"

"Look, are you going to tell me what you came here for or not?"

Nat looked smug. "Sure, but then you gotta tell me what's up with Travis." Before I could answer, he continued, "Do you remember what I told you about Charlie Ambrose? Didn't I say that he'd be busy cooking up some story as soon as we left?" He punched me in the arm. "Well, I was right."

I sensed this wasn't about Nat getting the axe. "Okay, so tell me, or else I'm going to go back in my office right now."

"Don't get in a snit. The esteemed senator demanded that I have an audience with him this morning, and he was charm

261

itself. Seems he wanted to give me the scoop that he's going to run for the U.S. Senate this fall against Senator Bartlett, the incumbent."

"Okay, but you already told me that was the rumor. What does it have to do with our trip to his house?"

"Hold your horses and hold on to your hat. He's also announcing today that he has appointed Dottie O'Dell as his campaign manager. She ran his soon-to-be opponent's campaign six years ago and has been running Senator Bartlett's Colorado office ever since. In other words, Ambrose is stealing O'Dell away from Bartlett, and the announcement's going to be in tomorrow's paper — with a byline by you-know-who."

I realized where this was going. "So you're saying that he wasn't having a fling with another woman while his wife was out of town. He was having a hush-hush political meeting with Dottie O'Dell at the Rendezview that night."

"Bull's-eye. He said the only reason he'd been secretive about being there was that he didn't want word of the meeting to leak out until Dottie accepted the job."

I was busy trying to reassess the senator's place on my list of suspects. It seemed to be slipping.

"And get this," Nat said, "Ambrose was suddenly Mr. Nice Guy. He asked what I'd been able to find out about the poor woman who'd been killed. He even confirmed what Joy's boyfriend said about seeing a light-colored car leave the parking lot that night."

"God, I hope you didn't ask him a leading question about the car." I was still smarting from Nat's criticism of my interview technique when we'd talked to Tom Jones.

Nat ignored my dig. "The senator said he thought he heard a scream outside the restaurant, but when he looked out the window, all he saw was a light-colored coupe tearing out of the parking lot."

"So have you told the State Patrol what the senator said?"

"Better yet. I'd already told them what Tom Jones said, but while Ambrose was in such a cooperative mood, I suggested that he could really help me out by putting in the call himself. After all, he represents the district where the accident took place.

"Anyway, it turns out the Patrol's accident reconstruction team had already found traces of yellow paint on the right rear fender of her car." He punched me on the arm again. "And here's the real zinger. I was talking to a neighbor of Joy's, and she said Joy was pregnant and had been planning to tell her boyfriend about it that night."

I had to admit that was a zinger, and it made her death a double tragedy. It also could have accounted for the glowing look on Joy's face in Laura's photo, as well as what her boyfriend said about her hoping to go to Las Vegas. She'd probably wanted to get married.

"Tom's gotta be the number one suspect in her death," Nat said, "so I'm sure the authorities will be talking to him soon."

"But he didn't go after her in his car. Remember?"

Nat's excitement couldn't be quelled. "He could have hired someone to run her off the road."

I doubted it, not unless Tom had found out about the pregnancy earlier, but I wasn't going to argue about it. "I have to get back inside," I said.

"Not until you tell me what Travis is up to."

I was well aware that I hadn't agreed to tell Nat anything, but I didn't see what it could hurt. "Mack hired him to try to find Ricky Monroe, Carol's ex-boyfriend, since she has never shown up since that night." I punched Nat in the arm, just to get even. "And get this, Malone is supposed to be short and skinny, just like the guy outside the window at the Rendezview."

"So did Travis come up with anything?"

"I don't know. You barged into the office before I could find out."

Nat shrugged. "Well, it sounds like a wild goose chase to me, now that we know about Joy."

"But Carol is still missing."

"Doesn't matter. She probably decided to shack up for a little one-on-one with this Ricky guy. The key to the whole thing is that someone was out to get Joy. Besides, Joy's probably the one who started the coat mix-up in the first place."

"Oh, come on. You're the one who told me Joy was wearing a black leather coat, not Laura's car coat."

Nat was unperturbed by my reminder. "I've got that all figured out. See, Joy takes the wrong coat, then someone else takes Laura's coat when hers is missing. It's kind of the Case of the Musical Chairs, only with coats."

"That's way too complicated."

"No, it isn't. Remember what her boyfriend said. He arrived at the restaurant before she did, so he didn't know what she'd been wearing when she got there. Then she started drinking, so when she left, she could have grabbed the leather coat and left her red one on the rack by mistake. Ergo, the person who owned the leather coat took Laura's coat when she couldn't find hers."

This wasn't getting us anywhere. "I have to go."

He shrugged. "But you still owe me. I'll call you later to find out what Travis had to say."

I wasn't going to argue with him about it right then. I started back into the office, but I thought of something else. "By the way, I was trying to call you last night. It's not like you to turn off your cell phone."

"Not unless I'm in love." He broke out in a silly grin. "And this time, I'm sure Laura's the one."

I shouldn't have asked.

He glanced at his watch. "Anyway, I gotta get back to work and write my exclusive on Ambrose. Ciao."

With that, he turned and left. I went back into the office.

"How's Nat?" Mack asked.

"Everything's okay." I returned to my desk.

"Travis thinks he has a line on Monroe." I could tell from the pleased look on

Mack's face that he felt exonerated for having hired the PI. "I'll let him tell you about it."

"Well, Mack didn't give me a lot to go on, but I think I've found a Ricky Monroe who's a likely candidate. There's a man by that name who works at an auto body shop called Denton's over in West Denver. He fits the general description Mack gave me, and he has a record for a lot of petty crimes and con jobs."

"Did you talk to him?" I asked.

"I tried, but he didn't show up for work today."

"How long since he was there?"

"Just today, but I have an address for him."

Mack interrupted. "Travis says the place where he works is a suspected chop shop."

"And from what Mack tells me," Travis said, "that could explain the different vehicles that were involved in your hit-and-run accidents."

I had to admit that was a much more logical explanation than Mom's idea about the rentals.

"Ricky could either be knocking out the dents and repainting the cars after using them, or he could be using cars that were scheduled for the chopping block," Mack said.

I was more convinced than ever that Carol was the key to everything, since she and Ricky obviously hadn't gone off someplace together.

"What are you going to do now?" I asked.

Mack had an answer for that. "Well, Travis is thinking of staking out his place, but we really need a better description than what I was able to give him. Didn't Laura's roommate show you a picture of the guy?"

"Yes." Why did I have the feeling that this admission was leading me someplace I didn't want to go?

"So we thought maybe you could go with Travis to get a fix on the guy if he shows up."

I started shaking my head even before Mack finished. He was the one who'd thought it was too dangerous for me to go looking for Carol's boyfriend. Did he really think it was a good idea now, or was he merely trying to finagle me into the prolonged company of Travis, feeling sure that this would bring us together?

"Things are pretty well under control here at the plant today," Mack continued, "and I'll take care of any emergencies that come up."

"But I —" I tried to think of what I'd

been planning to do. Checking out car rental agencies sounded dumb now.

"Okay, it's settled," Mack said.

"So we might as well get going." Travis stood up.

I had to admit that I was curious about this Ricky Monroe, and even though my curiosity had gotten me into trouble more than once, I found myself getting up, grabbing my newly cleaned coat, now free of the smell of Chinese takeout, and going over to the door. Fortunately, I already had on my boots, but I grabbed the knit cap I'd worn the night before and stuffed it in my pocket.

It wasn't until I was in Travis's car that I began to wonder what the devil I'd been thinking. What were we going to talk about during the interminable time involved in a stakeout?

In the few minutes when we'd been alone in the office, I'd been so uncomfortable I'd blurted out the question about how he'd gotten the mysterious scar on his face. What would I do during several hours of confinement in his car? God help me from becoming so desperate that I would start babbling on with questions about his sex life and whatever happened to Loose Lucy, the gal who'd been glued to his back on the motorcycle back in high school.

CHAPTER NINETEEN

"Where are we going?" I asked as I fastened myself into the seat belt in Travis's Ford Taurus.

"Up near Thirty-second and Federal," Travis said.

It would probably take us half an hour to get there on the snow-packed streets. I decided the safest thing to talk about would be to ask him about Ricky Monroe.

"Did you find a lot of people with the same name?" I was thinking of the fact that there were apparently a lot of real-life Tom Joneses.

Travis nodded, which I guess is all the answer the question deserved.

"How did you narrow them down to this Monroe?"

Travis glanced over at me as if he knew I was desperately trying to make conversation. "From what Mack said, I figured the guy had a record. This one seemed to fit the bill. Besides, my friend at the police department said this particular Monroe was short and skinny." He paused for a minute. "I gathered from Mack that he was interested in tracking the guy down because Ricky's girlfriend is missing, and it might have something to do with your friend's hit-and-run accident."

I just nodded back at Travis. I really didn't want to get into all the confusing details until I'd had a chance to sort them out.

"Mack also said that you got hit over the head at your friend's apartment, so he didn't want you going out on your own to look for the guy."

"I guess that pretty well covers it." Under my breath I was cussing Mack out for acting so overprotective and at the same time sending me out with Travis to check on the guy he'd been protecting me from. Talk about a double standard. It was a case of his desire to play Cupid overriding his paternal feelings.

"Just now Mack told me that you were involved in a hit-and-run accident yourself last night with a pickup truck." Travis looked over at me with what I thought was exaggerated concern. "You know, I hire out as a bodyguard, too, if you're interested."

"No thanks," I said. If the bicycle fiasco back in high school was an example, he'd probably bring his current girlfriend along just to enjoy my discomfort.

He grinned. "Okay, I just thought I'd offer."

I couldn't think of anything else to say, and we rode along in silence for an excruciatingly long time. When we reached Eighth and Downing, the silence may have begun to bother Travis, too.

"How come you never called me back last October?" he asked.

"Excuse me?"

"You heard what I said."

"You mean when I hired you to do the background check on that neighbor of my friend who was murdered?"

"More like when I rescued you when the owner came home unexpectedly to that house you'd entered illegally."

"Oh, that." I didn't like to be reminded that Nat had talked me into going into my old friend's house with a key we found by the back door.

Travis looked downright smug. "You know I'm not always available to come to your aid on such short notice."

That had been the last time I'd seen him — after he announced that he was "off the clock" and unexpectedly gave me a kiss, forcing me to respond in kind.

"I never got the message," I said. "I would have remembered." Oh, yes, I definitely would have remembered, and it crossed my mind that he was simply putting me on right now.

"I called the cleaners, and someone said she'd give you the message. When the woman asked me if it had something to do with my dry cleaning order, I said no, and she said 'Okey-dokey,' and hung up."

Maybe he was telling the truth, after all. The person who'd answered his call had to be Ann Marie, who'd forgotten to mention the monogram on O.J.'s lucky but still-missing shirt and who said "okey-dokey" with irritating frequency. I'd finally managed to impress on her the need to leave me written messages when customers wanted to speak to me about their orders. She wasn't so good about relaying personal calls, apparently planning to file them away to give me verbally at a later date.

"Why didn't you call again?" I asked.

Travis shrugged but didn't answer. The silence descended again like the low-lying clouds overhead that threatened more snow at any moment. Traffic was almost at a standstill when Travis turned onto Speer Boulevard, which would take us to Denver's northwest side, skirting the downtown area.

Somehow the quiet didn't bother me so much this time. After all, it gave me time to contemplate the fact that he actually had called after that final meeting and our steamy good-bye.

Eventually, curiosity got the better of me. "What did you want when you called?"

He didn't look at me this time. "Just to say thanks for paying your bill on time."

Oh, yeah, right, people always called to thank you when you paid your bills promptly. But if that's the way he wanted to play it, fine. I could wait awhile for the real answer now that I knew he'd called.

I have to admit I was feeling a little self-satisfied as the car arched over the railroad tracks and the Platte River. The rides at Elitch's Amusement Park — now part of the Six Flags family — just to the south of the viaduct were like giant Tinkertoys that had been abandoned to the snow and cold of winter. I was so caught up in my own thoughts that I didn't even notice until Travis began looking for a cross street off Thirty-second.

"It should be somewhere around here," he said, glancing up at the green street signs.

He must have found the street he was

looking for. He swung the car sharply to the right.

My smugness suddenly gave way to pit-of-the-stomach fear as we proceeded along a residential street with barren trees and not-yet-cleared snow.

"Please don't tell me that's the place we're going." I pointed to a house up ahead.

Five or six police cars and emergency vehicles were parked in front. I could see that the cinderblock building with an ugly facade of aquamarine paint was cordoned off with crime scene tape.

"Christ, I hope not." Travis pulled a slip of paper out of an inside pocket of his jacket and consulted it. "The address should be at the end of the block on the east side of the street."

That was the place, all right, and my stomach-wrenching fear percolated up into my throat. I could taste the bile as I thought of the missing Carol Jennings. Had the police found her body? Had she been stuffed away in this house since Saturday, and had the smell finally become so bad that someone called the police? Or maybe she'd been tortured for days and finally killed when she wouldn't tell Ricky what he wanted to know.

Travis pulled to the curb, plowing through a snowdrift, and stopped the car two houses south of the crime scene. "Monroe supposedly lived in a basement apartment around at the back."

Unfortunately, that was the direction two men were coming from with a bagged body on a gurney.

"It has to be Carol Jennings, Ricky's girl-friend," I said, my eyes filling with tears even though I'd never met her. I hoped to God the cops had caught Ricky, and that he hadn't taken off when they appeared.

"I see a detective over there that I know," Travis said. "You stay here. I'll go ask him what's going on."

I wasn't about to stay in the car while Travis went to see if he could get any information. I climbed out even before he'd shut his door. It crossed my mind that maybe I should stay away from the police, considering my previous encounters with them, but I quickly vetoed that idea.

The sidewalk hadn't been shoveled yet, and I tromped through the snow right behind Travis. When he turned around, I almost bumped into him. "I said to stay in the car."

"No, I need to find out if it's Carol, and besides, you're not my bodyguard. I'm not

276

even the one who hired you, so you can't order me around." I knew there wasn't any logic to what I'd said, but I couldn't seem to get over Mack hiring him.

He didn't argue, just turned back around and headed for the cinderblock house. I stopped dead in my tracks a few steps farther on. Maybe it was the tears in my eyes that had blurred my vision at first, but now I realized that Travis was zeroing in on a person I really didn't want to see — Detective Stan Foster.

Stan had been my on-again, off-again boyfriend for several years until he found a kindergarten teacher who had less of a penchant for getting into trouble than I did.

Don't tell me that Travis Kincaid and Stan Foster were bosom buddies? They didn't seem the type to be friends. I didn't see anyone else, though, that Travis could have been referring to when he said he saw someone he knew.

Right then, a clump of snow broke loose from one of the evergreen trees next to me. The snow cascaded down on my head and shoulders, turning me into a female version of Frosty the Snowman. I'd had just about all I could take of snow. When I finally brushed it off, I could see that Travis had reached Stan. The blond homicide detective nodded at him, but the mini-avalanche of snow must have drawn his eyes in my direction. I had a moment of panic. I was sure he'd spotted me.

Damn, I should have put on my knit hat. Not only would it have protected me from the full thrust of the snow, but it might have offered a partial disguise.

I tried to brush the snow out of my face and hair, and after the fact, I yanked the hat out of my pocket and clamped it on my head, pulling it down so far I could hardly see. No recognizing me now, and if ever there was a time to keep a low profile, this was it.

I did a quick detour into the surprisingly large crowd of cold but curious onlookers who stood just outside the crime scene tape and spilled into the street.

Forget about Stan, I told myself. Our breakup had been the result of a mutual loss of interest, so why did I care if he saw me? I guess it was because I wanted him to think I'd changed — that I wasn't sticking my nose into police business anymore.

Hidden away in the spectators and with the hat making me unrecognizable, I got back to business. "Do you know what's going on?" I asked a man in a jeans jacket with a collar turned up against the cold.

"*No hablo inglés*," he said.

I moved on and asked a woman this time.

She wrung her gloved hands in distress. "I keep telling my husband that we need to move. It's crime, crime, crime, all the time crime in this town."

I tried again to anyone who would answer.

"They just found someone dead in that house," a teenaged boy said. "We heard it was a murder."

I swallowed hard and asked, "Was it a woman?"

No one volunteered a response. Unfortunately, I was sure I already knew the answer.

Beyond the crime scene tape, Stan had turned to a uniformed officer and appeared to be giving him instructions. The cop took off on what seemed like a collision course with me. I moved deeper into the crowd and tried to make myself invisible.

"Anyone know whether the victim was a man or a woman?" I asked a new set of spectators.

Several people shook their heads and shrugged.

"We know the guy who lived back there was always having loud parties and getting into fights," a woman to my left volunteered.

I glanced toward the house and was

relieved when I didn't see the cop I'd thought was coming in my direction.

"Do you know the man's name?" I asked the woman.

She shook her head just as someone tapped me on the shoulder. It was the cop. He'd circled around from behind and caught me.

"Excuse me, miss," he said, motioning to Stan. "The detective over there would like to talk to you."

Guiltily, I started to move away from the throng of innocent bystanders, who I'm sure wondered if I'd had something to do with the crime.

I stopped. "First, would you mind telling me what's going on?"

"Sorry," the cop said. "I'm sure Detective Foster can answer your questions." With that, he told me to follow him to where Stan and Travis stood.

"At least tell me who was killed." I tried to pull my arm away from his grasp. He ignored my plea for information and held on.

"Hi, Stan," I said when we got to the crime scene tape.

"Hello, Mandy. What are you doing here?" Stan motioned toward Travis. "He says he's been doing a background check on Ricky Monroe, but he refuses to give me the name of his client. Is it you?"

I shook my head, pulling my hat up off my forehead so that I could actually see him.

"So what the hell are you doing here?" Stan seldom lost his temper, but I'd always seemed to bring out the worst in him.

"I was coming to check on Ricky Monroe, but I'm not anyone's client."

Stan's face turned red, and he shook his head in what I could only describe as disgust. In fact, his body language seemed to scream that he thought I was still the most annoying person he'd ever known.

Finally, he appeared to regain his composure. "Well, if you're looking for Monroe, you're about six hours too late. He was shot and killed sometime during the night."

CHAPTER TWENTY

Ricky Monroe dead. Not Carol Jennings. I felt a sense of relief, but it threw my whole set of assumptions out of whack. Don't tell me that the missing Carol had been shacked up with Monroe for a week and then killed him in a lovers' quarrel? If not, where was she?

Stan was saying something, but I missed it as all sorts of weird speculations whirled around in my head.

"Did you hear me?" he asked. "I want to talk to you as soon as I'm through here. Meanwhile, you can go to Officer Warren's car and give him a statement."

I figured it was worth at least one protest. "About what? I don't even know the victim."

"Just do it."

Okay, maybe it was time that I laid out everything and let the police try to rearrange all the crazy-quilt pieces of the puzzle into a logical pattern. I gathered Officer Warren was the cop who was still standing next to me as if I might flee the scene at any moment.

"Fine," I said, "but what about Mr. Kincaid?"

Whoops. From Stan's reaction, I guess I never should have mentioned my connection to Travis. "I'll talk to him later." Stan looked the private eye over suspiciously. "You're free to go for the time being."

Travis shook his head, but I wasn't sure if it was in disgust at my big mouth or simply in response to Stan's order. "No, I'll wait for Ms. Dyer."

Stan gave a tight little nod of his head. "And afterward, you might want to talk to your client and see if you can get *her* permission so you can tell me her name."

Her indeed. Stan obviously still thought I was the client. And why not? I'd come here with Travis.

"If you'll take the report now, I'll be over as soon as I can." Stan was talking to Officer Warren, who led me toward his squad car.

Unfortunately, it was to the north of the house, and when I got in, I could no longer see what was going on. I took one quick look over my shoulder, but both Travis and Stan had disappeared from view.

Warren started the car and turned on the heater. I was grateful for that, and I slipped off my knit hat that had turned out to be no disguise at all.

"Why don't you start by telling me how you knew the victim?" Warren said.

"I already said that I'd never seen the victim in my life."

He looked as dubious as Stan had a few minutes earlier. "Okay, then tell me why you're here."

"This is going to be confusing because it's really complicated." I started at the beginning with the coat mix-up and Laura's hit-and-run. By the time I finished, the poor policeman looked as if he wished he'd never asked. He asked me to repeat parts of the story and expand on others.

At some point during the interview, it had started to snow again. Warren finally turned on the windshield wipers as it became progressively darker in the car.

Finally, he told me to read the statement and sign it. I had to make some corrections before I put my name to it. I was not quite finished when Stan appeared at the driver's side door.

"Okay," he said to Warren as he waited for me to sign my name, "why don't you go back and see that everyone stays clear of the crime scene? I'll take it from here." He brushed the snow off his hair and clothing and slipped into the seat that Warren vacated. "It's really cold out there." He rubbed his hands together and then gave me the once-over. "You sure haven't changed much, Mandy."

I knew he was talking about my propensity to get into trouble, not any drastic change in my appearance since the last time we'd seen each other in June.

"I can explain," I said.

He stopped me with a shake of his head. "Let me read your statement first."

He took so long that I wanted to suggest he take a course in speed-reading, but I thought it might irritate him unnecessarily.

Finally, he glanced over at me and shook his head again. "Good grief, Mandy, why didn't you call about some of this earlier?"

I tried to point to the section of my statement that had addressed that issue. He moved the paper away from me as if I might try to snatch it out of his hands. "We did call the police on a number of occasions," I said. "Didn't you read that part? My friend Laura even turned over the color slides to the officer who investigated her break-in."

"So why did you hire Travis Kincaid?"

"I didn't hire him."

"Then who did?"

"You'll have to ask Travis."

"I'd watch it with him, Mandy. He's been known to take the law into his own hands sometimes."

Wasn't that what Stan always insinuated I did? By that standard, Travis and I should be well suited to each other.

"What do you know about Monroe's girlfriend?" Stan asked.

"Not much. She's a flight attendant, like I already said, and she lives in Laura's apartment building."

"Is she still missing?"

"She was this morning, but her room-mate didn't seem overly concerned."

"What about the coat?" Stan asked. "Where is it? Maybe it has something to do with all of this."

"It's at the cleaners, and believe me, we've gone over every inch of the coat. There's nothing there, not even in the lining." I pointed at the statement again. "And I already told Officer Warren what was in the pockets."

Stan mulled this over for a few seconds. "We'll need to talk to your friend Laura, and I'll send someone over to the cleaners to get the coat."

"Fine." Frankly, I would be glad to get rid of it.

"Okay, that's all for now. I'll talk to you later."

He got out of the car abruptly, but I could be just as fast. Before he could get around to my side of the patrol car, I opened my door and climbed out.

I couldn't imagine that Travis would still be waiting for me, but when I looked down the street, I could see the tan Taurus still in the same parking space at the curb. Only it wasn't tan anymore. It was covered with snow and looked like a giant sculpture of a car.

When I reached it, I could hear the motor running, but I couldn't see Travis inside. I cleared some snow from the passenger-side window and saw that he was leaning back in the driver's seat. He had a baseball cap he'd resurrected from somewhere pulled down over his eyes, but he wasn't moving. I panicked and fear rose in my throat, the way it had when I feared Mom, Betty, and I might be asphyxiated in the car the previous night.

I banged on the window and yanked open the door. "Travis, are you all right?"

He grunted and opened one eye. "It sure took you long enough."

"Oh, thank God, for a minute I was afraid you were dead."

He grinned. "It's nice to know you really care."

I ignored the remark, and as soon as I got inside, I saw that he'd cracked the other window. I wished I'd seen it before I said anything. Then he wouldn't have mistaken my panic for more than it was.

Thankfully, he didn't pursue the subject. "How'd it go?"

"They still think I'm your client."

Travis yawned and pulled himself up in the driver's seat. "And whose fault is that? I don't think Foster had made the connection until you confirmed that we were together."

"Can we just get going? I want to get out of here."

He squinted over at me from under the bill of his cap. "So you and Foster are old friends, huh?" he asked. "If you ask me, he doesn't seem your type."

I considered pointing out that no one had asked for his opinion. I even thought of telling him that Stan had warned me about him, too. I finally settled for asking, "And what type is that?"

"Oh, you know, you seem more adventurous than staid old Stan."

I have to admit that I was secretly pleased with the description. After all, I'd been the nerdy type back in high school.

I wasn't about to say this to Travis, however. Instead, I said, "I could say the same thing about you and Stan. Just how do you happen to know each other?"

He chuckled. "Let's just say we've had a few run-ins in which we developed a mutual respect for each other."

I hardly thought that "run-ins" and "mutual respect" were words that went together in the same sentence.

He was still looking at me with narrowed eyes and a slight arch to the left eyebrow that conveyed both cynicism and sexuality at the same time.

"Are we ever going to get out of here?" I glanced at my watch. It was already after noon.

He took off the baseball cap, ruffling his hair as if he'd just gotten out of bed. It made me wonder what my own hair looked like after I'd yanked off the knit hat. I tried to smooth the hair back carefully over my still-healing wound.

Meanwhile Travis tossed the cap into the backseat, started the car, and pulled away from the curb.

"Did you check with Mack to see if you could give Detective Foster his name?" I asked.

Travis stifled another yawn. "Sorry, I

had a late night last night." While I wondered what bimbo he'd been out with this time, he finally got around to answering my question. "I'm not going to tell Stan the name of my client. It's the PI code. But I will give Mack a report when we get back to the store."

"It's a plant, not a store."

He lifted his hands off the wheel. "Well, excuse me."

Why was I being so nitpicky? I even thought of apologizing, but Travis changed the subject. "How do you think this Carol Jennings fits into the murder?"

"I wish I knew."

Travis made a left turn on Thirty-second. "Do you want me to look into it for you?"

"Aren't you supposed to stay out of things once they become police matters?"

"Well, yeah, theoretically."

"Even though Monroe is dead, he could still have been responsible for the hit-and-runs," I said. "Everything points that way, since he worked at an auto body shop where he had access to different cars."

"So the big question is who killed him."

I scrounged around for possibilities. "I wonder who owns the business where he works."

Travis was on Speer Boulevard by this time. "I can find that out pretty easily, and I won't even have to put Stan's nose out of joint to do it."

I nodded, but I didn't ask him if he was going to charge me for his time. I figured that was a given.

We continued to speculate about Monroe's murder during the rest of the drive back to the plant. It was a lot less nerve-wracking than the ride out to north Denver had been. The snow had stopped again, almost like a spring rain, and there had been enough traffic on the roads that the icy conditions had improved so the trip wasn't as slow.

I even filled him in on some of the details that Mack hadn't been privy to, mainly what Nat had found out about Joy Emerson's crash and the yellow paint that had been on her car. "So it could have been another hit-and-run with yet another car involved."

When we got to the cleaners, Travis whipped into a parking spot in front and put his arm on the back of my seat.

"Want to try going out on a date again some time?"

The question threw me. "Again?" Surely he didn't think of this as a date.

"I said 'try,' " he said. "The last time I asked you out, you stood me up. Remember?"

"That was in high school."

"So what about now?"

"Well, sure. Why not?" My answer surprised even me, but I felt I had the upper hand now that I knew he'd called last fall.

"Okay, I'll give you a call to set something up."

"Fine." I started to get out of the car. "Aren't you coming in to talk to Mack?"

"Oh, yeah, right." He turned off the ignition, and when he joined me at the door, he looked downright embarrassed. "I guess I had other things on my mind."

Maybe he actually had forgotten about his plan to give Mack an update on Monroe, and that's why he'd parked in front instead of driving around to the back of the plant. Unfortunately, this way we had to run the gauntlet of my crew, who were always looking for something to gossip about.

I opened the door to the call office. Inside, my morning counter manager, Julia, hailed me even though she was in the middle of waiting on a customer.

"Before I forget," she said. "Ray Hardesty called. He said you owe his mark-in lady a hundred bucks."

My heart did a little leap. I'd given up on all the calls I'd made earlier to other dry cleaners. None of the owners had seemed interested in helping me track down the owner of the red coat. Several had even laughed in disbelief and said it was too tedious a job, even when I offered a reward.

Maybe I was finally going to get lucky, at least about the owner of the coat.

"Oh, yes," Julia said, pointing to the upholstered gold chairs by the front window. "This gentleman is waiting to see you."

I looked around, and Alex Waring was just getting up from one of the chairs. He was wearing a black leather coat over gray slacks and a maroon turtleneck sweater, and he looked as if he'd only recently stepped out of *GQ* magazine. He was hatless, and his thick dark hair was styled and sprayed neatly into place.

It made Travis seem downright unkempt by comparison. His hair, which he'd never bothered to comb after his nap, was still ruffled, but I decided Travis was just as good looking, even if in a more *Police Gazette* sort of way.

"I was in the neighborhood, and I thought I'd stop by," Alex said as he came up to where Travis and I were standing. "How are you?"

"I'm fine, thanks," I said, and to Travis, "Why don't you go on back and talk to Mack?"

Travis didn't move, just gave Alex one of his piercing looks, as if he were trying to size him up.

Alex reached out his hand and introduced himself, and I had no choice but to introduce Travis to him. I didn't explain who Travis was, but since he'd been looking into this whole thing for Mack, I figured he needed an explanation about Alex. "This is a neighbor of Carol Jennings," I said. "He was the one who told me that he hadn't seen her for a while. Did she finally show up?"

"Not as far as I know," he said. "In fact, she borrowed a book of mine, and I've been trying to get it back, so if you hear when she's coming home, let me know."

I was going to ask what the title was, since he hadn't mentioned a book when I'd seen him at her door. However, his next remark threw me completely off the track.

"That's not really why I'm here, though," he said. "I wanted to get your mother's phone number. She called yesterday and wanted to know if I could arrange with the manager to pick up Laura's mail and bring it to them. Only trouble was my answering machine ran out right then and she didn't say where they were staying."

Well, good for modern-day technology or the lack thereof. At least Mom hadn't revealed her and Laura's whereabouts to Alex. Besides, I had a feeling the call had been a ruse to get him over to the hotel to see the transformation she'd made on Laura. I was sure she was working over-time to fix Laura up with someone she deemed more suitable than Nat. Didn't these middle-aged meddlers ever quit?

"Anyway, if you could give me their address, I can run the mail over to them right now," Alex continued.

"That's kind of you, but you don't have to bother. Just give it to me, and I'll take care of it."

"Sorry. It's back at my apartment."

"Then leave it with the manager, and I'll stop by and get it this evening. I need to go see Mom, anyway." To give her a tongue-lashing, if nothing else — not just for the trip to the Rendezview, but also for trying to play Cupid with Laura, at least until her attacker was found.

Alex was gracious and probably relieved about not having to act as courier for the mail. He said good-bye with a parting promise to tell Carol we were looking for her, should he see her before she contacted us.

When he left, I led Travis through the door to the back of the plant. I pointed to where Mack was working. "I'll see you later. I have to return a call." I veered off toward my office.

Even though I was interested in hearing Mack's reaction to Monroe's death, the call to Ray Hardesty took priority. At my desk, I grabbed my Rolodex and rifled through it until I found Hardesty's Cleaners. I punched in the number, but I had to wait while a woman summoned her boss.

"Hardesty here," the owner said a few minutes later.

"It's Mandy. I can't believe you really found out something."

"You've got the weather to thank for that. With all the snow lately, business has been so slow that I had to find something to keep my employees occupied."

"So what did you find out?"

"Now mind you, this might not be the person you're looking for, but a customer did bring in a red coat to have cleaned a couple of months ago, and the lot number we used to clean it matches the one you gave me."

"Okay," I said, barely able to contain myself. "Just give me the name."

I held my breath while he apparently sorted through stuff on his desk looking for the information. "Damn. Now where did I put it?" I waited an agonizing few minutes, hoping he hadn't lost it. "Oh, good, here it is." He paused for a few more seconds. "We looked up the name on our computer, and she'd only been in a few times, so she wasn't a regular customer."

"The name, please," I said, trying not to sound too abrupt. "Just give me the name."

"I wouldn't know her if I saw her again, but her name is Carol Jennings."

CHAPTER TWENTY-ONE

It's strange how a person can suspect that something's true, yet be shocked when it really is. I felt that way about the coat, and it took me a moment to find my voice.

"I really owe you one, Ray," I said finally.

"So the name means something to you?" he asked.

"Yes, and unfortunately the reason she hasn't claimed the coat is because she's missing."

"Dear God," Ray said. "Do you think something happened to her?"

"I don't know, but I'll let you know if I find out. And I'll get a check in the mail right away for your mark-in person."

He spelled her name for me, and we said goodbye and hung up. I sat back in my chair and stared at the red coat hanging on the back of the door. Had Carol met with foul play, or had she deliberately gone missing with the stamp?

I needed to call Laura and tell her about the coat and the fact that the police would be contacting her. She answered on the first ring. Luckily, Mom wasn't in the room, so I didn't have to deal with her right then. Laura had already found out from Nat about Ricky Monroe's murder, Ricky's connection to Carol, and Joy and the yellow car. Still, she was stunned to hear about the coat.

"Look, can you keep a secret?" I asked. I told her how I'd been at the crime scene where Ricky died and that the police would be talking to her. "I don't want Nat to know I was there just yet. I'll tell him later."

She vowed not to tell him, even though she was going out with him again that night. I knew that wouldn't make Mom happy, so after I hung up I made a mental note to call later and suggest a mother-daughter dinner — with a little scolding on the side.

Before I did anything else, I needed to talk to Mack, to try to sort out all the mismatched bits of information that were floating around in my head. Right now, it was as if someone had mixed up two jigsaw puzzles so that the pieces couldn't possibly fit together. How could Joy Emerson's death have anything to do with the missing Carol Jennings, for instance? Had Laura's burglar been looking for the coat, the film she'd shot at the restaurant, or both?

I found Mack at his regular place in the cleaning department. He was spotting a wine stain on a wedding gown. Travis was gone by then, and I was relieved about that.

"Wow, that was a shock, wasn't it?" Mack said.

I knew he was talking about the murder of Ricky Monroe, not the fact that I'd agreed to go out with Travis. That information might have slipped out if Travis had still been here. I didn't want Mack to have a chance to gloat.

"I just found out something else, and I was wondering if you had time for a quick lunch over at Tico Taco's," I said, glancing at my watch. It was already one-fifteen. "I'll buy."

"I already ate, but for this, I'll take another break," he said. "Just give me a minute on this dress, then Kim can handle things for a little while."

Kim, Mack's Korean assistant, nodded his head.

I still had on my boots, and I'd grabbed my heavy jacket as I left the office, so I was ready to go. While Mack finished up on the gown, I went to the front counter and told Theresa, who'd just arrived for the afternoon shift, that I'd be gone for a while. I explained that the police might come by to get the coat that was hanging on the back of my office door. I told her she should give it to them and be sure to get a receipt.

Mack was waiting for me, wearing his old navy pea coat, when I returned to the cleaning department. Together we made our way across the parking lot to the Mexican restaurant that was in the strip mall behind our stand-alone cleaners. I was glad to see that the snow removal service we business owners hire to clear the parking lot after snowstorms had finally been here. At least I wouldn't have to dig my car out that night.

Tico Taco's was quiet now that the lunchtime rush was over. Manuel Ramirez, the owner, greeted us at the door like long-lost friends.

"I haven't seen you for a while, Mandy," he said.

I thought about telling him that I'd been staying away because I didn't want to become known as "the woman who dined alone." Instead, I said, "Sorry, I've had a lot to do lately."

"Didn't I just see you here?" This time he was talking to Mack, who said he liked the place so well he couldn't stay away.

Manuel beamed and led us to our favorite booth in the back where we were away from the few remaining diners.

"The usual," I said, meaning the cheese enchilada plate and coffee.

"I'll just take coffee," Mack said.

"I'll be back with your salsa *al momento*," Manuel said. He always threw in a few words of Spanish so no one would forget he was the proprietor of an authentic Mexican restaurant. No Tex-Mex for him.

"What's this new information you have?" Mack said as soon as he was gone.

"Ray Hardesty just called and said he cleaned a red coat with the same color tag and lot number as the one in my office. It belonged to Carol Jennings."

Mack gave a low whistle. "I've got to hand it to you, Mandy. I didn't think you'd get any other dry cleaners to go back through their files looking for the coat."

I agreed with him that it had been a long shot. "And then to have it belong to someone who's involved in all of this." As I finished, it occurred to me that I should probably call Stan and tell him what I'd found out.

"So what does it mean?" Mack asked.

"That's the problem. I don't know. I was actually hoping that the coat belonged to someone we'd never heard of before. That would probably mean Laura's hit-and-run and break-in were because of the film, not the coat."

Manuel was back almost immediately with our coffees and the complimentary chips and salsa. "Bon appetit," he said, mixing languages as easily as he mixed drinks.

Mack nodded his thanks but waited until Manuel left to continue, "I don't mind telling you I was blown away when Travis told me that Ricky Monroe was dead. Now we find out that his missing girlfriend owned the coat."

"If there'd been something of value in the coat, like this stamp she was supposed to have, maybe I could understand it, but there wasn't."

"Someone could have thought there was, however."

I tried to think why Carol would have grabbed another person's coat when she left the restaurant Saturday night. "Maybe," I said, "she thought she could disguise herself so that someone — Ricky, for instance — wouldn't recognize her when she went outside. And obviously she took whatever she was trying to sell with her when she left or it would have been in the coat."

"What if she got away but someone realized she wasn't wearing her own coat and still thinks there's something in it?" Mack said.

I shook my head. "That doesn't make sense. Unless someone knew she didn't have the item on her, why would the person be after the coat? More likely, she's hiding out and may resurface now that Ricky's dead."

Mack wasn't yet willing to give up the idea that the coat was somehow mixed up in this. "And she'll know exactly where to get the coat — either in the restaurant's lost and found department or from Laura."

"That's assuming she knew she had grabbed Laura's coat. I'll have to ask Laura about it tonight."

"Even if she didn't know Laura would take the coat, I'm sure Laura left her name when she called the restaurant about it."

"Frankly, I'm beginning to think Carol doesn't even want the coat and never plans to claim it."

"So who do you think killed Monroe?" Mack asked.

"Carol's beginning to seem like the most likely candidate, isn't she?"

"Well, Monroe sure sounded like the one who was involved in the hit-and-runs," Mack said.

"I was thinking he might have had a falling-out with a partner who killed him," I said. "Travis said he'd try to get a line on Monroe's boss at the auto body shop."

I should never have mentioned Travis's name.

"How'd it work out with you and Travis?"

Right then, Manuel returned with my enchilada plate. "You haven't even touched the salsa."

"Sorry." I grabbed a chip and dipped it into the bowl of salsa to pacify him. Mack followed suit.

"That's more like it," Manuel said, winking at us.

"Where were we?" I asked once he departed, hoping to get back on the subject of Monroe.

"We were talking about Travis. I wondered if the two of you got along okay."

"We survived," I said. "Unfortunately, because I was with Travis, the police think I'm his client."

No sense telling Mack "the police" was Stan. He had about as much use for Stan as Mom did for Nat when it came to them going out with friends and family.

"Why didn't Travis tell them it was me?" Mack asked.

"Client confidentiality, like a doctor-patient relationship."

"Well, I'll call him right now and give him my permission." Mack made a move to get out of the booth.

"Never mind. It probably won't come up again." I was sure it would as long as Stan was involved, but at the same time, I didn't want Mack to become the focus of his inquiry.

Mack settled back in the booth, and I noticed that Manuel was glancing our way, probably wondering why I hadn't touched my enchiladas. I cut into one and lifted a forkful to my mouth. As I ate it, I gave him a thumbs-up to let him know that it was delicious.

Mack dug into the salsa, but I could see his mind was elsewhere. "Now we're back to square one. We still don't know if the burglar was looking for the coat or Laura's film when he broke into her apartment."

"I think it had to be the film," I said. "The receipt for the film was missing, and don't forget, when I got to the photo lab, it had been broken into during the night."

Mack went on the alert immediately. "You never told me that. It's just like I said — Jimmy Stewart and Grace Kelly all over again."

I knew, of course, that he was talking

about *Rear Window* and how the disabled Jimmy had talked Grace into being his "legs" to try to get the goods on his murderous neighbor.

"So doesn't it sound as if the color slides were what the burglar was looking for?" I asked.

Mack was still shaking his head at my foolhardiness. "Maybe it was both."

I sighed. "That's the trouble. There are too many loose ends. In fact, one of Carol's neighbors was here a few minutes ago. He'd met Mom and Laura Wednesday, and he said Mom called and asked him to bring Laura's mail to them, but his tape ran out before she said where she was staying."

"I hope you didn't tell him."

"Of course not — especially because the only reason she did that is because she's a busybody, like some other people I know, and she's trying to set him up with Laura." I assumed Mack would know I was making a veiled reference to him and his flagrant attempt to bring Travis and me together.

He chose to ignore my remark. "Just what exactly does this guy have to do with Carol?"

"I don't know. I met him outside her door the first day I stopped by her apartment. I had the impression he hardly knew her, but today he was asking if I'd heard from her. He'd loaned her a book and wanted to get it back."

Mack took a drink of coffee. "I don't think you have to be close friends to lend someone a book. Unless maybe if it's a valuable first edition."

Suddenly I flashed back to the books I'd seen in Alex's apartment as I stood outside his door. The books had all been huge volumes with identical covers. From a distance, I'd thought they looked like law books. Maybe they were all hiding first editions, and Carol had taken one of them and been trying to hawk it along with the stamp. No, that was getting way off track. I tried to shut off the image of the books, but something about them bothered me.

"What are you thinking about?" Mack asked.

"Nothing," I said just as Manuel appeared again.

Any time he saw that people weren't talking, he was like the perfect host at a dinner party, ready to jump in with a new topic of conversation. He topped off our coffee and chatted for a few minutes about the weather.

Mack waited until he left to greet four

new customers. "By the way, you never told me what Nat wanted this morning. He didn't get fired, did he?"

"No, far from it. When he met with Senator Ambrose this morning, the senator wanted to give him a scoop about why he'd been at the restaurant Saturday night." I outlined the information about the senator's new campaign manager and the hush-hush dinner that led up to it.

"Remember how I told you that Joy Emerson's boyfriend said he saw a yellow sports car leaving the restaurant just after she left? Well, Ambrose apparently noticed it, too, and at Nat's urging reported it to the authorities. Turns out there were flakes of yellow paint on her car, and Nat also found out from a neighbor that Joy was pregnant."

Mack whistled, louder this time, which I feared would bring Manuel rushing back to our booth, but it didn't.

"I gather the authorities will be talking to Joy's boyfriend," I added, "but he stayed at the restaurant after she left, so he couldn't have run her off the road."

"Could he have hired someone to do it?"

"That's what Nat thinks, but I don't see how. Joy was apparently going to tell him about the pregnancy that night. Besides, even if Joy seems to be the focus of the investigation, I can't help thinking that her death and Carol's disappearance are somehow tied together."

"What about the skinny little guy that Ambrose claimed was outside the window that night?" Mack asked. "If it was Ricky Monroe, what would he have had to do with the dead girl?"

I nodded, as confused as I always was when I considered the disparate parts of the story.

"And, of course, there were the blurred images that you told me about in those first pictures Laura took of the restaurant," Mack continued. "What did the figures actually look like?"

"Like ghosts," I said. "Like wisps of fog that had somehow taken on human form."

"But they looked like men, didn't they — not women?"

"Yes, and Laura thought so, too, even though she didn't get a good look at them when she yelled at them to get out of the picture."

"How tall were they?"

"Well, one was taller than the other one. That's really all I could tell." Suddenly something else struck me. "Bless you, Mack. I bet they were the same two guys

Mom and Betty saw in the parking lot outside the restaurant last night."

I hated to admit it, but when we were looking at the slides, Mom had diverted Laura's and my attention to the mysterious item in the chair that disappeared along with the ghostly images before the time exposure was over. It was time to refocus on the men, now that Mom, in her meddlesome effort to help, had decided the item on the chair wasn't a cat.

Mack looked pleased. "Yeah, the short guy could have been Monroe, and the tall one could have been his partner — the guy with the big head."

"The Afro." I couldn't help smiling at how Betty had kept correcting Mom. Frankly, her description sounded a lot more plausible than "a big head," and we were definitely on the right track if Travis found out Ricky's boss at the auto body shop was a guy with a lot of hair.

However, there was something about the description that still didn't ring quite true. Where had the Afro been in the foggy image at the back of the restaurant? Wouldn't it have shown up like some sort of giant mushroom cloud above the tall guy's shoulders?

For a second, I felt as if I were close to

311

another explanation for the big head, but the thought was as ephemeral as the images on the color slide and evaporated just as quickly.

CHAPTER TWENTY-TWO

I went up to the front of the cleaners as soon as Mack and I returned from Tico Taco's. I was intent on searching for O.J.'s missing shirt, but first I told Theresa that I was back from lunch.

She nodded and said she needed to talk to me as soon as she finished waiting on a customer.

"Hi, Mrs. Riley," I said to the woman on the other side of the counter. Knowing your customers and addressing them by name is the best public relations there is.

We chatted for a few minutes while Theresa went to collect Mrs. Riley's cleaning from the conveyor and then completed the cash transaction.

Once we were alone, Theresa turned to me. "The police were here, and I gave them the coat the way you told me to do." She was whispering as if she thought Mrs. Riley might hear us from outside the door. "And here's the receipt the policeman gave me." She pulled it out of a drawer. "I was afraid I might lose it if I didn't give it to you right away."

I guess she had a point. After all, we'd lost O.J.'s lucky shirt. I took the receipt back to my office and placed it in my filing cabinet under *C* for coat. Surely I wouldn't forget where I'd put it.

I stared at the blank spot on the door where the coat had been. I felt a sense of relief that it was no longer there, but I knew I should call Stan and tell him that I'd found out the identity of the coat's owner.

I sat at my desk for several minutes, trying to work up the courage to phone him. Finally, I rationalized that if I hurried he would still be at the crime scene. I could simply leave a message on his voice mail, thus fulfilling my duty as an upstanding citizen while retaining my status as a first-class coward.

I rifled through my Rolodex for his numbers, strangely pleased that I'd forgotten his extension. That was a good sign. It meant I was finally over any feelings for him, ambivalent or otherwise.

I punched in the number for the police administration building and asked for his extension. I was confident that I'd be switched over to his voice mail after a few rings.

"Detective Foster," a voice said before

the phone had barely rung once.

Damn.

I thought of hanging up. "This is Mandy," I said finally. "Mandy Dyer." I wondered if I was afraid he wouldn't know me if I didn't give my full name.

"I recognized your voice," he said.

I cleared my throat and tried to sound as if I were all business. "The reason I'm calling is that I found out the name of the owner of the coat — the one your officer picked up a little while ago. It's Carol Jennings, the woman who is missing."

"And how did you discover that bit of information?" His words fairly dripped sarcasm.

I explained my methodology for tracing the owner of the coat. While I was at it, I pointed out that I'd started the process long before I knew that the coat might become part of a police investigation.

"Okay, I'm sorry. Thanks for the information."

He seem to mellow once he heard my explanation of how I'd traced the coat. Maybe he'd even realized that I was just an innocent bystander at the crime scene this morning. Then again, maybe not.

"But I don't want you to do any more snooping on your own," he added.

"No, of course not," I said and started to hang up.

"Good. We'll need you down at headquarters to go over your statement. Say about ten o'clock tomorrow."

I sighed and resigned myself to the fact that he was going to make this as difficult for me as possible. "Okay, I'll be there."

"By the way," he said, "as long as I have you on the phone, I thought you should know that I'm no longer engaged."

Why was he telling me this? Surely it wasn't to renew our relationship.

I scrambled around for a response. "I'm sorry to hear that," I said finally. "I'll see you tomorrow."

Once we hung up, I wondered about his broken engagement, but I quickly concluded that I didn't want to think about it right then. I considered calling Nat to tell him about the coat, but I needed to look for the missing shirt. That would give me a good excuse to clear my mind of all but the most mundane thoughts.

As I started to the front of the cleaners again, I tried to figure out the best procedure for finding the shirt. Going through each slot on the conveyor hadn't worked, mainly because I hadn't been able to finish after the plant closed, thanks to Mom and

Betty's joyride to the mountains. Now the conveyor was in periodic motion as Theresa and Elaine came back to pick customers' orders off of it.

I finally settled on the idea of looking at the lot numbers attached to the tickets on the individual garment bags as the conveyor was moving. We'd been working on a lot that used yellow tags the day Owen Jeffries brought in his clothes, so I would look for other orders with yellow tags stapled to the tickets on the garment bags. My theory was that the shirt had been misfiled with another order that was cleaned and finished the same day.

About twenty minutes later, I got lucky. Was I good or what? I'd solved one mystery, even though I'd be darned if I could solve the larger one about Laura, the coat, and her rolls of film.

I repackaged O.J.'s lucky shirt in its own separate bag and told Theresa that I was going to personally deliver it to his place of business. "I should be back by five."

With the hanger looped over one finger, I returned to the back of the plant. My cleaning and pressing crew was getting ready to quit for the day, and Betty was just coming out of the laundry department. I almost ran into her.

"See, you *can* find a needle in a haystack." I held up the shirt triumphantly.

"I said you can't find a needle under a bunch of other needles," Betty corrected.

That wasn't exactly what she'd said, but I didn't want to argue about it. "Whatever," I said. "All you have to do is keep digging and you'll uncover what you're looking for eventually."

"Whatever," Betty countered, apparently unimpressed by my inspirational lesson for the day.

I grabbed my coat from my office and went to my car, where I hung the shirt on a hook in the backseat. All my efforts were rewarded when I finally reached Owen Jeffries's office in the realty firm where he worked. He was ecstatic about the return of his lucky shirt. He even tried to give me a twenty-dollar tip, but I declined.

"Okay, but you'll have my undying loyalty forever," he promised.

That's what I was after. Something far better than a onetime tip.

Once back at the plant, I was working at the front counter with Theresa when the phone rang. It was almost seven o'clock by then.

"Dyer's Cleaners," I said.

"Why didn't you tell me the coat belonged

to Carol Jennings?" It was Nat, and he'd clearly been talking to Laura.

"I figured Laura could tell you," I said.

Although he'd sounded irritated, he was apparently willing to forgive me. "Hold on to your hat and sit down in the nearest chair," he said, using his usual mix of hackneyed expressions. "I've got big news. The cops found the body of Ricky Monroe this morning at his apartment. He'd been shot."

Obviously, Laura had been true to her word and hadn't told him about my presence at the crime scene. I tried to act surprised by gasping loudly.

"I just thought I'd give you a call to bring you up to speed," he continued. "See, you didn't need that jerk Travis after all."

That was the main reason I hadn't wanted to tell him. He would have gone on forever if he knew I'd been there with Travis. Come to think about it, I was surprised that Nat hadn't shown up at the house while Travis and I were there.

Nat kept on talking. "So what did Travis have to say when he talked to you and Mack this morning?" I could hear the sarcasm in his voice.

"He found out that Monroe worked at an auto body shop on the other side of town and hadn't shown up for work this morning. That was about it."

"See, I knew Travis wouldn't come up with anything worthwhile." Nat added that the police didn't have any suspects in the murder at this point and gave me a few of the details about the case, most of which I already knew. He probably added them to show that an ace reporter was privy to more information than a private investigator.

"Gotta go," he said abruptly. "I'm on deadline, and I've got a hot date with Laura tonight. See you."

I held on to the phone for a few seconds, irritated that he refused to listen to me when it came to getting involved with one of my good friends. I knew it wouldn't last, and what then?

Theresa had been on another line while I was talking to Nat, but she hung up before I did.

"That was Betty," she said when I put down the receiver. "She wanted to talk to you, but I said you were on the phone. She said it was *really* important, but when I told her to hold on, she said she couldn't wait. She would talk to you later."

"How important could it be if she wouldn't wait?" I said.

Little did I know.

CHAPTER TWENTY-THREE

When I closed up at seven, I tried returning Betty's call — just in case she did have something important to say.

Arthur Goldman, who looks like a Kewpie doll, and coincidentally runs a doll hospital, answered the phone. For reasons I would never understand, he'd been attracted to Betty and now they lived together.

"I'm sorry, Miss Dyer," he said in his chivalrous way, "but I had to deliver a doll for a child's birthday party, so I just got home a few minutes ago. Betty wasn't here, but I'll tell her you called when she gets in."

"Thanks, Arthur," I said.

We hung up, but I couldn't shake the uneasy feeling that something strange was going on. I called Mom at the hotel.

"I know Laura is busy tonight," I said, "but what about the two of us going out for dinner?"

"That would be nice, dear," Mom said. "I'm just sorry Laura can't join us."

Of course she was sorry. She'd expressed herself often enough about Nat and even gone so far as to invite Alex Waring over to the hotel.

"That reminds me," I said. "*Your* friend Alex stopped by today and said you'd called him about picking up Laura's mail. What were you thinking? We were supposed to keep your whereabouts to ourselves."

Mom was silent for a moment, and I could hear voices in the background. Maybe Nat had called from the hotel.

"Fortunately, Alex said his tape ran out before you told him where you were staying," I said.

"On second thought," Mom said, her voice dropping to a whisper, "maybe we better just skip dinner tonight."

"Why? What's going on? Who's there?"

"Just Laura and me. She's waiting for Nat to show up, but of course he's late as usual." I could hear the disapproval in her voice.

"No, someone else is there. I can hear people talking in the background. Is it Betty?"

"Why would you think it was Betty?" Mom sounded aghast at the thought, but I knew better.

"Are the two of you cooking up some new kind of mischief?"

"I can assure you Betty is not here."

I was not to be denied. "Okay, who is it?"

"If you must know, it's the bellhop — uh, returning my dry cleaning."

"What?" I yelled. That was the last straw. She was having her cleaning done at the hotel.

"Remember, I accidentally got nail polish on my white slacks when I was doing Laura's nails," she said as if that were the most logical explanation in the world.

No, I didn't remember any such thing.

"You know, I'm really tired, Amanda." She yawned dramatically into the phone. "Why don't we just skip dinner until to-morrow night, and I'll order room ser-vice?"

I could tell she was irritated, because she'd called me "Amanda," not "dear." But there was more to it than that. Mom was up to something, and I needed to know what.

"Okay, but don't call Alex anymore. I'll pick up the mail and bring it over tomorrow."

Before she could respond, I hung up. I could be sneaky, too. I had no intention of waiting until the next day.

I put on my cold-weather clothes over my uniform and left. I set a speed record, at least for icy streets, getting to Laura's apartment.

I went to the manager's office to pick up the mail, but no one was there, so I proceeded to the seventh floor. No one answered at Alex's apartment, either. While I was there, I checked at Carol Jennings's door, just in case she might have resurfaced. I was batting zero.

Having failed to make contact with anyone, I hurried on to the hotel, skidding on the ice as I turned into the underground parking garage below the hotel. It would have cost me less to park somewhere else, but I decided that this came under the heading of an emergency.

I knocked on the door of Mom's hotel room. No one came to greet me, but I could still hear voices inside.

I lowered my voice an octave. "Room service," I yelled.

"Just a minute." Mom opened the door. "I didn't order —" She looked decidedly put-upon when she saw me. "I told you not to bother coming tonight."

I pushed my way into the room. Aha. There was no bellhop. No Nat. And my premonition that it was Betty was wrong. It was worse. Alex, still wearing the clothes he'd had on at the cleaners, was sitting in a chair at the back of the room talking to Laura.

No wonder Mom hadn't wanted me to come.

"I'm sorry I didn't call you," Alex said. "Your mother phoned again and told me where she was staying, and I thought I'd just run the mail over here myself. It wasn't any trouble."

"And Alex has been kind enough to invite me out to dinner," Mom said. "It's too bad Laura can't come along."

Obviously, I still wasn't her choice to be fixed up with Alex, but I decided not to take it personally. In fact, it was rather nice not to be the focus of her matchmaking efforts for once, and if anything, her interest in setting Alex up with Laura had only intensified since Laura started going out with Nat.

"Your mother was just telling me about the coat mix-up and how you found out the coat belonged to Carol," Alex said. "No wonder you were looking for Carol that day."

Everything was spinning out of control, and I would have screamed at Mom if we'd been alone. Instead, I took a deep breath and said, "Mind if I tag along to dinner? I haven't eaten since —" Well, actually, I'd had that late lunch with Mack. My voice trailed off.

Mom frowned at me, but Alex gave me one of his 120-watt smiles. "We'd be glad to have your company."

At least this way, I figured, I could monitor Mom's conversation.

"Where's Nat?" I asked, turning to Laura, who was sitting in an upholstered chair across from Alex.

"He was supposed to be here at seven, but he's running a little late."

Welcome to Nat's world. She'd have to get used to being stood up when he was on the trail of a fast-breaking story. I was tempted to give Laura a few words of warning, but this wasn't the time.

I went over to her and Alex. Once I got there, I didn't know what to do. There wasn't another chair, so Mom must have been sitting on the bed when I interrupted their conversation.

I stood in front of them and tried to think of something to say that could be said in front of Alex and my mother, the blabbermouth.

"How's the leg?" I asked finally.

"It's itching under the cast," Laura said. "Otherwise, it isn't too bad."

I noted that her bruises were all but gone, although Mom's hand could still be seen in Laura's carefully applied makeup. I was sure she'd done it for Alex's benefit, not Nat's.

"Maybe you and your boyfriend would like to come with us, Laura," Alex said. "I know a great steak house just a couple of blocks from here."

"Thanks for asking, but Nat and I are going to eat here at the hotel," Laura said. "He says it's still too dangerous for me to go out on the icy sidewalks on my crutches." There was something about the way she said it that made me think she was actually falling for Nat. I should have warned her about him long before this.

"Nat's a police reporter friend of Mandy's," Mom said, even though I didn't think there was any need for an explanation. "I think he's just trying to squeeze information out of us about Laura's accident."

Laura looked hurt, and against all odds I found myself coming to his defense. "Nat's able to keep things to himself, especially if the information's off the record."

Laura suddenly rose from her chair, much more agilely than she had that first day after the hit-and-run. She grabbed her crutches and headed for the bathroom. "I have to get some Kleenex," she said, and then in a whisper as she walked by me, "Can we talk?"

I followed her to the bathroom but didn't shut the door. I wanted to know what was going on in the other room.

"What is it?" I asked in a low voice.

Laura perched on her good leg. "I can't take much more of this, Mandy. Your mother insisted on dragging Alex over here with the mail, and then she started talking about the coat. I didn't tell her anything else, but I guess I shouldn't have told her about the coat, either. I was giving her dirty looks all the time, but she just ignored me."

I nodded my head. "I understand, but maybe it won't be for too much longer. Things seem to be happening pretty fast now."

Laura nodded. "I can hardly wait to get back to my apartment."

I had one ear trained on Mom and Alex's conversation in the other room. They seemed to be talking about the weather, so I concentrated on Laura. "Tell me one thing, Laura. It's important. Did Carol Jennings know what kind of coat you were wearing at the Rendezview that night?"

Laura closed her eyes as if to re-create the scene at the restaurant. "Come to think of it, she did. I'd gone to the entryway to get another roll of film out of the pocket of my coat when she was on her way to the restroom. She stopped for a minute as I was searching through the pockets for the film. She said she'd about decided the mystery man she was supposed to meet wasn't going to show up."

So Carol did know what coat Laura had been wearing. That must have meant Carol took the coat deliberately, knowing that she could get her own back later. I would even have assumed that Carol might have left something valuable in her own coat, except there hadn't been anything of value in it.

All of a sudden I heard Mom mention Carol's name from the other room. I turned and charged out of the bathroom, but I didn't even bother to hear what she said. All I wanted was to move the conversation around to something totally innocuous.

"Well, isn't it about time we get going to dinner?" I asked. "I'm starving." Actually, I was still stuffed from gobbling down all those enchiladas at Tico Taco's to keep

Manuel at bay while Mack and I talked.

It was disgusting. Even a small fib and I began to itch. My personal barometer for telling me when I'd strayed from the truth didn't seem to make a distinction between a whopper and a little white lie that was of no consequence.

Alex stood up. "That sounds like a good idea. Does steak sound good to you, Cecilia?"

Mother nodded. "But you don't like beef very well, do you, Amanda?"

It was clear that she didn't want me along. "I'm sure they'll have chicken, too," I said.

She frowned and went to get her high-heeled boots and fur coat from the closet. I was already dressed for winter, although I wished now that I'd taken the time back at the plant to change from my uniform into something more appropriate for dining out. Mom was wearing gray slacks, a white silk blouse, and a lot of turquoise jewelry the way people from the Southwest do.

When we got down to the lobby, Alex asked, "You don't mind walking, do you? It's only a short distance, and my car is parked just about as far away."

I could tell that Mom wasn't keen on the idea of a walk to the restaurant, but what could she say? I wasn't about to volunteer my car, carefully tucked away below us.

We didn't have to hassle with traffic as we crossed Sixteenth, the main street through downtown Denver. It has been a pedestrian mall for many years. The only motor vehicles allowed are small trams that passengers can ride for free. It's a great place to hang out in the summer, with a number of outdoor dining areas attached to its restaurants and coffee houses. However, the whole area was almost deserted at this time of year. I didn't even see a tram; I'm sure Mom would have jumped aboard if one had come along just then.

She was lagging behind Alex, who had a long stride, and I couldn't help but feel sorry for her. I finally dropped back to keep her company.

"How much farther did you say it was?" she puffed.

"We're here," Alex said.

And not a moment too soon for Mom, apparently. "I was getting cold," she said, snuggling into her fur coat as we were ushered to a table.

I was relieved that we didn't encounter any antifur activists on our way. I was also glad there wasn't a coat check at the door or even a rack the way there had been at the Rendezview. I didn't particularly want to walk by the other diners in my uniform, but I did take off my coat when we got to the table. Mom didn't.

I ordered prime rib, and it wasn't just to prove that Mom was wrong about my taste for beef. I actually like it. Alex and Mom ordered steaks.

"So why do you think that Carol traded coats?" Alex asked.

I shook my head. "I have no idea."

"I thought you felt she might have left something in the coat that she wanted to retrieve later," Mom said.

"There wasn't anything in the coat, Mother." It was obvious I was going to have to take control of this conversation or it was going to keep getting back to Carol and the coat.

Mom wasn't to be denied. "Have you really checked it thoroughly, dear?" She looked over at Alex as she finally shrugged out of her fur and dropped it over the back of the chair. "Mandy has been keeping it at the cleaners in hopes of finding the owner."

"Speaking of the cleaners, something funny happened today," I said.

Alex and Mom both looked at me with interest. Maybe they thought I had some more snippets of information about the coat.

"A man came in several days ago and said a shirt was missing from his cleaning order," I said. "And get this, he said it was his lucky shirt." I emphasized the "lucky shirt" by curling my fingers in the air like quotation marks.

I could see my companions' interest flag immediately. I knew we were in for a long evening if I was going to keep the conversation off the coat. I pressed ahead. I managed to take us through the salad course with my convoluted story of how the customer had finally revealed to me that the shirt had an embroidered monogram on the pocket.

"Well, duh," I said. "It would have been a great help in finding the shirt earlier if the employee who took the complaint had only told me about the monogram in the first place."

"Are you finished?" Mom asked. She put up her hand and yawned. This time I was sure it was genuine, unlike the time on the telephone when she'd said she was tired.

"No," I said as our server replaced the salad dishes with the entrée. "There's more."

I then regaled them with the information that the shirt was monogrammed with the initials *OJ*. "Can you believe the customer would think that those initials were lucky?"

Alex laughed politely, but a few seconds later I thought I saw him yawn, too, behind his napkin.

I moved on, telling Mom and Alex of the efforts to find the shirt: how we'd checked to see if it had mistakenly been folded and packaged in one of our special shirt boxes and how we'd then started the laborious search of every space on our conveyor to see if it had been misfiled.

Mom was throwing darts of irritation my way by then. "I'm sure it's interesting to other dry cleaners, but —"

"Oh, I haven't gotten to the really interesting part yet." I told them about checking with the women in our shirt laundry. "One of them said, 'Looking for a shirt in a shirt laundry is like looking for a needle in a haystack,' and Betty — you know how she is, Mom — she said 'No, it's like looking for a needle in a box of needles.' Isn't that funny?"

Nobody laughed or looked even slightly amused.

"Actually, this afternoon she said it was like looking for a needle under a bunch of other needles."

Still no laughter, but suddenly something occurred to me. What if . . . ? No, it couldn't be, or could it?

I'd persevered until I found the shirt, or the needle under the other needles, and there was one place Mack and I hadn't looked when we thought something valuable might be hidden away in the coat. What about a stamp underneath another stamp? More precisely, what about a small but valuable stamp underneath a thirty-seven-cent stamp on an envelope addressed to the IRS? Was it possible? It seemed unlikely, but I knew I wouldn't be satisfied until I checked it out.

CHAPTER TWENTY-FOUR

I had to force myself to stay put at the table. As much as I wanted to get up and bolt from the restaurant, I still had Mom to contend with. I wasn't about to leave her here alone to spill her guts to Alex.

"Is that all there is to the story, Amanda?" Mom asked, clearly irritated and hopeful at the same time.

"Yes, that's about it, except that I found the lucky shirt." I glanced at both her and Alex's plates. They'd managed to eat most of their meal while I rambled on ad infinitum. Thank God. Maybe they were as anxious to leave as I was.

Alex must have noticed me checking their plates. "You've hardly touched your food."

"I think I'll just take everything home." I raised my hand and said, "Server." It sounded dumb compared to saying, "Waiter," but anything to be politically correct.

The man was at our table before I'd had time to lower my arm. "I'd like a doggy bag."

"Right away," he said. "Would anyone care for dessert?"

I shook my head. So did Alex.

"What do you have?" Mom asked.

The waiter rattled off a list of desserts that made the menu at House of Pies seem paltry.

Mom put her index finger to her cheek and considered the possibilities. "Would you mind repeating that list again?"

She was apparently determined to extend the meal as long as possible. It was probably my fault. Now that I'd concluded my tale of the lucky shirt, she might have been thinking that it was her turn to talk.

I couldn't let that happen. I waited until she ordered the chocolate mousse and Alex asked for coffee. "Tell us a little about yourself, Alex," I said.

He gave me another bright-enough-to-read-by smile. "Well, let's see. I'm thirty-seven and single. That's about all there is to it."

Of course, we already knew his marital status, but that didn't stop Mom. "I can't imagine that a man of your charm isn't married by now." I guess she still hadn't considered the possibility that he might be gay, thus negating her efforts to bring him and Laura together.

"Well, it's true, Cecilia, but I'm still looking." Alex looked right past me, however, toward the door as if he wanted nothing more than to get away. He'd obviously decided I wasn't even in the running after my incredibly dull story about the shirt. Who could blame him?

"I'm hoping that Laura can get back into her apartment soon," Mom said.

The waiter returned with Mom's dessert and the coffee.

"Sure you don't want any coffee?" Alex asked me.

I shook my head. I was riding on an adrenaline high, and I didn't need any caffeine to keep me going. All I wanted was to get out of there and take a look at that empty envelope back at the cleaners that was addressed to the IRS.

"Laura's such a lovely girl, and she hasn't been in Denver long," Mom continued. "Maybe the two of you should go out for dinner sometime. I'm sure you'd hit it off." Talk about being obvious.

"What do you do for a living, Alex?" I asked.

He looked uneasy, but I wasn't sure if it was from Mom's suggestion or my question.

"I'm in the antique business," he said after a moment's hesitation.

Okay, so maybe that explained the decor of his apartment better than the idea that he was gay or trying to get in touch with his feminine side. It really wasn't important except to Mom's efforts to fix him up with Laura.

"About that book that you were trying to get back from Carol, what kind of book was it?" I asked.

"You know, it's embarrassing that you should mention that. I finally found it. I'd completely forgotten that she'd returned it to me, but there it was. I'd simply misplaced it."

"So what was the book?" I asked. After all, Mack and I had thought it might be a first edition that would put him on the suspect list for all the mysterious goings-on.

"It was just a travel book about the Caribbean. I've been thinking of taking a trip down there, and I wanted to check out some places to stay."

At that point, a lot of things occurred to me that were just as good as a first edition. Offshore banking. Secret account numbers. Maybe Carol had fled to some tropical island once she'd collected the money from her stamp. And maybe Alex was her secret lover who was planning to join her there at a later time.

The idea shot holes in my theory that the Jenny Invert might be hidden away behind the stamp on the envelope we'd found in the coat. It wasn't going to stop me from taking one more look, and in fact, the idea that Carol was waiting for Alex at some Caribbean hideaway was full of a lot of holes itself. Why wasn't he already there if they had planned to flee the country together? Why would he mention a travel book if it might point the way to his lover's secret hiding place?

Alex began to tell us about a few of his previous trips to the Caribbean. To be frank, the stories were as dull as my tale of the missing shirt. I couldn't help but wonder if the travel lectures were meant to deflect any more questions about his private life.

Mom must have gotten bored, too. She finally proclaimed that she was ready to leave. Alex insisted on paying for dinner, but he agreed that I could leave the tip.

He said his car was parked nearby, and we parted company at Sixteenth and Tremont Place. First, he handed Mom a business card. "Here's my cell phone number. If I can be of any more help, please don't hesitate to call."

I waited until Mom and I were back in

the lobby of the hotel. "Why'd you tell me the bellhop had just returned your dry cleaning when I called?"

She looked as if that were the dumbest question in the world. "Well, I couldn't very well say Alex was in the room when you'd just scolded me for calling him. I guess it was a mistake to mention dry cleaning, though. You're so sensitive about it."

"Well, *yeah*." I prepared to scold her some more. Fortunately, she was saved because my cell phone rang. I checked the ID. It was Nat's number. "I need to answer this."

"Are you coming up to the room later?" Mom asked.

"Hold on," I said into the phone.

I didn't want to tell Mom my theory about the stamp. She might want to come. I don't know why I didn't just say I needed to get home instead of weaving a half-truth about what I was going to do.

I covered the mouthpiece of the phone. "Sorry, Mom. I just remembered I have to run back to the cleaners. I have a tax bill that I forgot to send to the IRS." I rubbed the tip of my itching nose as I continued to cover the phone. "I need to get it in the mail tonight or the tax police are going to come after me."

Mom seemed relieved that I wasn't coming up to the room. She probably suspected that I wasn't through chewing her out.

"Very well," she said. "I'll just go to the gift shop and get something to read."

I waited until she left, then turned toward the entrance before I spoke into the phone. "What's going on, Nat? I hope you aren't calling to give me some feeble reason for why you stood Laura up. You need to tell her, not me."

"Well, ex-*cuuuse* me," Nat said from the other end of the line. "The reason I called you is that I thought you might want to know that some cross-country skiers just found a body up in the hills near the Rendezview."

I clamped the phone to my ear so hard it hurt. "Who was it?"

"No ID, but I'm sure it's Carol Jennings."

My whole body turned numb, and the phone felt as if it were frozen to my ear. "When will you know for sure?"

"The coroner is trying to find her roommate right now to see if she can identify the body."

"Where are you?" I envisioned him at the coroner's office.

"If you must know, Laura and I are having dinner in the hotel."

I glanced around. Sure enough, I could see them beyond the divider that separated the lobby from the restaurant. They were facing away from me. I headed toward them, but the hostess tried to stop me.

I covered the phone with my hand again. "I just need to speak to my friends." I motioned toward Nat and Laura.

"What did you say?" Nat asked.

"I said, 'I'm here.'" I sat down beside Nat as I shut off the phone, ringer and all. Frankly, I didn't feel like getting any more bad news that night.

"Jeez, why don't you sneak up on people and scare them to death?" Nat said.

"That's not funny, Nat." Laura looked pale behind the blush Mom had applied to her cheeks, and I knew it wasn't because of me sneaking up on them. "Can you believe this, Mandy? Won't it ever stop?"

I realized I was as shaky as Laura looked when I tried to stash the cell phone in the pocket of my coat. I pulled out my hand and grabbed the edge of the table for support.

"Why would you think it was Carol if she didn't have any ID?" I asked.

"Because I asked them if the woman had on a coat that matched the one Laura had been wearing that night. Bingo. They said she did, even though it no longer had an exposed roll of film in the pocket. Obviously, whoever killed her removed the film because he was afraid of what was on it."

I didn't say that it was more likely he thought a stamp was hidden in the canister. Instead, I shook my head at the news. Only moments before, I'd decided Carol was sequestered on a tropical island.

"Why don't you go out to the coroner's office, Laura? You could identify the body." I immediately realized that was the wrong thing to say.

Laura leaned toward Nat as if he were her protector. "I'd really rather not."

"Yeah," Nat said. "Laura has been through enough already."

This must be true love. Nat wouldn't have taken no for an answer under any other circumstances. In fact, he would have dragged her out to Jefferson County with him, if for no other reason than he wanted to stay on top of the story.

"Do you want some coffee or maybe a drink?" Laura asked. "You look as if you could use something."

I could, but I declined. Nat's news put a whole new spin on my desire to get to the cleaners and take a look at the envelope. I talked to them for a few more minutes, then said I had to go.

Normally, Nat would have asked me why I was in such a hurry to leave and where I was going. He couldn't have cared less now. He was patting Laura's hand and looking at her as if she were the only person in the restaurant. "It's going to be okay, babe," he said. "I'll take care of you."

"I'm leaving now."

Laura said good-bye, but Nat didn't even seem to notice my departure.

As I headed to the elevator that went to the underground parking garage, I glanced around the lobby. Mom was nowhere in sight. In fact, the only person in the lobby was seated at a round cushioned area near the entrance and all I could see was the back of his head.

He was wearing a bright, frizzy red wig the way clowns do. It seemed late for a kiddie party, but it takes all kinds. Maybe he was even a she — a stripper dressed as a clown instead of a policewoman and waiting for a ride to a bachelor party somewhere.

I was on Speer Boulevard, halfway to the cleaners, before I thought of something. I hit the flat of my hand against my forehead. "You stupid jerk," I said aloud. "You turned the coat over to the police."

That meant I couldn't check what was in the pocket. It took a few more minutes before I realized I'd never put the envelope back in the coat when I looked at it after I'd talked to Carol's roommate, Sally. I'd put it in my desk.

Stan Foster wouldn't be happy that I'd forgotten to give it to him, but right now I didn't care. I mentally apologized for calling myself a stupid jerk. It was almost as if I'd known that I would want to check the envelope later. Maybe I even had some form of adult-onset ESP. Or else it was just a serendipitous event.

I was going to feel foolish if my theory was wrong, but at least then I could give up the envelope, knowing Mack and I had gone over every inch of the coat and what was inside.

When I reached the cleaners, I parked at the back door and raced into the plant, stopping only long enough to attend to the alarm. I unlocked the door to my office, and as soon as I reached my desk, I yanked open the top drawer and removed the envelope. My hands were shaking the way they had when Nat told me about the body up in the mountains. I rubbed my fingers across the thirty-seven-cent stamp with the pastoral farm scene on it. Yes, it felt as if there could be something underneath.

As soon as I could get my hands calmed down, I took hold of an edge of the stamp. Fortunately, it was one of those self-adhesive stamps instead of the kind you lick. Maybe I wouldn't have been able to peel it back as easily otherwise, but it began to come loose from the envelope.

Hot damn, as Nat liked to say. In fact, hot double damn. I could see something was under the stamp. It was in a little glassine protector, the kind you get when you buy a sheet of stamps at the post office, only this one was cut down to the size of what it was protecting. The glassine was stuck to the back of the stamp that was covering it. I pulled at the top stamp until I could see the one underneath. And there it was. An upside-down airplane, just like the one I'd seen in the stamp newspaper in Filmore's office.

I began to pull back the rest of the stamp that was covering it, but before I could, there was a banging at the back door. I didn't move. I didn't breathe. No one should be here this time of night, unless maybe it was Manuel from Tico Taco's checking to see why I was still at work.

I prayed for the person to go away. I even

thought about dousing the light, but the banging came again. In a panic, I pressed the top stamp back down over the Jenny Invert, grabbed my cell phone out of my coat pocket, and went to the door to shoo away whoever was there.

"Who is it?" I yelled, ready to turn on the phone and call the police if the person sounded suspicious.

"It's your mother," Mom yelled back.

I couldn't believe it. Worse yet, I knew she wouldn't go away, so I went over and shut off the alarm before I unlocked the door. "What are you doing here?"

Mom stepped across the threshold. "I have a surprise for you."

Great. Just what I needed. Another surprise. Frankly, it would be hard to top the one I'd just discovered a few seconds before.

"Go to your office and close your eyes."

"Mother," I said, drawing the word out in disgust.

"Just humor me. This is going to break the case wide open."

I could tell I wasn't going to get rid of her until I played her silly game. I went back to my desk and waited.

"Are your eyes closed?"

"Yes." What a person wouldn't do for her mother.

"Okay, you can open them now."

I did, but I thought I was hallucinating. It was the clown in the red wig that I'd seen in the hotel lobby. Worse yet, the clown was Betty. The only thing missing was some white makeup and a red nose.

She didn't even need to paint thick lips on her face. She was grinning from ear to ear. "The moment I saw this gall-derned wig, I knew it had to be the answer," she said. "The guy with the big head was wearing a wig."

"Isn't that wonderful?" Mom said. "We figured it out."

I suddenly flashed back to the first night I'd seen Alex Waring when he let me into Laura's apartment building. "No, I don't think it was a wig," I said, jumping up from my chair. "I think it was a big fur hat."

Betty looked crestfallen. "Why the dickens do you say that?"

I didn't answer. I was too busy putting the pieces together, now that they were beginning to fit. For one thing, it hadn't been a cat in the chair in Laura's time exposure at the restaurant. It had been the fur hat that Alex's ghostly silhouette had retrieved, bumping into the chair as he grabbed it and ran.

"You can come in now," Mom said, sounding as disappointed as Betty. "The surprise seems to be over."

That's when Alex, the guy I'd just tapped as the killer, came through the door.

CHAPTER TWENTY-FIVE

I tried to get control of myself. "Why'd you bother Alex with this?" My words came out as if I were trying to disguise my voice by squeaking like a mouse.

"I never picked up another rental car after you ran the other one into the mountain," she said.

"But why not just call me here at the plant?"

"I tried your cell phone, dear, but you must have shut it off."

I glanced down at the cell phone that I'd dropped on my desk when I'd played her silly game. To my horror, I saw the envelope right beside it. Why hadn't I hidden it when I went to the door? The thing that was really scary was that I noticed I hadn't managed to press down the top stamp completely. It was loose at one edge.

"Alex had just given me his number, if you remember," Mom continued, oblivious to my panic. "I explained that you'd gone back to the cleaners to finish a tax report. He returned as soon as I told him why we wanted to see you. I'd decided it would be fun to see your reaction to the wig."

"Yeah, and you really did look wigged out." Betty snickered at what she'd just said.

Mom had also interpreted my shocked expression as having to do with the wig. "You should have seen the look on your face."

I glanced at Alex. I could tell that he'd heard what I said and knew I'd connected him to the "big head." I dropped my eyes, but I tried not to look at the desk.

I thought of something else. All those dark green books in his apartment that had reminded me of a law school library must have been stamp albums. They were the same size and color as that album Cedric Filmore had been poring over when I visited him in his office.

Alex must have wanted Carol's stamp enough to kill for it. If he only knew that the stamp was hiding in plain view on my desk.

I had to do something before he came over and grabbed it. Mom said she'd told him I'd needed to complete a tax return. I decided the best thing to do was be obvious about it, so I sat back down at the desk.

"Just give me a second to finish these taxes," I said.

I grabbed a handful of papers from the top of the desk, folded them in thirds before anyone had a chance to see that they were bills, and jammed them in the envelope. I pressed the top stamp down as I turned the envelope over and tried to lick the flap on the back. I didn't have any saliva. My mouth had gone dry.

I tried to summon some moisture by puckering up and imagining that I was eating a dill pickle. It still took three attempts before I managed to seal the envelope. Now that I knew where the stamp was, I was afraid I might damage it if I put the envelope in my purse. Instead, I slid it over by some other papers on the desk.

"I believe you're right about the wig, Betty." I stood up again, glad that I'd been able to create enough saliva that my voice no longer squeaked. "Why don't you let Alex get out of here, Mom? I'll take you home, but I have a few more things I need to do first."

"I thought you'd be a lot more excited," Mom said.

Betty bobbed her red clown's hair up and down. "Yeah, when I saw the wig in one of those funky costume places, I knew it had to be the answer."

Alex was still staring at me.

"I'm sure you solved the mystery, Betty." My mouth had dried up again.

"Mandy, may I talk to you outside?" Alex asked.

"Sure." I almost choked on the word.

Mom and Betty looked puzzled as I followed him to the door. He closed it behind us, took hold of my elbow, and led me around the corner to the dry cleaning machines.

"You figured it out, didn't you?" he asked.

"Figured what out?"

"You know damned well what I'm talking about — the fur hat." He hadn't admitted that he'd killed three people, but he might as well have. Now he would never let us go.

"I need the coat." He gripped my elbow so hard it almost brought me to my knees.

"What coat? What are you talking about?"

"Carol's coat. I need something that's in the coat, and if you don't give it to me, I'll have to kill those two sweet little ladies in your office."

"Sweet" was not a word I would have applied to either of them, but I got the point.

Come to think of it, no wonder he'd put up with Mom's matchmaking efforts. He'd wanted to pump her for information.

He motioned inside his expensive leather coat. "I have a gun, and I'm not afraid to use it."

"But I don't have the coat." I'd almost blurted out that the police had it. Either way, I knew it was the wrong thing to say. I searched desperately for some other explanation. Even though he hadn't said what was in the coat, I decided to go for it. "But I know where the stamp is."

He pulled back from me in surprise. "So you found it. I knew it had to be in the coat as soon as I heard about it."

I didn't dare tell him where the stamp really was or it would all be over for the "sweet little ladies" and me. I needed to come up with another location, but for the life of me I couldn't think of one right then.

"Mom and Betty don't have a clue about this," I said. "If you let them go, I'll take you to the stamp."

He didn't hesitate. "Good. The way your mother's been trying to fix me up, I'll tell her we're going out for a nightcap. That ought to make her happy."

I wasn't so sure about that, but I nodded.

He grabbed my elbow again and steered me back to the office. When he opened the door, he almost knocked Betty off her feet. She'd obviously been attempting to eavesdrop, but I knew she hadn't heard anything because we'd been too far away.

"Look," Alex said, "Mandy and I have decided to go out for a drink. You don't mind, do you?"

Betty shrugged. "It's no skin off my nose."

Mom didn't respond, but she looked irritated. I could almost guess what she was thinking: How could her matchmaking arrow go so far afield after she'd had Alex earmarked for Laura?

I tried to look as if I were thrilled about the prospect of going out with him. I'm not sure Betty bought the whole thing, but Mom didn't seem to have a doubt in the world that I was beside myself with joy. That's what I got for having a mother who had been married six times, enjoyed any type of male flattery, and was a lifelong romantic.

"Okay, let's go," Alex said.

I was still wearing my coat, but I needed my purse. I went to the desk, grabbed it, and dug the car keys out for Mom. "Take my keys and go on home," I said. "I'll pick up the car tomorrow."

"But Cece and I ain't good night drivers," Betty said.

Mom frowned at her. "I am, too, when I'm down here in civilization, not out in the wild someplace."

Betty gave in finally. "Okay, if you really can drive at night and aren't going to turn all wimpy about it."

I would have liked to grab my cell phone, too, for all the good it would do me, but I was afraid of what Alex's reaction might be.

He gave my elbow another viselike squeeze and escorted me out of the office.

"I need to tell Mom how to set our alarm," I said.

Alex ignored the request and pushed me out of the plant to the passenger's side of his car. He told me to get in and slide across to the driver's seat. Not an easy thing to do with the console for drinks in the middle, but I managed it.

"You're going to drive," he said as he got in beside me and pulled out his gun.

All I'd had time to see from the outside was that his car was a fancy silver four-door sedan that looked brand-new. The smell of the leather interior confirmed it. But it wasn't like any of the cars that had tried to run us down or off the road. Ricky

Malone must have been his partner in crime, and I wondered if Alex had killed him when he became an inconvenience.

"Don't try anything funny," he said. "I'll have the gun pointed at you the whole time."

I needed to figure out some place to take him. If I knew where Travis lived, I would have taken him there. After all, Travis had offered to provide me with protection, and right now I'd have paid him double time to be my bodyguard.

Alex handed me the keys, and after some difficulty finding the ignition, I started the car. I pulled out of the parking lot and turned west on First Avenue, which feeds into Speer Boulevard. I still couldn't think of where to go. My brain felt numb with fear.

"I think someone's following us," Alex said after we'd gone about a mile. For the first time, he sounded worried. "The car's been back there since we left the cleaners. Did anyone else know you were there?"

"No."

I glanced in the rearview mirror. All I could see were the headlights of another car a half block behind us. Frankly, I thought it was all in Alex's head, but I decided to play on his paranoia. "Maybe it's your friend Ricky Monroe."

"Can't be," he said.

If there was ever a time to go on the offensive, this was it. "Why not? He's the one who ran Laura down, isn't he? He's the one who forced Joy Emerson's car off the road and rammed my mother's car when I was driving. He was using cars from the auto body shop where he worked, wasn't he?"

"You figured that out, huh? Smart girl." Alex turned and glanced out the back window. "We're going to drive around for a while until we lose the car back there."

"So why don't you think it's Ricky? He could be following us to see that you don't double-cross him when you get your hands on the stamp."

"Because he became a liability and I had to kill him." Alex's voice was as calm now as the cold, overcast night.

I gripped the steering wheel to keep from shaking, but I didn't dare quit now. "What if he's not really dead? I've heard of wounded people doing incredible things."

Alex's voice was louder than it had been before. "No, he was dead. I know he was dead."

"But it *does* look as if someone's following us, the way the driver is keeping the same distance behind us all the time." Actually, I could see three sets of headlights behind us now, but I didn't point that out. "Who else could it be?"

"I don't know, but we'll take care of it."

He reached over and yanked the steering wheel to the right. We slid on the ice and bounced into a curb as we rounded the corner to a side street. Unfortunately, there were no police cars around to come to my rescue. All but one of the vehicles behind us continued on Speer. The other car seemed to have disappeared.

"God damn it, back up and get us out of here," Alex yelled.

It took me a while to find reverse. When I did, I finally got us off the curb and headed north on the side street. A few seconds later, another car came around the corner. Alex saw it, too, and he tensed beside me. His paranoia was giving me a false sense of hope. Maybe there actually was someone following us.

He jammed the gun into the side of my head. "You're going to do exactly what I say, do you hear? You're going to see that we lose that guy."

Anger welled up in me. "And I suppose you're going to kill me if I don't. Big surprise. You're going to do that anyway as soon as I hand over the stamp."

"As soon as I get the stamp, I'll be out of here. You and the old ladies will be safe."

Oh, sure, as if I really believed that. However, this was not the time to make a stand. I needed to do it when I had at least a chance of getting away.

He withdrew the gun to show what a nice guy he was. "Turn right at the next corner," he said.

I did.

He continued to give commands until we were heading south in the direction we'd just come. The light turned to yellow when we reached Sixth Avenue. "Ignore it," he said. "Keep going." The light changed to red, and I barely missed the oncoming traffic.

"Good," he said. "I think maybe we've lost him. Keep going."

For a moment I thought he might be taking us back to the cleaners, and I prayed that Mom and Betty would have left by then. At Fifth, he ordered me to turn east, then south again on Steele, and east on Fourth.

He gave a yank on the wheel when we got to an alley a few blocks later. This time I managed to keep the car from plowing into a fence as we careened down the alley.

"Now stop," he shouted.

I slammed on the brakes in front of a graveled entrance to a garage.

"Pull over in the driveway and turn off the lights."

I'd never been convinced that we were being followed, and I hadn't had a chance to look behind us after we ran the light at Sixth. But if we had been, I was sure we'd lost the tail by now. Any faint hope I had of being rescued faded away.

"I said to shut off the damned headlights."

I switched them off.

"Now cut the engine."

As soon as I did, Alex turned to look back to the street where we'd just been. A car passed the entrance, and Alex let out a sound halfway between a grunt and a gasp.

"The guy's looking for us," he said. "I don't think he spotted us, but we'll have to get out of here if he comes back around the block."

He kept looking at the street behind us, but apparently no other cars came by.

"Why did you think you had to get rid of Ricky?"

Alex never took his eyes off the back window. "He was a loose cannon."

And now I was a loose end. Unfortunately, so were Mom and Betty.

"None of this would have happened if he hadn't been such a wild card," Alex said. "He killed everyone."

I decided to play dumb, for all the good it would do me. "What are you talking about? Who else is dead?"

"Carol. That woman, Joy, who was run off the road."

"Carol? You mean she's dead?"

"Yes, but I doubt if anyone will find her body until spring."

I decided to tell him what I'd learned from Nat. "I just heard that some cross-country skiers found a body up near the restaurant. Do you suppose it was her?"

That seemed to shake him. "Well, I didn't kill any of those people."

"But you said you killed Ricky."

"That was different. He was out of control, completely over the top."

"So what if the police have made the connection between you and Ricky? Maybe it was an unmarked police car back there that had you under surveillance."

"That's impossible." But I could tell he was worried, because of the slight tremble in his voice.

We heard the sound of an engine somewhere ahead of us. Alex swung his head around. Headlights of another car went slowly by on the street in front of us.

"Damn, he's circling the block looking for us," Alex said. "Get down." He yanked me toward him and held me down.

"What if the car comes through the alley?" I asked when I managed to get up.

"We'll have to make a run for it," he said. "Otherwise, you'll have to ram the son of a bitch."

The sound of the car faded away, and an unnerving stillness settled over the neighborhood. It was strange how quiet it could be on a cold winter night. I was freezing, and I was sure he could hear my teeth chattering and my heart trying to pound its way out of my chest.

"Can I start the car so we can get some heat?" I asked.

He ignored the request. "The police can't find any connection between Ricky and me. I hired him to set up the buy when Carol showed me the stamp, but we were always careful about being seen together."

"Until that night at the restaurant," I said.

"When Carol suggested meeting at the restaurant to the buyer, I liked the idea because the place was isolated. No one was even supposed to be there when we got to the restaurant, especially a photographer."

"So why didn't your buyer show up at the restaurant?"

Alex glanced over at me, but it was too dark to read his expression. Besides, it was starting to snow again, and the windshield was getting covered. "Are you crazy? We had to call him off when we saw your friend Laura taking pictures. It was scary enough that she'd almost caught us on film. We sure didn't want any record of the sale."

I had to keep him talking, if for no other reason than I still needed to come up with a plan for what to do next. All I could think of was to play on his rationalization that this whole thing was Ricky's fault.

"So what did Ricky do that spoiled everything?"

"He couldn't let it alone. He kept going over to the window to see if Carol was ever going to leave. I guess she spotted him, and when she finally came out, he jumped her and demanded the stamp.

"The next thing I knew he was strangling her, and this other woman, Joy, heard the struggle. She must have passed out in her car, but she sat up, saw what was going on, and took off like someone possessed. I told Ricky to stop her, and then I had to clean up his mess."

"You mean get rid of Carol's body?"

Alex shrugged. "I think we lost the tail. We need to get going."

I started the car, turned on the windshield wipers, and moved out of the alley, still unsure what to do next.

"You know, if it hadn't been for your damned friend Laura none of this would have happened."

That finally gave me an idea. What about taking him to Laura's photo studio? I still had the key that she'd given me when I picked up her notebook. I thought about the bolt I'd thrown across the door of her darkroom and the phone inside. If I could slam the door on Alex and lock him out, I could call the police from Laura's phone.

And if that didn't work, I even thought of a backup plan. I remembered the total blackness when I first entered the darkroom, and how I'd had to grope around forever before I found a light switch. If I could dive into that black hole while Alex was looking for the light, I could grab one of the huge jugs of chemicals I'd seen under her worktable. If those chemicals could ruin clothes, they ought to be equally hard on eyes. All I had to do was grab one of the jugs, twist off the lid, and hurl the contents in Alex's face when the lights came on, then flee to the bar I'd seen next door for help.

"Okay," Alex said as I headed south. "It's time to get the stamp. Where is it?"

"It's at Laura's photo studio."

CHAPTER TWENTY-SIX

"Where's this studio?" Alex said.

"It's south of here off University."

"That's not the way you were heading when you left the cleaners."

I floundered around for a response. "I didn't want to say anything about it, but I thought maybe Ricky was following us, so I decided to go a longer way. I didn't want to get mixed up in a fight between you and him."

Surprisingly, the answer seemed to satisfy Alex. He leaned back in his seat and appeared to relax.

"Why did Ricky go after Laura?" I asked. "She'd already dropped Carol's coat off at the cleaners."

"That was him acting crazy again. He went nuts about the pictures. He thought if he knocked your friend out of commission, he'd have an easier time finding the film in her apartment." Alex gave a short laugh. "Little did he know that the thing he really wanted was the coat she'd just left at your store."

No wonder we'd been confused about the whole thing.

"So it was Ricky who attacked me when he broke into Laura's apartment," I said.

Alex nodded.

I moved closer to the windshield so I could see as the snow began to come down harder. "I presume he also broke into the photo lab," I said.

"See how out of control he was? He was obsessed about those pictures. It wasn't until I heard you talking in the stairwell about the unrecognizable image of us in the color slides that I was able to convince him to back off. Believe me, it gave me a scare for a while, too."

"And I don't suppose you were really trying to get a book back from Carol when I ran into you at her door."

"That was another of Ricky's screwups. He still had a key to her place, so he went in looking for the stamp, but he couldn't find it. I was going to give it a try myself, but you surprised me. That worried me, so I figured you'd buy the explanation about the book I'd loaned her."

We were on University by then, not too far from the studio, and I'd run out of anything else to ask. I was almost out of time, too. The fear I'd been trying to keep in abeyance suddenly overwhelmed me. My plan seemed foolhardy now, but I didn't know what else to do.

I decided the only edge I had was to play on his paranoia again. "Are you sure one of those cars back there isn't following us?" I asked, even though I could barely see the cars behind us because of the snow.

He must have glanced in the side mirror, because he didn't turn around. "No, I think we lost him."

Damn. I guess I'd actually hoped one of the cars was a tail. I didn't care who it was. I was so paralyzed with fear by then that I wasn't even sure I could make the turn on Louisiana to get over to Laura's studio. I gripped the wheel and managed to get around the corner. Another car turned when I was almost at the next block. I didn't say anything about it this time, because I was living on false hope. I made another turn and slid into a parking spot in front of Laura's studio, where a new layer of snow covered the ground. The car behind us had disappeared.

All the other businesses seemed to be closed for the night. There were no pedestrians and only a few parked cars on the street. Still, a neon Budweiser sign blinked like a beacon in the window of the otherwise darkened bar next door. I prayed it was still open. It had to be open if my first plan failed and I had to resort to Plan B.

Alex slid his gun into his pocket before he got out of the car. "Slide across the same way you got in," he said.

I crawled out, and he gave a little motion with the gun in his pocket toward the entrance of the studio.

He looked at the sign by the door. "Golden Moments Photography. No wonder Ricky couldn't find this place."

I fumbled inside my purse to find Laura's key. When I pulled it out, my hand was shaking so hard that the key looked like a shiny silver blur amid the snowflakes.

"Hand it over," Alex said. "I'll open the door."

"No, I can do it." I found the keyhole and managed to unlock the door. I didn't lock it behind us, just in case there actually had been someone following us. Alex was so anxious to get the stamp that he didn't seem to care.

"I think it's best not to turn on the light out here. Just follow me."

There was enough light, reflected off the snow outdoors, that I could work my way behind the counter and down the hall to the darkroom. I never had a chance to put

Plan A into operation. As soon as I opened the door, Alex pushed me headlong into the room.

I kept going in the general direction of Laura's worktable, as I tried to remember exactly where I'd seen the jars of chemicals.

"Where the hell's the light?" Alex yelled.

I found one of the jugs and twisted the top as hard as I could. The lid was stuck on tight. I tried again. I couldn't budge it. I grabbed another bottle just as the single overhead light came on.

"What the hell are you doing?" Alex waved the gun at me.

"I'm looking for the stamp. We hid it on the bottom of one of these jugs over here."

"Let me have it."

I would if I could only unscrew the lid.

"The stamp must be under one of the other bottles." I bent down under the counter, trying to shield the jar from Alex's view as I twisted the lid with all my strength. I still couldn't get it open, and my last hope faded.

"What's that?" Alex asked, suddenly on alert.

It sounded as if the outside door had opened. "Maybe the wind blew the door open."

We both listened for another sound, but I was afraid his paranoia and my wishful thinking were playing tricks on us.

A floorboard squeaked in the hallway.

Alex cut the light, and I thought of making a dash for the door. I didn't dare. He'd be able to shoot me as he saw me pass across the threshold.

I didn't know where he was. I didn't know who was outside. I gave another yank to the bottle top, but it still wouldn't give.

The door swung open. I could see a silhouette, backlit from the light that the person had turned on at the front of the studio.

I didn't know who it was, but anyone was better than Alex.

"Hold it right there, or I'll shoot," Alex said.

In the light from the other room, I could see that he'd moved away from the light switch, and his gun was aimed toward the door. I lifted the jug over my head and sent it crashing down toward his arm. I heard something pop as I made contact with his wrist. The gun went off as it left his hand and clattered across the floor. The jar slammed into the floor, breaking glass and spewing out the chemicals inside.

The person in the doorway went down,

and Alex let out a scream of pain.

"Turn on the damned light, Mandy." I knew the voice.

I went over to the wall and turned on the switch.

Travis was on the floor, holding his left leg with one hand and pointing his own gun at Alex with the other.

"Oh, my God, I'm sorry," I said as soon as I saw the blood soaking through his pants. "I'm really sorry." I started toward him but thought better of it as Alex made a move toward his gun. He was holding his wrist in obvious pain.

"Don't even think about it, Waring," Travis said.

Alex froze, and I could see the chemicals dripping down the front of his sharply pressed pants. Well, that was one pair of pants that no amount of dry cleaning was going to save. I didn't know about any burns to his skin.

"Get his gun, Mandy," Travis said.

I cut a wide swath around Alex and went for the gun. It had slid underneath the worktable. As soon as I retrieved it, I pointed it at Alex and kept it there as I went to the phone on Laura's desk and called the police.

"Send an ambulance, too. There's a man

who's been shot." I turned and looked at Travis. "I'm really, really sorry."

"Will you stop with the 'sorry'?" Travis said. "If you hadn't whacked him with that bottle, I'd probably be dead by now."

CHAPTER TWENTY-SEVEN

The police led Alex away, but they didn't handcuff him because of his broken wrist. I don't know where they took him, but Travis left in an ambulance for Denver Health Medical Center. I was eventually hauled away in a squad car to be interviewed at the police administration building downtown.

What I'd really wanted was to accompany Travis to the hospital. No matter what he said, I still felt responsible. I would have liked to call Mack and ask him to go to the hospital, but I was rushed into an interview room when I got to police headquarters.

Stan arrived soon after, and he didn't take kindly to the fact that I'd failed to give him the envelope with the Jenny Invert on it when he'd sent an officer to collect the coat earlier in the day.

"I'll be taking Ms. Dyer to the cleaners to get the stamp as soon as this interview is over." I guess he was talking to the video camera or a tape recorder when he spoke of me as if I weren't in the room.

And frankly, I wished it were true. I thought the interview had turned into more of an interrogation once Stan arrived.

"What made Travis Kincaid come to your friend's photo studio?" he asked, turning back to me. "Was he using you as bait to get to Waring?" I could hear the disapproval in Stan's voice.

"No," I said, but for the life of me, I didn't have any idea why Travis had shown up.

Stan kept pushing. "So why was he there?"

"I don't know." And it was one thing I still needed to find out.

When the interview was over, I asked Stan if I could make a phone call. He frowned, but he finally motioned to the phone at his desk.

I called Mack and told him what had happened to Travis. He said he'd get right down to the emergency room and see what was going on.

"I warned you about Travis, didn't I?" Stan muttered when I hung up. "He must have been using you as a decoy to get to the killer."

"My relationship with Travis really isn't any of your business," I said.

I guess that was the right thing to say.

Stan was silent for most of the trip to the cleaners. When we arrived, I opened the back door with my key. At least the "sweet little ladies" had remembered to lock the door, but there was no need to shut off the alarm system, because it wasn't on. I turned on the lights and led Stan to my office. I flipped on the desk lamp and reached for the envelope with its valuable stamp.

"Oh, God. It isn't here."

Stan looked as if he were going to erupt.

"The envelope was right here," I pointed to the spot on the desk where I'd left it.

"Well, you damned well better find it. It has to be around here someplace, doesn't it?"

I wasn't so sure, and now I was shaking. Maybe Alex had a third partner in crime — the unidentified guy who was supposed to have been the buyer, for instance — who had broken into the cleaners. Once the security system was off, there would have been no silent alarm to alert anyone about a burglary in progress.

I checked through the other papers on top of the desk and looked in all the drawers. The envelope wasn't anywhere.

"I'm going up front. I need to check to see if someone could have broken in." I got out of my chair.

Stan followed me, but the call office was secure. No forced entry through the door. No broken glass in the windows.

"So where's the envelope?" Stan asked.

I had one more idea, but I really hated it. I called Mom at the hotel and asked the desk clerk to ring through to her room even if it was the middle of the night. "It's an emergency."

Laura finally answered the phone.

"I need to speak to Mom."

"But she's got on some sort of beauty mask, and she's wearing her earplugs. I'm afraid to wake her up."

"Do it anyway."

Finally, Mom came on the line. "What are you doing calling me this time of night, Amanda? You know how much difficulty I have getting back to sleep."

I ignored her complaint. "I need to know something, and it can't wait. Did you happen to put that tax envelope in one of my filing cabinets before you and Betty left?" Even as I asked the question, I had a pit-of-the-stomach fear about her answer.

"No, certainly not, Amanda." She paused. "I knew you were in a hurry to get it mailed, but you must have been so excited about going out with Alex that you forgot all about it." I gritted my teeth, not only at Mom's interpretation of my "date" with Alex, but also at what I was afraid she was going to say next. "Anyway, I put your return address on the envelope and dropped it in a mailbox on my way back to the hotel."

I covered the mouthpiece of the phone and told Stan what Mom had done. He wrenched the phone out of my hand and identified himself to her.

"Where did you leave the envelope?" he asked. "I need to know right now."

I couldn't hear what Mom was saying, but I would bet it was something vague. Every time she tried to help me, it was a disaster. Why should it be any different tonight?

After several more questions, Stan hung up. Actually, he slammed down the phone without saying good-bye. When he finally turned to me, his words came out as if each syllable were a painful effort. "She doesn't remember where she mailed it. She drove around and put it in the box with the earliest pickup time she could find. It's probably already on its way to God knows where."

I tried to be helpful. "I think the envelope was addressed to Dallas."

He called homicide and notified another

detective to contact the U.S. Postal Service in an effort to intercept the letter before it started on its way to its destination.

"Is your car here at the cleaners?" Stan asked when he was through.

"No, Mom has it."

"Okay, I'll take you back to your apartment." He still sounded angry but resigned to the fact that he couldn't get rid of me just yet.

"Could you drop me off at Denver Health instead? I need to find out about Travis."

Stan looked as if that were the last thing in the world he wanted to do. I guess it was because that's where he was going himself, and he didn't want me tagging along.

When we arrived at the hospital, we were directed to the surgery department. The first person I saw when we got to the waiting room was Mack.

"Travis is still in recovery," Mack said as soon as he saw me, "but he's going to be okay."

"Thank God."

"The bullet hit a blood vessel in the upper inside of the leg, but the doctor said he was able to repair it. Travis should be able to go home on crutches in a few days, then there'll be several weeks of recovery."

While I was talking to Mack, Stan went up and flashed his badge to an attendant on duty. He disappeared into the recovery room, but I barely had time to bring Mack up-to-date on what had happened before Stan returned to the waiting room.

"I can't get anything out of him," he said. "I want to see if he'll talk to you."

I followed Stan back to a cubicle in recovery.

Travis seemed to recognize me even if his eyes were still a little glassy. He grabbed my hand. "I love you," he said.

That was nice to hear, but a little embarrassing under the circumstances.

"He's obviously still out of it," Stan said, turning to leave. "I'll have to come back later."

A nurse came over to check on Travis. "I love you," he said to her.

Stan looked smug. Okay, so Travis really was out of it. I headed back to the waiting room, too.

Mack offered to drive me home, and I took him up on the offer. I didn't feel like hearing any more snide remarks from Stan about my relationship with Travis. For that matter, I wasn't keen about hearing any dire predictions from Mack, either. "Someone's going to have to help Travis when he gets home," I said, "so I don't want you to say one more word about *Rear Window* or Grace Kelly and Jimmy Stewart." He didn't.

Instead, he said he'd get someone to cover for me at work for the Saturday shift so I could get some sleep. No matter what, I loved this guy.

As soon as I got to my apartment, I fed Spot. The next thing I did was call Nat. Before he had a chance to wake up and start telling me how wonderful Laura was, I said Alex Waring was under arrest for the murder of Ricky Monroe.

"Holy friggin' cow," he said. "Did he kill Carol, too? The roommate just ID'd her body."

"Apparently, Ricky killed her and Joy Emerson both," I said.

"I guess that gets Tom Jones off the hook," Nat said.

"The whole thing had to do with a valuable stamp that Alex wanted to get his hands on."

Nat was wide awake now. "Where's the stamp?"

"I don't know." I was telling the truth, but it still felt like a lie. I began to itch, and I scratched the side of my nose as I continued, "You'll have to ask Stan Foster about that."

When we hung up, I called Mom's hotel room. Laura answered, and I explained about Alex Waring and the stamp and told her it was safe for her to return home.

"But why did Carol leave her coat at the restaurant if it had a valuable stamp inside the pocket?" Laura asked.

"I'm guessing that she saw Ricky outside the window and realized the whole thing about selling the stamp was a setup. She didn't want him to get his hands on the stamp, so she wasn't about to have it with her when she went outside to confront him.

"She knew which coat was yours, so she must have decided to borrow it. She probably planned to come back and return it to the rack after she finished telling him off, but I guess we'll never really know."

"I wonder why she didn't just stick the envelope in my coat?" Laura asked.

I was guessing again. "Maybe she thought you would throw the envelope away. After all, it didn't have anything inside."

Apparently Laura was satisfied, but she wasn't willing to wake up Mom now that she'd finally gone back to sleep. "She was really upset after she talked to you before," Laura said. "Her exact words were 'You try to help out your daughter, and what do you get? Heartache.' "

I told Laura that perhaps, under the circumstances, I would wait and talk to Mom when I picked up my car later in the day. After that, I collapsed on the sofa.

By the time I woke up, it was almost noon. I showered, put on jeans, a sweatshirt, and the coat I'd worn the night before, and took a taxi to the hospital.

Before I went to Travis's room, I bought the largest bouquet of flowers I could find at the hospital gift shop. It was so large, in fact, that I couldn't even see the patient when I got to his room.

"This is for you," I said, finally finding a place to set the flowers on the stand by Travis's bed. "They didn't have a very good selection this time of year." I pointed at the scraggly mix of mums and carnations and realized that I was starting to ramble.

I glanced over at him, and this time I couldn't help but notice his leg, which was sticking out from under a blanket all swathed in bandages. I cringed.

"I'm sorry," I said.

"Good. That ought to score me some points." Travis had the audacity to wink at me. I assumed he'd been winking at all the nurses, too, since he'd been so free earlier with the I-love-you's to every woman he saw.

Forget about it, I told myself. I pulled a chair close to his bed. "What I need to know is why you happened to follow Alex and me to Laura's photo studio."

Travis grinned. "That's what your boyfriend, Stan Foster, wanted to know, too."

I couldn't help myself. "He's not my boyfriend."

"That's right. Mack said he was your ex-boyfriend."

Mack had obviously been here at the hospital after he took me home. I'd have to have a word with him about that later. "So are you going to tell me or not?"

"Sure. After you introduced me to Alex yesterday afternoon, I did some checking. Turns out he's in the antique business, and he did the decorating at the restaurant where your friend was taking pictures. I figured that was way too much of a coincidence to be accidental."

"Why didn't you call me about it?" I asked, reeling from the information.

"I tried, but I couldn't get you, so I decided to go looking for you instead. Imagine my surprise when I got to the cleaners and saw you in the driver's seat of Alex's car. Frankly, I was a little hurt that you would prefer him to me, but I decided to follow you, anyway. When you tried to lose me, I knew something else was going on."

"I guess I owe you for that."

"Ohhh, yeah," Travis said.

Just then an attractive blond nurse came into the room. "Mr. Kincaid really needs to get some rest. He's had company all morning."

I was glad to see that he didn't wink at her. Instead, he motioned for me to lean down close to him.

"Now that you've got me in bed," he said, "why don't you come back later and join me?"

"In your dreams," I said. "That's not what I meant by owing you one."

As far as dreams are concerned, sometimes they come true in ways a person doesn't even expect. I kept dreaming that the police located the envelope with the valuable stamp on it, but they didn't. It seemed to have slipped through the cracks at the post office.

But a week later, the mailman returned a letter to me. Apparently, I'd stuffed too many bills in the envelope before Mom mailed it, and it came back marked RETURN FOR ADDITIONAL POSTAGE.

Mom was home in Phoenix by then, and she insisted on taking back her apology for screwing up. "Betty said it didn't have enough postage on it," Mom said. "Aren't you glad I never listen to her?" Betty almost popped a seam when I told her it was her comment about needles that gave me the idea of where to find the stamp.

I turned the envelope over to Stan. Eventually, the stamp will be sent to what Filmore called a "stamp expertizing service" to see if it's an authentic Jenny Invert or a fake. If it's real, I've been told, it may take months to trace the provenance and find out if Carol's uncle was the real owner or if it had been stolen.

Instead of dreaming about the stamp any more, I've started to have sexy dreams about Travis. Who knows? Maybe they'll come true someday, too, but not for a while. In the immortal words of Mack the Movie Buff, I'm too busy right now playing Grace Kelly to Travis's Jimmy Stewart.

MANDY'S FAVORITE CLEANING TIP

If you get nail polish on a garment, the way Mandy's mother claimed she did (chapter 23), use the obvious — nail polish remover — to get it out. First stretch the fabric over a glass bowl with a rubber band and then drip acetone-based polish remover through the stain, gently sponging the remover over the back of the fabric. Keep doing this until the stain fades away. Do not use on silk, acetate, or Arnel fabrics. If some color remains on a white or color-fast garment, try a combination of half hydrogen peroxide and half water on the stain. Place it in the sun while keeping it moist with the peroxide solution.

Nonwashable garments should always be sent to a dry cleaner.

ABOUT THE AUTHOR

DOLORES JOHNSON is a former newspaper journalist and freelance writer who interviewed many dry cleaners as a field reporter for *American Dry Cleaner* magazine. She is the author of six previous Mandy Dyer mysteries and lives in Aurora, Colorado, where she is at work on her next novel. Dolores enjoys hearing from readers at doloresdjohnson@cs.com.

The employees of Thorndike Press hope you have enjoyed this Large Print book. All our Thorndike and Wheeler Large Print titles are designed for easy reading, and all our books are made to last. Other Thorndike Press Large Print books are available at your library, through selected bookstores, or directly from us.

For information about titles, please call:

(800) 223-1244

or visit our Web site at:

www.gale.com/thorndike
www.gale.com/wheeler

To share your comments, please write:

Publisher
Thorndike Press
295 Kennedy Memorial Drive
Waterville, ME   04901